DANCING IN THE FIELDS OF GOD

Janice Imbach

To Michelle
I treasure you!
Much love and many
blessings.
Grandma Jan

AmErica House
Baltimore

© 2001 by Janice Imbach.

First printing

ISBN: 1-58851-404-8
PUBLISHED BY AMERICA HOUSE BOOK PUBLISHERS
www.publishamerica.com
Baltimore

Printed in the United States of America

In memory of my father
who understood better than most
the sacred syntax of Love.

Prelude

Journal Entry:

June 4, 2005
Beginnings and endings. Gain and loss. Joy and sorrow. Delight and despair. Such were the years in which I consciously began my inner journey.

I have often pondered the first sign of this odyssey of the soul. It seems to me, in retrospect, that the true beginning came with my first shattering experience of death. Or was it when I first met Douglas Cameron? Or was it, instead, the birth of my beautiful daughter that propelled me into a continuous years-long search for the key to life.

The expression "key to life" leaves a good deal to be desired. I knew, even as an unseasoned youngster, that there was really no magic key that would open the doors of life and flood them with meaning. I intuited even then that only by slowly and painstakingly refining my own belief structure and constructing my own philosophy of life could I hope to gain clarity, and yet I felt at some subliminal level that there had to be something, some kind of pattern that made sense of the chaos, the conformity, the ambiguity, indeed, the absurdity of life as most people live it. As I matured, I searched for gnosis: direct knowledge of spiritual truth. I am still searching, or at the very least, refining. A task that is, I suspect, never ending.

June 5, 2005
As a child of the 20's, I went with my mother and father every Sunday to the neighborhood Episcopal Church. Cleanliness was a requirement for Godliness and church attendance was a requirement for community acceptance and prestige. Very few of that generation failed to avail themselves of that genteel Christianity, of that impetus to belong. I must have been no more than five or six the summer our rector, dear sweet man, went on vacation and left us, by some astonishing twist of fortune, in the clutches of a fire-eating, hell and damnation preacher. My parents were not amused; I was not convinced. My young soul refused to be persuaded by his pyrotechnics. My father, so my thinking went, was a kind and generous man who would never, ever judge others so harshly. Surely then, God would not be more mean-spirited than my father. For me, that was the end of the matter.

My parents were nominal Episcopalians; my mother by way of

7

birth, my father by way of marriage. His family, a generation back, had been Catholic. My grandfather, a young man newly training to be a priest, had become badly disillusioned and cynical about some of the non-priestly activities that he had observed while in seminary, such as conducting mass sans confession. He summarily left, disgusted with what he considered to be the blatant hypocrisy of the church. He said goodbye to his family in Derry, caught a ship to America, and after a short season as a brick layer, managed to get himself hired into a banking institution where he remained, with stunning success, for the rest of his life.

All in all my religious training was quite unexceptional. I attended Sunday school in yellow organdy and white Mary Janes, exchanging them in the winter for a thick coat and black Mary Janes. We walked to the Christmas Eve service each year. I still can feel the delicate, delicious crunching of new snow under my feet as I held my father's hand, fiercely aware of the grace of his presence and protection. At the end of the service, each child received a red net stocking filled with hard candies and a large orange, bright symbol of sunshine in our frozen winter world.

Our religious life, as a family, was more tradition and social imperative than conviction, though many years later, I came to understand that my father had a very powerful and private interior life. My own developing spiritual nature as an adult was a rather surprising anomaly in my ordered life.

June 6, 2005
I ask myself why I write this journal now, why I sift through the particulars of my life like a small animal scrabbling through the leaves on the forest floor. In truth, I'm not sure. Perhaps I am seeking an inner validation of the life that I have lived, of the choices that I have made.

Perhaps I am having a dress rehearsal for the review that supposedly comes to each one of us when we cross to the other side; a review of the joys and the triumphs, the hurts and the sorrows, the love given and the love withheld as we lived our lives. Perhaps this is a kind of house-cleaning of the spirit.

I have long loved Walt Whitman's line: "Death is different from what anyone supposes, and luckier." I look with some interest to finding out if that is true. My heart tells me that in time I will be returning to my true home

I laid aside my journal–scribbling I call it–and slowly walked to the kitchen to prepare something for dinner. Early dinner. As I age, I seem to want all tasks completed at an early hour. I'll get ready for bed–turn the covers down, wash my face, put on my nightclothes just as soon as I'm through with my simple meal. A little indolent, a little embarrassing, I suppose, if anyone should drop by, but that's highly unlikely. If Dylan or Gentry should stop in, it won't matter. Anyone else knows to call first. Anyway, at eighty and then some, I surely have long left behind any concern for what other people might think. This way, whenever the spirit moves me, I'm ready for bed. Ready for sleep. Ready to dream the dreams of my youth. And, just maybe, ready to meet Douglas again while I sleep.

Leitmotif

Chapter 1

My life as a woman began the night I met Douglas Cameron. At that time, I was a coltish, skinny and somewhat unkempt fourteen-year-old, interested primarily in bicycles, swimming and roller-skating. Very nearly fifteen, I was mostly tomboy, only occasionally slipping into an uneasy feminine adolescence. I had yet to learn to be comfortable with my rapidly developing body. I was something of a loner, a dreamer, certainly a romantic. I was shy, yet inwardly confident that somehow, some day, I would be someone special. My mother, her North Carolinian heritage firmly imbedded in her soul, must have been a bit appalled at this daughter who skinned her knees and tore her clothes and disdained social niceties. In her serene way, she gently chided me into appropriate behavior as best she could. She was a finely drawn watercolor in contrast to my vivid coloring. I adored her.

When I could find the time, I practiced my piano lessons and attempted to write short stories and poetry, all very fanciful and jejune. I had a flare for words and deep in my heart I wanted to be a writer, a secret I kept well hidden from everyone, even Matthew Parrish, my constant companion and confidante. From the day I had moved from Chicago to the San Fernando Valley at the age of nine and had seen the skinny redheaded boy who lived across the street, Matthew and I had become inseparable.

It was a rare day we weren't together. When we were young, we had rolled in the sweet summer grass, savoring the smell of new-cut lawn. We had stolen sticky, sun-honeyed apricots from the neighbor's ancient tree. We had played ball and chased Charlie, my black and tan shaggy mongrel, around our spacious back yard. As we got older, we went swimming in the community pool; we biked to the library together and to the movies and to the ice cream parlor, Charlie following at our heels as often as we would allow.

One evening in early spring of 1939, Douglas Cameron, the son of my dad's old college friend, stopped in unexpectedly to say hello to my parents. He was in Los Angeles for a job interview with the Times.

I had been out as usual with Matthew. Completely unaware that Dad and Mom were entertaining, I impetuously rushed in, disheveled and rumpled, interrupting a comfortable adult conversation. A tall young man, strange to me, immediately got to his feet and offered me his hand, assessing me with penetrating eyes.

"You must be Kathleen. I'm Douglas Cameron."

His spontaneous courtesy startled me. From a grown-up, such attention was rare. Clumsy and inarticulate, I muttered a timid hello and extended my hand to meet his, painfully aware of my untidy and over-heated state. Thoroughly embarrassed, I managed a self-conscious smile as I noted his lean frame, his brown hair crisply curling at his broad forehead, his firm chin. His features had a pronounced austerity about them, but a dazzling smile gentled his expression and softened his startlingly intense blue eyes. I was transfixed, almost paralyzed by an emotion I could not name.

My father, a broad-shouldered man with an open face, eyes twinkling with humor, invited Douglas to stay for dinner, and Mother, turning quickly to our guest, reinforced the invitation.

"We have plenty. We're having a simple supper, but we would immensely enjoy your company. Please stay."

Without fuss, Douglas quietly assented.

My mother, Catherine, delicately pretty, presided over our meal with the same inherent dignity and grace that she brought to all of her undertakings, and Dad, with his usual social expertise, kept the conversation stimulating and interesting. My father had been appointed to a judgeship the year before, and I took a proprietary pride in his new title, Judge Stephen Quinn Curran.

As the conversation drifted from one subject to another, I watched and said little, surreptitiously studying Douglas as I ate. He had a confident, compelling way about him. I guessed that he must be twenty-four or twenty-five though something about his bearing made him seem older. He seemed to be of a serious disposition, a little aloof and detached. I stared, fascinated, at his beautifully modeled mouth, noticing the mole on his upper lip. He caught me scrutinizing him and gave me a quick smile. Dropping my eyes in flushed confusion, I fumbled for my glass. He quickly sensed my discomfiture and skillfully turned the table conversation to the tense situation in Europe.

"Well, Judge Curran, what do you think of Chamberlain's latest action?"

"Ah, to my mind, it's disastrous, and, furthermore, I'm really disturbed by Hitler's interest in Poland."

"Yes, I am, too. Chamberlain's conciliatory approach won't work. He's making a grave mistake in thinking that he can appease Adolph Hitler's voracious appetite by throwing him a bone. His timidity will ultimately be the undoing of us all." Douglas spoke with quiet authority. I stared at him, fascinated. He was surprisingly well informed for one so young and he was not at all reticent in expressing his views.

"There's no question in my mind that Germany is intent on having the whole of Europe under its thumb," Dad said. "In time, the betrayal of

Czechoslovakia will haunt us all. I see no way in God's earth that we can escape involvement."

"I'm afraid you're right," Mother agreed. "People like Kaltenborn and our British ambassador have been advocating strict neutrality in European affairs." She sighed. "They may be espousing a very naïve point of view. I find the whole thing confusing and downright frightening."

"Most people are considerably more comfortable believing rather than questioning powerful voices," Douglas remarked with a shrug. "Of course, no one wants war, but I'm convinced that the isolationists are dead wrong. Europe is on the brink; it's only a matter of time until the whole thing explodes. We're surely going to be caught up in it. This is a cancer that won't be contained."

Silence fell as we contemplated his chilling words. With mature perception, he turned out to be right. War did come that fall of 1939. Chamberlain could not hold the peace and the world was soon aflame.

Mother skillfully steered the conversation to lighter, happier topics. "You mentioned that you had other interviews coming up, Douglas, one with a newspaper in Chicago and one in radio?"

"Yes, and I'm darned lucky to have a shot at three really good journalistic jobs."

"Which would you really prefer? Print or radio?"

"I don't know; either would be fine. Your question reminds me of a most unusual dream I had a few nights ago. My mother, now dead for several years, came to me in my sleep. She looked just as she did before she became ill, maybe a bit younger. In silence, she pointed to a radio." He paused, uncertain of how we were taking his comments. "Then she showed me a black box and said, 'This is your future, Douglas.' I knew at once that the box was a television set. Then I abruptly woke up. What do you think? Should I pay any attention to this?"

Dad leaned forward. "I read somewhere recently that a dream not understood is like a letter that's not opened. I think that's from the Talmud. Some psychoanalysts–Jung, for instance–take dreams very seriously. They suggest that they can contain important messages from our unconscious."

"It's strange; I really never thought I'd be influenced by the say-so of an invisible consultant," Douglas laughed. Then, shrugging deprecatingly, he went on, "I very well may not get any of these positions anyway, but should I be so lucky as to have a choice, I'll pay close attention to that dream. I have a strong feeling that television will be the wave of the future."

"Do you really think so?" Mother queried. "I know next to nothing about it and I'm no scientist, but television sounds like a fantasy to me. Pictures sent over airwaves? That seems beyond the realm of possibility."

"It does sound incredible, doesn't it? I was lucky enough awhile back to see a demonstration; it was truly amazing. I don't know whether or not pictures and sound can be transmitted well enough to be commercially viable, but technology is expanding at such a rate that the impossible soon becomes the ordinary."

"True enough." Dad stared into space. "I've seen changes since I was a boy that I would never in my wildest imaginings have dreamed possible–the beginning of the automobile and air flight, the proliferation of electricity, radio's incredible growth, the movies–so much in my generation alone. It boggles the mind. There seems to be no end to what man can envision."

Soon we finished eating and returned to the living room. Douglas settled beside me on the couch. As his eyes wandered appreciatively around, I tried to see the room from his point of view. A grand piano stood close to the bay window, music piled up on the bench. Charlie lay in comfortable slumber by the fireplace that was flanked on each side by a glassed-in bookcase. The room had a comfortable lived-in feel. Bright pillows, an elegant bouquet of calla lilies, a sculpture of a woman's head, a few paintings graced the room. It had welcoming and embracing warmth.

My mother's doings, of course. She was an elegant and lovely lady who possessed a keen and discerning eye for beauty. Her dark hair, combed straight back, accentuated her rather high, white forehead; to my romantic imagining, the patrician delicacy of her features suggested noble breeding.

As my mother called my father out of the room for a phone call, Douglas courteously turned to me and asked about any future plans I might have. I told him about my intent to go to college and, completely captivated by his intense interest, furiously flushing, I confided my desire to be a writer.

He studied me a moment. "You know, you can do anything that you really believe you can, Kathleen. So many just drift along without any conscious direction. Listen carefully to the voice of your spirit. It will never steer you wrong."

"The voice of my spirit?"

"Yes. If you really listen, you'll hear it deeply inside of yourself. My mother taught me that." His eyes were fastened on mine as if he were willing me to understand and remember. Then, as if to lighten the moment, he added, "Ah, forgive me, Kathleen, I tend to preach."

As our eyes met, I felt a sudden shift within from girl to young woman. My childhood silently vanished into yesterday as I recognized and willingly embraced my budding femininity.

Douglas soon said his goodnights to everyone and, taking my hand in his,

16

he stared down at me seriously. "Don't grow up too fast, Kathleen." With that, he left.

That night, I had a dream, one that was to be replayed in one variation or another for many years. I was dancing with Matthew in a boundless place without walls, without floor, with no discernible height or depth. It was as if we were waltzing in the clouds, happy, unencumbered and free. As we circled around and around, my dress suddenly transformed itself into a beautiful white ball gown fit for a fairy princess and Matthew faded away to be replaced by Douglas. I woke with a start. The dream left me disturbed and shaken.

I didn't see Douglas again for many years, but that night changed me irrevocably. It also brought about a marked change in my relationship with Matthew. He was no longer the comfortable, rough-and-tumble pal to me that he had been for so many years, for I had suffered a sea change and could not go back to simpler, more innocent days. Matt, a year older, mirrored my awakened sexuality. Friends before, we both became aware of a new dimension of feeling for each other, a feeling that we hardly knew how to handle.

"You're so beautiful, Kat." Matthew flushed, cautiously eyeing me to see what my response would be.

"Beautiful! You're crazy! I think you need glasses, Matt."

"You're the one who needs glasses. Don't you ever look in a mirror?" He pushed me backward on the grass, part shove and part awkward embrace. We stared at each other in silence, neither of us quite sure how to manage this new rampant physicality. He experimentally brought his mouth down on mine in an innocent kiss and then quickly changed the subject. "Hey, Kat–will you help me with my English paper tonight?"

"I'll help you to get started, if you want, but you're the one who has to do the work." I felt a surge of affection for this smiling boy in his rumpled blue shirt. He and I were different as shadow and sunlight. He excelled in math; verbal skills were my strength. He focused his attention on the outward aspects of life, I, on my mind's inner landscape. He was gregarious, I, a loner. He focused on practicalities, I, on possibilities.

Laughing, he pulled me up. "Come on, I'll buy you an ice cream cone."

Later that night, I studied myself in the mirror, trying to find any sign of the beauty Matthew had insisted was mine. As far as I could see, I was completely ordinary looking: leggy, skinny and unprepossessing. My father had told me many times that I was the image of his maternal grandmother, reputed to be 'the most beautiful girl in all of Derry and the surrounding countryside as well.' I dismissed this as transparent fatherly pride. I looked

17

again at myself. I recognized that my dark shining hair was a dramatic contrast to my porcelain skin, that my chin was firm, that my large eyes were a clear aquamarine blue. But, alas, I possessed a singular lack of curves. Would I ever have a bosom? I thought about Matthew's fumbling kiss and was thrilled that he, at least, liked the way I looked.

Jumping into bed, I turned off the light and let my thoughts drift back through our early days in California. My mother, delicately fragile, had tolerated the Chicago cold poorly, so, on the advice of her doctor, we had quite suddenly moved to a quiet neighborhood in Encino where Dad became a partner in a friend's law firm. As for me, I had been delighted to come to the land of sunshine and Shirley Temple.

Matthew, who lived across the street in a low, white house, had been welcomed into our family immediately, frequently joining us in a family picnic at the beach or in a casually shared lunch or supper. He was in and out of our house constantly. The two of us shared our secrets and our dreams. I couldn't ask for a better friend, and I thanked God for his presence in my life as I drifted into sleep.

Our constant companionship, encouraged by my parents, had not come cheaply for Matthew. His mother, a relentlessly unhappy woman, nagged him mercilessly about me. Alice Parrish was a disappointed woman—a shrew, full of spite and convoluted pride. She was censorious and prickly, quick to take offense and slow to embrace the new, whether new ideas or new people. Her whole life was defined by the litany: 'what will people think? what will the neighbors say? Matthew, how could you?'

Her anguish over others' opinions was hard to understand. She disliked all of her neighbors out of hand—especially, I was all too aware, she disdained my mother and father and me. She knew very well that we had made every effort to invite Matthew into our family life. I could almost read her thoughts. Who did those Currans think they were, fawning over her son, spoiling him with their fancy ways? As if she couldn't provide everything he needed without interference from them? She wouldn't stand for his getting above himself. In her fury, she tried mightily to separate Matthew and me, but in this one thing, Matthew proved to be infuriatingly intransigent.

His father had worked for a farm implement company. He had been gone for long stretches of time when Matt was young, traveling up and down the state. When his son was six years old, to no one's surprise but his wife's, Mr. Parrish just kept on traveling and never came home again. To his credit, he faithfully sent money every month, even through the hard years of the depression, but that was the extent of his involvement. I think Alice Parrish felt righteously justified in her bitterness. She was incapable of recognizing that her mean spirit was the prime cause of her unhappy circumstances.

We Currans weathered the depression years in much better style than most. I was aware of the grace of my life. During that difficult period, I saw men with gray, dull faces and slumped shoulders, broken despairing men, wandering listlessly about town. My mother, bless her always soft and gentle heart, was quick to give each man a task to be done in exchange for a sandwich or a hot meal.

In sharp contrast to these wandering ones, I myself had a lovely home and my father provided for all our needs, including many luxuries. I took piano lessons from the best teacher in the area and was given an occasional delicious trip to the Los Angeles Philharmonic, at that time under the baton of Otto Klemperer. We enjoyed frequent dinners at fine restaurants. We took long, lazy summer trips. I knew that my dad was fairly prosperous and I couldn't help but be aware of my good fortune.

My parents were adamant that those who had more should be generous with those less fortunate. In the same way, they were unstintingly generous with Matthew. They liked him; they were sorry for the dearth of emotional support given him, and they did their best to include him in our easy, affectionate home life. Much of my father's business had been connected to the burgeoning movie industry. He was well respected for his integrity and his astuteness in law. I was enormously proud of him.

My mother, not at all well, took pains to keep her health problems from me, her only child. She smiled her quiet smile, lavished affection on me, and went about her life with simple dignity. She gave me a lovely sixteenth birthday party–dancing and cake and chocolate ice cream. As we jitterbugged on the back patio, I was aware of my mother's smiling face as she watched us from the doorway. We were so young and innocent, all of us–the girls, pretty and fresh in full-skirted pastel dresses, the boy's, self-consciously stiff in their Sunday clothes. We laughed and danced and exchanged innocent kisses under a full moon. A night to remember with gratitude and fondness.

Life for me was sweet and uncomplicated. Loving family, friends, and my best friend in the world, Matthew, surrounded me. I wrote poetry at night, tucked in my narrow white bed. I memorized favorite poems: Browning, Milllay, Wordsworth, Emily Dickinson. I was genuinely fond of my crotchety, elderly piano teacher, though I practiced with considerably less enthusiasm than she would have liked.

One tranquil green and gold spring evening, just as twilight was falling, I strolled into the living room to play the piano for a bit. To my consternation, I found my mother slumped over in her chair, her needlework fallen to the floor beside her. She was white and alarmingly still.

19

Terrified, I ran to her. As I touched her, her hand fell heavily off her lap, hanging grotesquely in space. I hesitantly touched her face. Instinctively, I knew that her spirit had left her body. I screamed in horror; I screamed for my father; I screamed at a God who did not answer.

"Mother–Mother–you can't go. Come back–don't leave me–oh, please–oh, God–please, please."

Touching Mother's face yet again, I buried my head in her lap and sobbed uncontrollably as my universe silently spun out of control.

I became dimly aware of my dad feverishly feeling for her pulse, then rushing to the phone to call the doctor. In a bit, he gently lifted me up and held me to him for a long time. Making strange noises in his throat, he lovingly stroked my hair.

"There, there, Kathleen. She didn't suffer. Your mother has been tired out for a long time. She was ready to go."

He led me to the couch. "Lie down, sweetheart. I have to wait for the doctor."

His face was drawn and tight and unshed tears glistened in his eyes. I closed my eyes and sank into exhaustion.

* * *

After my mother's death, I felt completely abandoned, betrayed by life's precarious fragility. It had never occurred to me that my mother would not be there for me always. I had never been faced with the death of a loved one, never even been to a funeral. Her death was shocking and starkly horrible to me. Why had I not been more perceptive? Why had I not sensed that something was amiss? I was old enough, I berated myself, that I should have realized that she was ill. I should have helped her more. I should have told her how much I loved her. The intense guilt that I heaped on myself chained me to my sorrow.

I'm sure my parents wanted to shield me from the harsh realities of life. They both knew my mother's weak and overstrained heart was failing. At that time, there were no miraculous cures for a defective heart. Apparently, she had been fortunate to live as long as she did. Both were well aware that, had I known, the specter of her inevitable early death would have robbed me of any chance of natural childhood happiness. To my sorrow, I had had no warning to soften the blow.

Her death completely shattered me. I felt abandoned and lost. The tears I shed on finding my mother dead were the last I shed for a very long time. Closing off that portion of myself that was too painful to deal with, I became withdrawn and aloof. The spontaneous joy within that had bubbled up naturally for so many years lay, a frozen, undigested mass at the center of my being.

My life eventually went on, but I never really recaptured the carefree insouciance that I had enjoyed before my mother's untimely death. I now clearly understood the fleeting fragility of life. My dad, buoyantly optimistic in the past, also became quiet and withdrawn. He asked my Aunt Peggy, his youngest sister, to come and live with us. She was a good choice. Her practical and affable personality was a calm benediction for a mourning household.

Very, very slowly, my father regained his indomitable spirit, and, in time, he, in tandem with Aunt Peg, and lovingly supported by Matthew, coaxed and cajoled me into an acceptance of my unpalatable reality. Wounded in a very deep part of my psyche, I finally reluctantly rejoined life, but somewhere along the way, I had lost the music of my soul.

Chapter 2

My resiliency was eventually my salvation. Slowly I abandoned my lethargy and regained an interest in life. I had never forgotten that special evening when I had met Douglas. He had been unstintingly kind to an unformed fourteen-year-old youngster. The intensity of his lapis blue eyes burned in my memory. I was still hopelessly fascinated by his charismatic personality.

Soon after his visit, he wrote to my parents that he had been offered jobs both at NBC and at the Tribune. "*Very lucky*,' he had written.

I decided on the position at NBC. I'm grateful that I've been sent to New York City because, after all, it's the heart of everything. I've been learning a lot and still finding time to enjoy this exciting town.

Real radio news is almost non-existent. I hope to do a little to make it more substantial and relevant. It's been a revelation to me to see what scant attention and money the powers that be give to it. Radio news lacks immediacy and depth. I wonder if it can ever compete with the newspaper. I plan to do all in my power to contribute to that end.

Be sure to give Kathleen my very best wishes. I hope to visit with all of you again some day.

With regards,
Douglas

I had eagerly listened to every word, quietly thrilled that he had thought of me. Setting the letter aside on the table, Dad had smiled. "New York City–good. It's not surprising. Douglas presents a remarkably mature and intelligent appearance and it's abundantly clear that he enjoys a challenge. That young man is destined go far."

Douglas' letter, thanking us for his evening with us and updating us on the outcome of his interviews, was the last we heard from him. Then one day, about a year after my mother had died, I came home from school, tired and dispirited, still achingly heartsick, to find a letter for me on the hall table. I recognized Douglas' bold handwriting. I fled to the privacy of my bedroom.

February 20, 1941
Dear Kathleen,
I have just heard the terrible news about your mother. I've been in Europe and out of touch for a while. I'm sorry I didn't know sooner.

*It's very hard to lose your mother. She was so young and vibrant.
I know there is nothing I can say that will take away the pain that you
are feeling. I'll just share with you my belief that your beautiful and
loving mother has walked through an open door into another realm of
being. Even though you can't see her with your physical eyes, trust
that she watches over you with the same love that she has always had
for you.*

*You have great gifts to develop, Kathleen. I hope you make the
most of your talents, thus honoring both your mother and yourself.
The quest to hone your abilities will ease the pain. Please let me know
how you are getting on.*

Your friend,
Douglas

His concerned words made me feel special and cared for, and a feeling of joy flamed through me as I sank back, enraptured, on the bed.

As I re-read his letter carefully, I felt a lightening of my spirit. Almost, I could feel Mother's love reach out and enfold me. Her lovely, loving presence seemed to shimmer just beyond my sight, caressing and comforting me, releasing a rush of new energy. The combination of Douglas' words and the otherworldly sense of my mother's benediction broke my spirit loose from its sorrow. With great clarity, I saw that I needed to do exactly what Douglas had suggested. I needed to become all that I could possibly be, wasting neither time nor talent in useless and self-involved grieving. Once again, Douglas had initiated a transformation in my perspective.

I immediately answered his kind letter. That was the beginning of an infrequent but wonderfully satisfying correspondence. I cherished our exchanges. I wanted to be close to him in any way possible; I wanted to learn anything that he chose to teach me; I wanted to be shaped and molded by his perceptions.

He soon got into the habit of sending me books he thought I might enjoy; the most prized was a beautifully illustrated copy of *The Rubaiyat*, sent from England. He was at that time officially stationed in London, well entrenched in the dangerous and compelling business of reporting news of the war that was by this time escalating daily in Europe. I have that lovely, exotically illustrated book still. Douglas also suggested poetry that I might find interesting: A.E. Housman, Walt Whitman's *Leaves of Grass,* and Rainer Maria Rilke, a German poet unknown to me. I eagerly followed any suggestion he might make. My mind was unformed clay waiting to be molded by his every word.

One day, a new package arrived from England. I impatiently tore it open to find, to my surprise, a large, impressive volume containing biographies of long-dead Christian saints, detailing accounts of their various religious experiences. Leafing through, I read names I had never seen before: St. Catherine of Siena, Teresa of Avila, Hildegard of Bingen. Now curious, I read a short entry from Julian of Norwich.

All will be well
And all will be well,
And all manner of thing will be well.

'All manner of thing will be well.' Simple enough to read the words, but what, exactly, did that evocative statement imply? It hinted at mysteries I could not quite grasp.

Because it was a gift from Douglas, I forced myself to read the unwieldy and sober book intermittently. Sometimes I was charmed; more often, I was repelled. I could see that those holy men and women kept nothing back in their abandonment to God. The idea of such radical devotion was bizarre and frightening. It was all too much, and yet I frequently found myself paging through the book, dipping indiscriminately, here and there.

From the time of our arrival in California, my family had faithfully attended the Episcopal Church down the street from our house. I had always loved the magnificent music; now, strangely and reluctantly fascinated by the saints I read about, bizarre though they seemed to me, I began seriously to listen to Father Broderick's sermons. Though I was completely unconscious of it at the time, my spiritual education had begun.

My tastes, under Douglas' long-distance tutelage, were slowly changing. They were becoming increasingly diverse and mature, my perceptions expanding exponentially. Not all of my more adventurous forays met with Aunt Peggy's approval. She considered it a part of her role as surrogate mother to monitor my reading as well as my comings and goings. She was a firm but just disciplinarian. I loved her and I listened for the most part to her words, but at times, I felt the need to assert my independence, particularly rebelling at any attempt to censor my reading.

"Does your dad know you're reading that'" Aunt Peg queried when she came upon me reading *Lady Chatterley's Lover.* "It seems to me you're pretty young for that book."

"Oh, Peg–don't be so stuffy. Dad wouldn't care. You know he wants me to be well-rounded."

"Humph, well-rounded, indeed. That's your stock reply when you don't want to listen." Shaking her head in frustration, she left the room.

In many ways, Peg was more like a sister than an aunt to me. She was only ten years my senior. At times, the responsibility of bringing up a youngster weighed heavily on her. After a few abortive attempts, she finally gave up on monitoring my intellectual life. Blessedly, I was left to my own devices, free to dip into whatever literary pools I wished.

I became increasingly interested in news of the war. Europe blindly staggered under that mad little mongrel, Hitler. Fanatically charging across skies and fields, he recklessly lay waste the fair green lands of an entire continent. England was on her knees; Moscow was reeling. Displaced humanity everywhere, in a terrified and frantic diapsora, was precipitately fleeing to uncertain and unknown sanctuary. In America, President Roosevelt was helping England, *sub rosa,* as much as he dared, given our country's extreme fear of becoming embroiled in a war it desperately sought to avoid.

I imagined where Douglas might be, what he might be experiencing during these perilous times. I was desperately afraid for him, for I knew that he would take whatever risk necessary to get any story he deemed important. He made every attempt to crack the insular view then prevalent at NBC. Ensconced in London, he had the responsibility of interviewing significant figures–politicians, ambassadors, and statesmen–in his weekly half-hour broadcast from Europe. Clearly, he was achingly frustrated at the kind of warmed-over news he was forced to broadcast to America. He longed to report live news as it was happening, to detail the intense daily drama of the European war as it unfolded before him.

In his infrequent letters to me, he expressed his exasperation. *"How can they give so little attention to a war in which thousands upon thousands of people, civilians and soldiers alike, are suffering and dying,"* he fumed. *"America will be all alone, the only country left to fight off Hitler if we don't act, and act soon."* Our obdurate head-in-the-sand attitude infuriated him.

Shuttling frequently from London to Paris to Moscow, he reveled in being immersed in the thick of the action. I worried constantly about his safety. Each Sunday, relief flooded through me as I heard yet again his deep, rather somber voice: *This is Douglas Cameron reporting to you from London.*

I recognize now, in the wisdom of maturity, that at seventeen, I was bent on acting out, in an unconscious way, the role of Galatea. Never mind that Douglas might not wish to be my Pygmalion. I had transferred to him, unknowingly, a goodly portion of the gold of my psyche.

* * *

Carter's ice Cream Shoppe was filled with laughing kids. Glenn Miller's *Moonlight Serenade* blared from the jukebox. Girls, peony pretty, with ribboned, shining hair, smiled at boys decked-out in clean cream cords and white shirts. Friday night chatter, flirting and table-hopping. Neon lights and noise and never-ending motion.

Matt and I sat in a back booth, isolated from the cheerful chaos. He reached over and took my hand, an intent look in his gray-green eyes. "Kat, you know how I've always been fascinated with airplanes?" I nodded.

"Now that I'm working, I'm thinking of taking flying lessons." His job in a grocery store had given him a little pocket change, though most of his salary went toward college tuition and books and insurance payments for his old Chevy coupe.

"It's something I've longed to do ever since I was a kid. Remember how we used to ride our bikes out to the airport to watch the planes take off?"

"I remember. You never wanted to leave, and I'd get into trouble for being late for dinner."

"Yeah, well, I talked to a fellow out there who teaches flying. It's pretty expensive, but I think I could swing it. 'Course my mother will have a fit." He shrugged his shoulders in resignation.

"She surely will," I agreed. "She'll scream bloody murder."

Mrs. Parrish was a master of manipulation and guilt; her hold on Matthew was fierce and unrelenting. I knew there would be an appalling scene. I thought it more likely than not, that his mother would dredge up some vague illness to keep her son in line. I had seen her use that trick more than once. Though he understood her dramas very well, in the end he usually deferred to his mother's wishes. It seemed to be beyond him to speak harshly to her. Gentle, unassuming Matthew. I hoped that this time he would stand his ground, even though the reality of his flying terrified me almost as much as it would her.

"I don't know how I'll convince her, Kat, but this is terribly important to me. I intend to learn to fly no matter what she says; I've always dreamed of this. I know we're going to get into the war. I just know it." He stirred restlessly. "When the time comes, I want to be ready to go into the Air Corps." He brushed back his dark mahogany hair impatiently. "Somehow I'll convince her. I'm just going to have to stick to my guns. After all, I'm almost nineteen. She's going to have to let go of me sometime. I need to do what I think is right for me." He paused. "But, gosh, it's sure going to be tough."

"Someone told me once that you have to follow your heart," I said thoughtfully. "An older friend told me that a long time ago. If that's what you really want, you'll make it." I pretended a calm I didn't feel. He was my best

27

friend; he needed my support no matter what, but his easy assumption that he would soon be a part of the slaughter raging across the sea chilled and frightened me to the core. I was deeply afraid for him.

That night as I lay in bed, my mind kept churning over Matt's plans. "My God," I thought, "nothing will be the same again. For the first time, where he's going, I can't follow. For the first time, I'll be alone." I shuddered. After twisting and turning for hours, I finally fell into a restless, troubled sleep.

Soon after Matt's announcement, I received a brief letter from Douglas, telling me that he was planning to marry an English girl, Rosalind Atherton. He had met her at a weekend party at the country estate of her father, Lord Atherton. He would be married by the time I received his letter. *In war-wracked London,* he wrote, *there's little opportunity for leisurely planning. I know you will wish me well.*

I dropped the letter to my desk and leaned my head on my arms, stunned by his news. A curious numbness spread through me and I had trouble catching my breath as an empty silence settled in my heart. Foolishly, I hadn't anticipated the grief Douglas' marrying would cause me. Indeed, I hadn't thought of such an outcome at all. I was too young and unsophisticated to have foreseen the inevitability of his doing so.

Chapter 3

"Good morning, Kathleen." My father looked up from the newspaper he was reading over a late breakfast.

"Morning, Dad." I dropped a quick kiss on his forehead.

My aunt smiled at me as she quietly stirred her coffee. "Morning, Peg. You do have a green thumb. December roses–they're so beautiful." Looking at the mixture of pink and cream roses in the middle of our golden oak table, I once again admired Aunt Peggy's unerring eye for artistic elegance. She effortlessly maintained the lovely, patrician ambiance of our home.

"That's just about the last of them, I think. It's time I cut them back." She picked up a fallen petal. "Sit down, Kathleen, and I'll get your waffle going." Carrying her empty plate, she headed for the kitchen.

Outside our French doors, I noted a sparkling day graced by a cloudless cerulean sky. The sun, streaming into a large bay window, slanted across a portrait of my mother, washing her delicate features in a golden glow. Bach's elegantly simple *Arioso* played softly on the radio.

Setting aside his paper, Dad studied me gravely. "We haven't had much chance to talk lately, dear. We seem to pass each other coming and going these days. Is everything okay with you?"

"Sure. Everything's fine. I leave pretty early most days. Lots of meetings."

"I know how busy you are. I'm really proud of you. Vice-president of your senior class, your excellent grades, all your extra-curricular activities. I miss you, dear, though I guess I'm not home much either." His eyes searched mine. "Are you enjoying yourself?"

I had been quieter than usual of late, and my preoccupation had not escaped his keen observation. I did my best to reassure him.

"I'm fine, Dad. Matt told me that he's almost ready to solo. Isn't that exciting? I admit I worry about him some–but he loves flying so much that I can't help but be thrilled for him."

My dad and I had always been close. From the time I was very young, he had read poetry to me as I sat cuddled in his lap. As I got older, he had made a point of discussing meaningful issues with me, doing his best to instill strong values and clear thinking in his daughter. Our conversations ranged from personal morality to philosophy to political issues. One topic of discussion that had come up again and again was capital punishment, an issue that brought him considerable anguish.

"There's nothing fair about the way the death penalty is handed down in this country," I remember his telling me one evening over dinner. "Wealthy people–particularly wealthy *white* people–have an enormous advantage over minorities and the poor in our system of justice. They often get totally inadequate legal aid."

"How can that be, Dad?"

"Here's an example. Just last year a young man, Martin Perez, was executed in Texas. His second court-assigned lawyer–the first one had already withdrawn form the case–didn't really investigate at all and was completely unaware of the deadline for filing a federal appeal. Believe me, that would never happen to someone who could afford a competent lawyer. The whole botched mess was appalling.

"To add to the confusion, every state has its own criteria. One can commit murder with impunity in some places and be sentenced to death in others, but, most dreadful of all, innocent people have been killed as Perez well may have been. Sometimes I feel helpless in my efforts to see that justice is served. If we default in caring for the weakest members of our society, we all become less. Remember that, Kathleen."

I had thought about his words for a moment. "In some ways it would be a worse fate to be imprisoned for the rest of your life, to be unable to escape the heinous thing you had done. No way out, no freedom, no choices–devoid of hope. Horrible!"

"Yes. There's another issue here, too;" Dad went on, "the perpetrator of the crime is given no opportunity to change, to grow, to understand the ramifications of his deed, perhaps to redeem his soul. Many feel that it's too costly to maintain a prisoner for life, but in actual fact, it's no more expensive than the legal costs engendered by appeals that can last for years. It's hard for me to understand how a supposedly civilized society can play God in this fashion. For goodness sake, Kathleen, we kill people in order to teach them not to kill. Where's the sense in that?"

On this December morning as we shared our breakfast, I sensed my dad's concern for me. I tried again to assure him that all was well. Sipping his coffee, he continued to study me. Just then, Aunt Peg brought my waffle to me. I was grateful for the interruption. Douglas' marriage was a source of sorrow that I was not inclined to share.

"Kathleen, I'm going Christmas shopping tomorrow. Do you want to come along?" Peg asked.

"I'm not sure. When are you planning to–?"

Suddenly a voice interrupted the music that was playing on the radio: *We interrupt this program to bring you a special news bulletin. The Japanese have attacked Pearl Harbor, Hawaii from the air, President Roosevelt has just announced. The attack was also made on all naval and military activities on the principal island of Oahu.*

An uneasy silence shattered our serene Sunday morning. I noticed, irrelevantly, that dust motes gleamed in the bright sunshine as they settled on the table. A pink petal dropped from a full-blossomed rose. A bird sang from somewhere far in the distance. A car went roaring by on the street. We sat speechless in our stunned surprise.

Finally, Dad found his voice. "This is it then. President Roosevelt will certainly declare war at once."

Silently, I bowed my head. I had no words, no prayers, only chaotic thoughts.

On Monday morning, December 8, 1941, the United States formally declared war against Japan.

* * *

We walked in the park on a brisk March day, our fingers entwined. Matt wore his old tan sweater, I, a bright red one. It was a lovely afternoon, ripe with the smell of earth and decaying leaf and crisp, cold air. A cool breeze lifted our hair, blowing it around our heads and sending errant papers skidding across the ground. We munched on tart apples as we loafed along and threw sticks for Charlie, who excitedly raced ahead, sniffing out tantalizing odors and digging in wet bracken, giving short barks of joy.

"Kat," Matthew turned to me. "I'm going to do it–I've decided–I'm going to join the Air Corps."

"Oh, Matt!" Horror surged through me. "Please don't. Please wait until you're drafted. You know that will come all too soon." I tried to keep the tears from my eyes. "Why do you want to rush into this terrible war? I can't bear it."

"Listen, Kathleen." Matt held me by my arm. "Just listen to me for a minute. I've had enough training that I could be a pilot fairly soon. Some Air Corps recruiters came to the campus a few weeks ago. They said that the country needs pilots–it needs them desperately. I've been thinking about this for a while." He took me in his arms and held me close, burying his face in my hair. "I know you're scared for me–hell, I'm scared, too. God knows, I don't want to leave you and Mom and my life here. Well–," he paused. "Well, that's not exactly true. I have to admit that I'm really excited. Sure, I want to stay here with you, but at the same time, I want to go. I *need* to go. Kat, it's what I've dreamed of–being a pilot. It's the chance of a lifetime. I'm

31

much more likely to be accepted into pilot training if I enlist. Who knows where they'll send me if I wait 'til they draft me." His eyes pleaded for understanding.

I struggled to be reasonable. "Matt, if they need pilots so badly, surely they'll assign you to the Air Corps. You've had six months of flying experience already. Can't you wait?"

He sighed. "Try to understand, Kat. It's something I've got to do. You know it's only a matter of time 'til I'm called. I'm already almost nineteen."

I saw the raw excitement in his eyes, his intensity tangible. I gave up any attempt to argue further. He had had more than enough of his mother's manipulation by guilt. I wanted no part of that game. I instinctively knew that he needed freedom–freedom from any demands from me, freedom to go wherever his spirit called him. I knew, too, that his acquiescence to my wishes would cost vastly more than a few months reprieve would be worth.

I forced a smile to my face, threw my arms around him and kissed him. "You'll knock their socks off, Matt. You're going to be a terrific pilot."

"Thank you, Kathleen. Thank God, you understand. I love you so much." Laughing, he waltzed me around and around on the hard packed path. "I'm giddy with relief. I'd hate to hurt you; it would be unbearable to go without your approval."

I struggled to control my expression. "You do have my blessing, Matt. I know how much flying means to you. I hate for you to go; I'm scared silly for you, but I do understand." I hugged him close. "When will you enlist?"

"Right away, before I lose my nerve." His lips brushed mine as arm-in-arm we headed back home.

* * *

I heard the telephone ring as I came into the house. I ran to answer.

"Kat, hi–it's Matt." I could sense the wide grin on his open face. "I've got a week's leave. Can you come and pick me up at the airport?"

"Sure, Matt. Terrific! What a wonderful surprise! Just tell me where to go. I'm so excited! I can't wait to see you."

"I can't wait either. I love you."

"I love you, too, Matt. See you soon."

To his great delight, Matt had been accepted into the Army Air Corps Pilot Training Program and had been shipped off immediately to Fresno, California for basic training. He was now officially a Cadet.

He had gone through a specialized course of study dealing with aerodynamics, meteorology, navigation and other such subjects, and, after many months of study and flight training, he was stationed at Marana Army Air Field, Arizona. He had written that approximately 40% of his class had washed out since basic training, adding that he had been limp with relief when he had drawn a position as a pilot. Apparently, he could just as easily have been assigned to be a navigator or a bombardier.

He had written often during those long months and had been home on leave once, but I had missed him dreadfully. I worried, too, about what the future would bring, for the war raged on relentlessly.

On the rare occasions that Mrs. Parish and I chanced to meet, I politely said hello. Her reply was invariably a brusque nod. That was the extent of our exchange and a clear bellwether of our relationship. Matthew's name never crossed our lips in all the time he had been gone.

I had been listening to the radio news assiduously for many months, struggling to keep up with the progress of the war and to catch, as often as I could, Douglas Cameron's weekly *Report from London.*

He had finally gotten his wish. He had begun with a fifteen minute broadcast every Saturday afternoon. Now that the United States was enmeshed in the war, he was finally given more airtime.

I made it my business to follow his career, but I heard nothing from him personally. To listen to his vibrant voice, his almost stoic, slow delivery filled me with an intense longing that I really couldn't understand. I knew that he was married–happily I sincerely hoped. I was years younger than he. I loved Matt dearly. Whence, then, this yearning?

* * *

I watched Matthew stride confidently across the tarmac. He wore a leather flight jacket and khaki pants, and I could see, even from a distance, that he looked trim and hard. He carried himself ramrod straight.

"Kathleen." His smile was brilliant as the morning sun.

"Matt, it's so wonderful to see you. You look terrific." I rushed into his arms. As I tipped my head back for his kiss, I saw that the planes of his face had subtly changed; his features appeared to be stronger and more sharply defined; his eyes held a new purposefulness. He was no longer the easygoing boy I had known for so long.

We spent every minute possible together those few days. The long months apart and the keen awareness of the few hours allotted us gave every word, every smile, every act an almost unbearable intensity. We knew that harrowing times were ahead, but we chose purposefully to forget them. I listened tirelessly as he talked about his training, about his instructors and his buddies, about his fears.

"You learn to fly by the seat of your pants, Kat. My instructor–you know, I wrote you about him–Mr. Whitten–he said you have to learn to be natural. It's all feel. In combat, you have to rely on your instincts. Did I write to you about the first time I tried a barrel roll? Hell, I was terrified. I was scared to death that I wouldn't be able to pull out of it. Now, I can do snap rolls, slow rolls, barrel rolls, almost without thinking. It's a thrill, Kat, such a thrill, to be able to slice through the sky like that, wheeling and diving and rolling, free as a bird."

His enthusiasm was contagious and incredibly endearing.

"You make it so real, Matt–almost, I can experience it, too. I wish I could see you fly some day. I know my heart would be in my throat, though. I'd be petrified for you."

It's really pretty safe if you know what you're doing. Actually, night flying, learning to ride a radio beam, is a lot trickier. It's a big black universe out there, and the street lights all look alike in that inky sky. It seemed an eternity the first time I tried it–sweaty palm time."

"I'm so impressed, Matt. All you've learned–and your courage." I sighed. "I love you so."

"You know I love you, too, Kathleen." He smiled. "Can I take you to lunch tomorrow? Somewhere special? The time is going so fast. Soon I'll have to head back to camp, and God knows when I'll see you again."

We held each other close as if our fierce clinging together could save our being pulled asunder by the chaotic, violent world in which we lived. Finally, Matt released me with a sigh, kissed me and said goodnight.

* * *

Fuchsia and geranium, purple and pink, rimmed the edge of the beautiful brick patio where we sat. Green umbrellas fluttered overhead. Eucalyptus stood, tall sentinels along a path that wound down to a small blue and green paradise: clear, shining water, lilies, grasses, fern leaning close as if to behold the reflected image of their beauty.

Matt pulled his chair closer to mine. "Kathleen." He brought a small wine velvet box from his pocket, opening it so that I could see a lovely diamond ring flashing in the sunlight. "Will you marry me? I love you so much. I guess I've always loved you. Would you do me the honor of being my wife?"

Matthew's proposal stunned me. "Marry you? I love you, too, Matthew,' I said slowly, "but I'm not sure I'm ready for marriage. We're both awfully young. And everything's so uncertain now."

"I know, Kat. I asked your father for his approval. He worries too that you're so young, but he said he'd give us his blessing wholeheartedly if it was what you wanted. Gosh, he said I was already very nearly a son to him. I was really touched by his faith in me."

"He loves you, Matt. I do want to marry you, but I wish we had more time. If only we could wait until we both were a little more settled and sure of ourselves. I don't question our love–that will never change–but it's all happening so fast."

"I know I'm asking a lot of you, Kathleen, but please say you will." His green eyes pleaded with mine.

I thought of the long separation that was inevitable for us. I thought of the danger he would face. "Alright, Matt. If it's what you want, I'll marry you."

His radiant face dispelled any lingering doubts. He slipped the ring on my finger and lightly kissed me. "You've made me so happy, Kat–so darned happy."

"What about your mother? She despises me. She's going to be really upset. I think she wants to keep you all to herself."

"It will be tough for her but she'll just have to get used to the idea. I'll tell her as soon as we get home." His face suddenly looked sad and drawn. "Some things she just doesn't understand."

"It's going to be awkward for me. Do you think I should go visit her after you go?

"Probably you should just leave her alone for a bit. Maybe in a week or two you could visit her."

"I'll ask her to dinner, but I doubt that she'll come." I was positive she would prove as obdurate as ever.

"I've been thinking a lot about this. I have several more months of training; then I'll get a leave before I'm sent overseas. Would you consider our getting married before I go?"

"It's such a big decision, Matt. Could I think about it for a few days?"

"Sure. I know I'm asking a lot, when here I am, on my way to shoot down German or Japanese planes. Good God, I don't even know where I'll be going, but I want this so much, Kathleen, even if we are sort of snatching at happiness."

Before he headed back to camp, I had promised to marry Matthew as soon as possible. I felt keenly that this brief time before he was sent overseas was all that we could count on. I felt that some unseen, giant hand could well snatch any future from us, willy-nilly. I consciously made the choice to share with Matthew whatever the future might bring, united body and soul.

As I had feared, Mrs. Parrish rebuffed my invitation to dinner and spurned every attempt I made to build a relationship. She pulled her dignity and her loneliness tightly around her, an armor of protection against a devastating and traitorous world. I felt sorry for her, for her fear and hurt, but I was deeply saddened that, for Matt's sake, we couldn't be friends.

Chapter 4

Images in chiaroscuro flicker across the screen of my mind; Matt and I exchanging vows, radiantly beautiful in our joy; friends and family happily celebrating our union; Matt's mother, a stiff, unsmiling presence; my dad's loving embrace as we dash to the car to begin our lives as Mr. and Mrs. Matthew Dylan Parrish.

In the two weeks we had, we saturated ourselves with each other, our bodies united, first tentatively and then passionately, in bliss. We didn't speak of Matt's imminent departure for England; to refuse to give it voice was to deny temporarily its stark reality. Our story was no different than that of untold other war time lovers; we were caught in a web of tragic circumstances over which we had scant control. We were determined to grasp what joy we could find in that fragile, fleeting time that was ours.

I drove Matt to the airfield where he would catch a flight to the east coast. He had already said his good-byes to everyone. We wanted to spend these last few priceless moments alone.

"My affairs are all in order, Kathleen. We both know my mom's damned difficult. I know you'll do the best you can with her."

"I will; I'll do my very best, I promise."

"It would be stupid to pretend that this isn't a dangerous job I'm heading for. Just remember, whatever happens, that I love you with all my heart." He kissed me and held me tight.

"I love you so much, Matt. Go with God." Determined not to cry, I managed a smile.

He tipped up my chin, looking deeply into my eyes. Then, kissing me once more, he strode through the gate without a backward glance. Tearful now, I turned away and headed back home, giving in to the sorrow that flooded my soul.

During those long months, while Matthew was fashioning himself into a fighter pilot, hop-scotching across the country to various Army bases as he learned his lethal trade, I had buried myself in my studies at UCLA, the Los Angeles campus for the University of California. I drove daily over the ridge of mountains in Matt's old coupe to the huge, impersonal campus in Westwood. When I had insisted that I wanted to live at home, Dad was hard put to understand. He had enjoyed his college days to the full and he thought that I was being cheated out of an important facet of life if I didn't go to the University of Southern California, join a sorority, and live the life of a carefree college coed. In his heart, he knew that I could not return to being that innocent girl I had once been, but his dream for me died hard.

My life had taken on a mature cast that colored all my thoughts and activities. The seriousness of Matthew's circumstances and the obvious scarcity of healthy young males on campus, a constant reminder of the deadly hell that engulfed the globe, precluded any such lighthearted diversion for me. I tried to lose myself in my studies. I worked hard and seldom took part in any social activities.

After our wedding, I returned to my classes. I had just finished my second year of college when I found that I was pregnant. Our wedding and honeymoon in early April seemed by now almost a dream. We had had so little time together after his enlistment that the reality that was Matthew seemed clouded and uncertain. I looked at the pictures on my desk; Matthew in his Air Corps uniform, so young, so vulnerable, so serious looking; I studied our wedding portrait; our smooth faces glowed with innocent joy.

With some difficulty, I tried to grasp the fact that in a short time I would give birth to a small bundle of humanity seeded and fashioned by our love. I wrote immediately to Matt, hoping he would be as delighted as I was–and I truly was delighted even though the prospects of our having a child seemed strangely unreal.

As was my habit, daily I closely followed the news. I was filled with joy and a rare optimism the day I heard Douglas reading a news bulletin on the radio:

Special Report From London: This is Douglas Cameron speaking. Under the Command of General Eisenhower, Allied Forces supported by strong naval and Air forces began landing Allied troops this morning on the northern coast of France.

After weary months, the invasion of Europe had finally begun. The good news encouraged my hopes that this worldwide insanity could not go on much longer. On the other hand, I feared that the danger factor for Matthew had risen considerably.

Letters from the front were always slow. Sometimes weeks went by and then, suddenly, two or three would arrive in close succession. The information Matt could send was very limited; generally it was heavily censored. I knew he was first stationed in England at Thruxton. I knew that after the liberation of Paris, he had moved to Laon, France where he was supplying air support for Allied land forces. I knew that his missions were frequent and dangerous, his goal, to smash railroad yards, take out bridges, destroy transportation systems. Much he could not tell me; much I pieced together from the newsreels I saw at the local theater and from radio and newspaper reports. I knew that his plane was a P-47, a Thunderbolt, the notorious 'jug' that not only bombed bridges and smashed railways, but often engaged in vicious dog fights with the enemy, wheeling and spinning and attacking far above the earth, either to come home in glory or to plummet swiftly to disaster.

I prayed for him every day, all the time questioning why God should answer my supplications rather than those of the many German wives and mothers who prayed as I did. I found it incredibly naïve to believe that God was somehow on 'our side'. I supposed that He must be righteously outraged at us all. We had crushed and despoiled the gift of life that He had given us. We had systematically destroyed huge portions of His beautiful earth. Yet, in my helplessness, I prayed.

Matthew's answer to the news of my pregnancy was a very long time in coming. His letter was filled with euphoric plans for the future but he had added a disquieting addendum:

> *I am so very thrilled that words can't begin to express my joy. I want you to know that, should something happen to me, I have willed to you the annuity my Grandmother Parrish left me. It will be enough that you can get along okay.*
>
> *This war seems endless; the cost in lives is staggering. Pray that it will soon end. You are my life. God bless you.*
>
>

With utmost love,
Matt
>

His words seemed uncharacteristically somber. My heart ached for my dearest love. I knew that in spite of my best imaginative efforts, I had no real concept of the hell that he endured day after day as he fought his lethal battles for supremacy of the sky. I prayed that he might survive this malevolent maelstrom. I prayed that he might return soon to my arms.

Through those long months, I attempted conscientiously to shape a relationship with Mrs. Parrish, who, self-involved as ever, displayed no discernible interest in her unborn grandchild. I regularly called to see if I could help her in any way, to tell her whatever I could of her son, to make some effort to lighten her loneliness, but she bitterly hung on to her formidable disapproval of me. It was an uphill battle, but I ignored her unpleasantness as best I could for Matt's sake.

* * *

One gloomy morning, a loaf of bread in hand, I rang her doorbell.

"Yes, Kathleen?" As the door opened a few scant inches, Matthew's mother peered suspiciously through the crack.

"Hello, Mother Parrish." I had chosen this stiff and formal form of address because she had never suggested any other I might call her. I knew better than to attempt a more intimate name without invitation.

"I brought you some bread that Aunt Peg made. Could I come in for a minute?" With reluctance, she opened the door wider and allowed me entry.

"I'm going to the grocery for a few things," I said. "Can I pick anything up for you?"

"Maybe a pound of margarine if you can find it, and there are a couple of other things. I'll get my list." She trudged off to the kitchen, leaving me standing inhospitably in the hallway.

"The news is certainly more encouraging these last weeks." I ventured. "Maybe now that our troops are on European soil, the war will be winding down. Do you suppose so?"

"Humph. Who knows?" She frowned. "I doubt it. It will never be the same as it used to be anyway. Matthew should never have been a pilot. He wouldn't be in such danger if you hadn't encouraged him to fly; he would've dropped the whole idea if you had asked him to," she whined.

Her unfair judgment hurt, but I brushed it aside. Anger wouldn't help. Her attempt to place blame on me for Matt's flying was an old song, sung again and again.

"And now you're having a brat," she continued. "Just don't expect me to help you take care of it. You young folks think of no one but yourselves. No one cares what I think or pays any attention to me. I might as well not exist."

Lost in self-pity, she seemed to forget that her polite, agreeable son had spent years catering to her whims. She also conveniently ignored the fact that the draft would have snatched him up willy-nilly anyway, catapulting him into horrible danger no matter where he served. She had to have someone to blame; I filled the bill perfectly.

I had learned early that the least said, the better. "Well, I have to go. I'll get the margarine for you, Mother Parish."

In unsmiling silence she shut the door.

* * *

"Go on, little one." A voice, the sweetest, most dulcet I have ever heard, pierced through my exhausted state. "Your mother will love you very much."

I knew that these words came from some celestial Being, some spiritual

40

entity not of this world. I had been in labor for seven long straining hours; my mind was tired but clear. Moments later, to my great relief, on a cold morning in early January, Dylan Catherine Parrish was born.

This sweet miracle, Dylan, filled my soul, stretching it wider than the sky. Ah, Matt, I thought, if only you could be here to see your darling daughter. She's beautiful beyond belief.

I longed to share with him the angelic voice I had heard so clearly; I longed to see his eyes light up as he held his daughter in his arms, to watch his face as he gazed at her for the first time. I sighed for the loss of shared moments–no hand to cling to, no arms to hold me, no words of love. This sacred event had been despoiled by the cruel imperatives of war.

My father and Aunt Peggy were ecstatic. They fussed over me, bundled me home to bed, and adamantly insisted that I should rest. First granddaughter; first niece; first in a new generation of Currans. Their pride was palpable.

Aunt Peg had insisted on furnishing and decorating the baby's room. With her usual impeccable taste, she had created a cheerful, pale yellow haven. A white wicker chest of drawers, a wicker rocking chair for me, a wicker bassinet, a sturdy white crib were perfection against the sunny walls. Sheer curtains of white and a muted hooked rug completed the room. At first, I insisted that Dylan sleep in her bassinet in my room during the night. She could enjoy her own room during the daylight hours.

I don't know what suddenly woke me a few weeks after her birth, but as I tried to orient myself, struggling to wake up, I saw a shadowy figure standing by her crib. As I stared, perplexed by this intrusion, I saw that a man wearing a flight jacket and a cap leaned over her. I caught my breath. Just as I was about to scream, he turned. As he faced me, I saw that it was Matthew. I could see him only dimly. His whole body seemed to be shrouded in a cloud. He looked pale, almost translucent. "Matthew," I cried. He said nothing. He just looked at me with great love, gave me a brilliant smile, and, touching the bill of his cap in farewell, he vanished.

No one had to tell me that he had died. I understood with every fiber of my being. He had held the energy of his spirit together long enough to see his daughter and to bid me farewell: his last good-bye, poignant and sad and infinitely devastating.

By the time that unholy telegram arrived, despair had already grabbed at my gut and torn at my heart. It confirmed for Dad and Aunt Peg, however, that I was not the victim of post-birth delusion.

Several weeks later I received a letter from First Lieutenant James Tolliver:

January 26, 1945
Dear Kathleen,

I hope you don't mind my using your first name, but Matt talked about you so much that I feel like I know you. I was his pal. He was a good guy and a hell of a pilot. I went out on the same run with him that night. We were on a strafing run on a German airfield. We had earlier tangled with six bandits and shot down four or five. Then, as we approached the airfield, I saw Matt's plane go into a tailspin. It took a hit from antiaircraft flak. I saw him go down in flame. I can't tell you how helpless I felt. I feel damned guilty that I couldn't protect my buddy. He was a gutsy guy. I thought you would want to know.

Yours,
Jim Tolliver

Sighing, I set the letter aside. Knowing the circumstances of Matt's death didn't make it any easier. I couldn't get the horrifying image of his plane, spinning out of control and smashing into the ground in flames, out of my mind. Nonetheless, I was grateful to First Lieutenant Tolliver. It was comforting to know that Matt had had a comrade who cared for him, who had perhaps shed a tear and wished him *bon voyage* when his plane, *Beau Chat*, had failed to return to the airfield. I said a prayer for Lieutenant Tolliver, asking that he might come safely home to his loved ones.

After that night when Matthew had appeared in my bedroom, a heavy silence, vast and oppressive, blanketed my psyche. My every impulse was to close down, to shut out the fear, the rage, the sorrow that flooded my soul. The whole world had become gray and shadowy. Depression battled for control of my mind. Dylan, the fragile reed to which I clung, was my only anchor to reality. Her small being became the lodestar of my existence. Because of her, I fiercely fought against the desolation and immobility that daily threatened me. Gradually, a faint spark intruded into my numbness, telling me that for her sake I must survive.

Mother Parrish, true to form, had no words of sympathy for me though I tried to extend them to her. I had gone over to her house several weeks after Matt's death to give her some pictures taken a few years earlier She looked through them, pointedly returning those that included me. She again berated me that her son had died because I had encouraged him to become a pilot. Her hatefulness had in no way diminished.

"I'm moving," she snapped. I'm selling the house as quickly as I can and am going to live with a cousin in Texas. I want no part of this place." Her words were hard. "There's nothing here for me. Now that my son has been stolen from me, I'll go. It's your fault, Kathleen. He should have listened to me."

I was suddenly enraged by her unjust attack. I no longer tried to contain my anger at her snide remarks.

"How dare you say that to me?" I snapped. "I've listened to you blame me all these months." My voice rose in frustration. "Go to Texas–go to Hell–I don't care where you go. All you can think about is yourself."

Turning on my heel and slamming the door in anger, I fled home.

In a few months, she was gone. I never saw her again. I was heartily sorry later for my outburst. She undoubtedly deserved it; yet I knew that harsh words were never a solution, no matter the provocation.

For Matthew's sake, through the years I regularly sent her pictures of Dylan, the grandchild she saw only once. I was relieved that she was no longer a part of my life.

In time, a very long time, an inner strength began to take root and eventually it grew to be a viable and sustainable force. I found a stability within that allowed me to turn my attention, at last, away from my sorrow to the pressing issue of creating a meaningful, new life for my daughter and myself.

Chapter 5

One crisp fall day in 1951, I drove to the University of Southern California to do some research for an article I was considering. I had been writing for various magazines for several years—sometimes on assignment, sometimes on whatever caught my fancy. Along with the annuity that Matthew had left me, I managed to make a comfortable living for Dylan and myself.

I decided to look into a series on post-war college life. Campuses were overflowing with a glut of returned veterans, eager to take advantage of the GI Bill. A steadily increasing number of women, intent either on finding a prospective mate or on earning a college degree, added to the burgeoning college population. I had already interviewed the Dean of Men, the Director of Housing and various students and dorm personnel. A gravely proud young lady in the required costume of sweater, skirt, saddle shoes and bobby socks had taken me on a tour of inspection of USC's brand new dorm, home to two hundred coeds.

I had a couple of hours to wait for my appointment with the Dean of Women. As I meandered along, enjoying the lovely flowers and trees and listening to the laughing, chattering students, I decided to walk over to Exposition Park. Desultorily strolling through the rose gardens, I noticed a number of people going into the Art Museum. Impulsively, I decided to follow them.

The paintings on exhibition took my breath away. I had never seen anything comparable. They were so achingly vibrant and alive that they seemed to draw me right into their swirling intensity, drowning me in pulsating seas of blues and greens and yellow and ochre. Vincent van Gogh.[1] I had heard of him; I had seen photographs of his work. I was as knowledgeable about art as most, I suppose, but none of my past experiences had prepared me for the impact these paintings had. I was literally stunned.

I stood transfixed in front of *Starry Nights*.

"Remarkable work, isn't it?" A man's voice pierced my attention.

"Indeed it is. I've never seen anything like it. I'm completely awed."

---

[1] The first exhibition of Vincent van Gogh's work, an exhibition of 155 paintings and drawings, loaned by the Van Gogh Foundation in Amsterdam, actually took place in 1958-59 at the Los Angeles County Museum of History, Science and Art in Exposition Park. It lasted for six weeks with an attendance of 120,000.

"Are you an art student?"

I turned to study him. Moderate height, short curly brown hair that made a halo around his head. He wore a fisherman's sweater and brown corduroy trousers.

"No, I'm not. These paintings are making me wish I were."

"Well, maybe you should give it a try– painting, I mean. You don't have to go to school, you know." He paused and held out his hand. "I'm Gentry."

His silver blue eyes held a softness unusual in a man. He had an innocent, unassuming quality. It was not my habit to strike up conversations with strange men, but I instinctively knew that there was no harm in him.

"My name is Kathleen–Kathleen Parrish. Do you paint?"

"Yes, I paint some." He studied me seriously for a moment. "Look, would you have a cup of coffee with me?"

"I have an appointment at USC in a few minutes. I'm sorry, I'd really like to talk to you about painting." I was surprised to find that I felt mildly disappointed.

"How long will your appointment last?"

"Well, I should be free by about 4:00." I looked at my watch. "I really have to go now."

"How about meeting me at the campus cafeteria when you're finished? I don't mind waiting."

Over coffee, Gentry convinced me that I should give painting a try. He helped himself to a page from my notebook and scribbled on it.

"Here. These are the things you'll need to get a start. Don't expect too much at first. Just get a feel of working with the colors and the way the paint goes on." He handed me a sizable list.

I looked at it with dismay. "Wow! It's a little intimidating."

Impulsively he reached over, took the list from my hand and with a leprechaun grin tore it in two. "Forget the list. Why don't we go together to get this stuff? I'd enjoy helping you. Is that okay with you?"

"I'd be grateful. I feel completely out of my depth."

"Done," he said. "Why don't we meet at that new art store in Westwood tomorrow at ten; do you know the one I mean?" I nodded. "Is that convenient for you?"

"Perfect"

That day I found a new friend and a new passion.

At that time, I still lived in my childhood home with Dad and Aunt Peg. Of course, they doted on Dylan and spoiled her badly. She was a sunny child, given to laughter and song. She had inherited her father's eyes, though hers were a mossy green, along with his red hair, considerably lighter and brighter than his.

Animals, large and small, fascinated her. I found her one day, studying a spider spinning a web on a low section of our huge camellia bush. Another time, she spent half and hour on her knees gravely inspecting a colony of ants coming and going. For her fourth birthday, her granddad–Granda to her–presented a ginger kitten to her. Charlie, our old dog, had died the previous winter. To our surprise, she held the kitten gently and stroked it carefully. She seemed to know without our telling her that this small creature needed to be treated with love and care. She quickly named him Sunny.

Living in my childhood home was a very happy arrangement for me. Thanks to Dad and Peg, Dylan and I had a loving family environment. At first I really needed their support, especially the first couple of years. Not all war widows were so fortunate. I was sometimes lonely; I missed Matthew dreadfully, but I was never required to be completely on my own.

I tried to convince Peg that we should get a baby-sitter for those times that I needed to be away, but she insisted that she wanted to look after Dylan herself when I wasn't there. Thanks to my aunt, I was able to make a slow beginning at freelance writing, free from guilt or worry.

Occasionally I saw several friends from high school and college, but on the whole I chose to stay at home when I wasn't working. My life with its attendant responsibilities seemed to be out of sync with their interests. I felt that I was years older than they–that we had very little in common anymore.

The one exception was Anne Wilder, a girl I had met in an English Lit class at UCLA. She was a bit older than I–a vivid copper-haired duchess not five feet tall who managed to pack considerable dignity into her diminutive stature. She had a mighty temper when she felt people were taking advantage of those less fortunate than she. On the whole, she was excellent company and a trusted confidante. I enjoyed her immensely.

I called her after my shopping foray with Gentry.

"Guess what, Annie? I'm going to start painting."

"You're *what*? I thought writing was your first love, with music a distant second."

"Well, I just added a new love. Have you seen the Van Gogh show at the Art Museum?"

"No, I don't know anything about it."

"I was absolutely carried away by his work. You really should see it. In fact, I'll go with you if you like. I'd like to see it again to see if it has the same impact the second time."

"Hey, sounds good to me."

"By the way, I met a very interesting fellow there. He helped me buy

47

some paints and canvases and stuff."

"You aren't wasting any time in getting started with this painting business, are you? More important, tell me about this guy," she demanded.

"There isn't much to tell. I met him; I liked him; he encouraged me to try painting. He's a painter himself. I really don't know much about him. His name is Gentry. That seems to be his only name; just Gentry."

"Hmm–interesting–what does he look like?"

"Well, he's not particularly handsome; he's maybe five foot eight–has a crop of curly brown hair and silvery eyes. He's very casual and he has a very expressive face and funny smile. He has an almost foolish look about him." I paused. "That's not a very kind thing to say, I guess. I'm not doing him justice; he's a thoroughly nice guy."

"If you're sure he's okay, I'm all for it. You really need to get out more. You're practically a hermit." Annie couldn't believe that I didn't want to find someone to socialize with.

"Not really, Anne. I have more freedom to come and go than most mothers. I just don't enjoy the stuff I see others doing. I'm not a party type. The few times I have gone out with someone, I've thought that I'd have had a better time if I'd stayed at home with Dylan."

"I understand. But a man in your life couldn't hurt, could it?"

"I suppose not. We'll see."

"Keep me posted, Kathleen," she said as she hung up the phone.

My first attempts at painting were disastrous. They looked very much like the work of an eight-year-old child. I had no idea how to mix colors or to put them on canvas. They were sterile, cramped, muddy pieces that I quickly painted over. All in all, they were embarrassing.

Gentry called every few days to offer encouragement.

"They're terrible, Gentry; downright terrible," I wailed.

"Don't give up, Kathleen. You have to give this a fair chance."

"Ugh, it's hopeless. Why am I bothering?"

"Because you would be more bothered if you quit," he replied simply.

With his encouragement, I persisted and soon came to understand something of the subtleties of painting. In spite of the impact of Van Gogh's work, I was not much interested in doing landscapes or buildings or still lives. The human face drew me, and the human form. I began to see, as I learned to observe more closely, that all faces had their own kind of beauty.

Gentry invited me to see his work. He lived in a big loft that was sparsely furnished. A bed, a dresser, a couch, a chair, a few tables and his easel and worktable were grouped in areas surrounded by paintings and lots of empty space. The furniture was upholstered in a camel color and the only other colors were the wine Oriental rug that defined the sitting area and touches of cobalt blue in the few well-chosen accessories. There was no clutter. The huge room was harmonious and pleasing.

His paintings seemed to me to be a mixture of fantasy and personal symbolism, with wild animals depicted in many of them. I didn't know enough to ask intelligent questions but I liked them immensely. The light in his studio was soft and pellucid, giving the room an almost otherworldly feel, and somehow he had managed to capture that same ethereal light in his paintings.

Gentry proved to be very different from anyone I knew. He was an enigma to me. He had a special quality that fascinated me but I couldn't quite define what made him so unique.

After a few months of struggle, I gave in to his request to see my work though I was nervous about showing him my beginner's efforts.

He silently studied my few paintings, holding them, one by one, to the light. I could read nothing from the expression on his usually mobile face. *Please, Gentry, say something,* I thought nervously. *Just say what you think and get it over with.*

After a long silence, he turned to me. "They show promise, Kathleen. You seem to have a good sense of color and composition."

I released the breath that I hadn't realized I had been holding. Relief washed through me.

"They're not too bad?" I surprised myself at how much I cared that he should validate my insignificant beginnings.

"No, not too bad." He paused. "You know, it takes time to develop a true vision."

"Vision! I'm just struggling to put paint on canvas in an intelligent way."

"Kathleen, of course technique is important. It takes a lot of time to learn how to use your brushes and your paint well, how to apply brush strokes in a meaningful way. But never, never lose sight of the fact that you must look beyond the facade of whatever you're painting. If you can't see the essence of your subject–if you don't look past the outer covering to the core within–your work will always be very ordinary."

"I think I understand what you're saying, Gentry, but right now it's my technique that needs shoring up. I'm in way over my head. Maybe I should take a few lessons?"

He didn't immediately answer. He sat silently for moments–uncomfortable moments for me. He seemed to have withdrawn his attention so completely that he was hardly present in the room. Then, as if he had shifted some inner gear, his face regained its usual expressiveness.

"I don't think it would be a good idea. For you, I think formal training would be a mistake. You should spend as much time as you can drawing–that would help you a lot–but experience and close observation are the only real teachers. Why don't you just keep on as you're doing for a while? You can always change your mind."

"Well, all right. I'll soldier on for the time being." I stood up. "Come on, let's go find Dylan and walk down to the drug store for some ice cream."

One night as I sat reading in the living room, my father, sartorially splendid, strolled in. I had always admired his excellent taste and fastidious grooming.

"Hi, Dad. You're on your way out? You're looking very, very sharp."

He was looking especially handsome, his well-tailored blue suit setting off his silver hair, a broad smile on his face.

"I'm taking Elizabeth to dinner tonight. We're going to Scandia's. That's one of her favorite restaurants."

"Mmm–mine, too."

My father had dated various women over the years. This was the first time he had centered his attention on one person for any length of time. Elizabeth Sheridan had been widowed a few years before. She was a tall, handsome woman with well-defined cheekbones and a wide mouth given to smiling. Her short dark hair was laced with silver. A few months before, I had invited her to dinner at my dad's request. I knew then that he must be very attracted to her.

"That should be fun. I'm sure she'll enjoy it." I regarded him thoughtfully. "You seem to be seeing a lot of her lately. She's a lovely person. I like her."

He hesitated a moment. "I'm going to ask her to marry me. I hope you approve. I've been alone for a long time now. Elizabeth is a wonderful lady and I think we could be happy together." He looked at me anxiously. "How do you feel about my getting married again?"

I threw my arms around him and gave him a hug. "I think it's absolutely great, Dad. I couldn't be happier for you. You deserve a wonderful wife. After dinner, why don't you bring her back to the house for a glass of champagne? I really want to get to know her better."

A few months later, Dad and Elizabeth were married in a quiet, private ceremony. Both had urged me to continue to make my home with them. I knew, though, that it was time for me to find a place of my own. Aunt Peggy and Dad and I talked it over.

"Well, I wish I could convince you that we'd love to go on here just as we've been doing. Elizabeth loves all of you," my father argued.

"No, Dad, I don't think that's a good idea. You need space for the two of you to begin life together alone. Anyway, it's about time I have my own home. I'd like to buy one."

I had been thinking about that possibility for some time.

"Peg, I'd love for you to come with me. We could work something out. We don't need anything this large. What do you think?"

"I'd like that, Kathleen."

She turned to Dad. "Steve, you've been so very generous to me–insisting on a monthly salary along with providing this beautiful home for me all these years. Thanks to you, I have a fair amount of money saved. I'd like to join forces with Kathleen and–maybe this sounds crazy–but I'd dearly love to go to college."

"Oh, Peg, have you held back for me all these years? I feel so guilty."

It had never occurred to me that Peggy, so self-sufficient and contained, might have other dreams for herself, that perhaps she had sacrificed considerably to look after first me and then Dylan. I was appalled at my lack of sensitivity.

"No, no," she hastened to assure me. "This is something that I've just recently thought of. I wouldn't have traded being here for you and Dylan for anything in the world. You are the dearest of dear to me, the daughter I never had. Now that Dylan's a little older though and you're well established in your work, I'm sure we could arrange something that would work out for both of us."

Dad put his hand on mine. "Kathleen, I want to do something for you. Don't argue, please. I've never given you a wedding present as I would have if Matthew had returned. Now I'd like to help you find a home and put a down payment on it for you. I can easily afford it."

"Dad,"–I felt tears come to my eyes–"that would be wonderful. Thank you so much."

"My friend Barney will find you something–just leave it to me."

Just before Dad and Elizabeth got married, Peg, Dylan and I moved into our new home. Barney had found us a comfortable ranch style house with wood siding just a few blocks from my childhood haven. It was perfect for the three of us.

Gentry and I slipped into a very comfortable relationship. We haunted art galleries and antique shops. We frequently went to the theater or to some musical event. His quiet, puckish charm made every adventure magical, as his quicksilver mind slipped back and forth from seeing the humor in life to contemplative silence.

We walked out of the theater one night into a light, fresh-smelling rain.

We had just seen *An American in Paris.* Both of us had delighted in Gershwin's music. We had been awed by the muscular grace Gene Kelley had displayed in the ballet scene.

As we walked along, Gentry suddenly disappeared from my side. Soon he was skipping along the curb in a pseudo *Singing in the Rain* style, his impish face wreathed in smiles.

"How'm I doing?" he asked. "Good as Gene?" It bothered him not the slightest that a few pedestrians turned and stared at him.

"Sensational," I laughed. "But right now, I'd rather have something to eat than a dance recital, though you *are* awesome."

We ducked into our favorite Italian restaurant, laughing and shaking drops of rain from our coats.

"Ah, you are wet," Alfredo smiled. "I have just the table for you by the fire." He seated us with his usual flourish.

"Thanks, Alfredo. We just want some dessert and wine, please."

"Ah, the zabaglione is perfect tonight, Signor Gentry. As beautiful and fresh as the Signora."

Gentry grinned at his lavish expressiveness. "How about it, Kathleen? Does that suit you?"

"Hmm–perfect. With a glass of Chianti."

As we sipped our wine, I lifted my eyes to meet Gentry's. I studied him a moment in silence.

"I've known you for almost a year, Gentry. I enjoy your company immensely, but I don't think I understand you any better now than I did when we first met."

"In what way do you not understand, Kathleen?" he asked quietly

"Well, for one thing–you never mention any family–anything about your background."

"I have no family–my mother and father died a few years apart some time ago. I do have an aunt and two uncles and several cousins who live in the area. They're very friendly, likable folk but in the main part I choose to disengage myself from their lives."

"But why? Don't you get lonely?" I couldn't imagine deliberately separating myself from Dylan or any other of my family.

His silvery eyes studied me with interest "No. I'm really quite solitary. I like being alone–in fact, I need to be alone much of the time."

"You seem very different from most people I know. I'm being impossibly inquisitive, but do you mind telling me why? Why you need to be alone, why you've disengaged from your family?"

"Well–that's really two questions. I guess the simplest way to answer is that I'm more drawn to interior reality than to the consensus reality that shapes our world. In order to have an interior life, you need time alone–and you have to cut down on outside distractions." He sat quietly for a moment. "It takes time and commitment and silence to develop the faint whisperings of the soul. I've pretty much cut myself off from relationships so that I can minimize distractions. The other reason is more subtle; it's harder to explain."

"Oh, please try. I'd like to understand." I sensed a deep, rich vein running through Gentry that set him apart from any others I knew. He never wasted words, he never complained or explained, he never gossiped or judged. He seemed to be supremely comfortable with himself and his life.

"Most people don't realize it, but we are in great measure defined by others' expectations of us," he finally said. "Those expectations act as a suppressant to growth and change. Families and old friends, having known us for so long, have firm convictions about who we are–who we *should* be–that are almost cast in stone. Those perceptions limit us; they tend to bind rather than to free."

"I don't understand. That seems a bit hard-hearted and I know you're the most loving person I've ever met. I must be missing something."

"It's hard to explain in a way that makes sense. Who we are is not a son or a daughter–a sister, a brother. Who we are is much more magnificent than that. Others' perceptions, unless we are very strongly centered, constitute a gentle tyranny; they keep us ordinary, keep us bound to the image that they have of us. Does that make any sense?"

"Yes, I think so. I can just catch a glimpse of what you're driving at. You're different because you're focused primarily in an inner reality unknown to most people. Is that correct? And to be focused in that place you can't allow the distractions that most of us depend on to shape our lives. I sense that you have a solid core that is non-existent in most people. It's most appealing."

"Thank you, Kathleen. Let me explain further. Society is engaged in an unspoken conspiracy. One of its primary functions is to keep us asleep, unaware. It hasn't much use for the true original–the eccentric, the free thinker, the non-conformist. It's generally leery of genuinely creative people–artists, musicians, writers–anyone who dares to wander outside the fold of conventional wisdom. All of these originals are a threat to its structure. Society is terrified of people like that, and in subtle ways it undermines their very existence. That's why it conspires to kill its saints and its prophets. It kills its very best."

I noted the passion that flared in his silver eyes. "Why have we not talked about any of this before? These ideas clearly mean a lot to you. Did you think I wouldn't be able to understand?"

"Oh, no–I knew you'd understand. I was just waiting for you to ask. I don't discuss such things arbitrarily." He searched my face. "Did you think that my approaching you at the Art Museum was coincidence?"

I nodded.

"There's no such thing as coincidence, Kathleen. Something told me to strike up a conversation with you. I spoke to you that day because I was prompted to."

"Prompted by what?" I was fascinated by his words.

"By my inner voice"

"Hmm–that's interesting." A quick vision of Douglas Cameron, of his intense blue eyes holding mine, flashed through my mind. "A friend from long ago talked to me about an inner voice; he said that I should listen carefully to the voice of my spirit. I was very young and didn't quite understand him."

"He probably sensed the same thing about you that I sense."

I looked at him questioningly. "What? What's that?"

"That you're one of the few, Kathleen, who has the potential to encounter God directly. There aren't many who have any desire to do so."

"Me?" I looked at him in astonishment.

I couldn't come to grips with what he said. My mind flashed back to the book about Christian saints that Douglas had sent me long ago. I remembered my dual fascination and repulsion back then. I wasn't sure I had any wish even now for such a seemingly esoteric experience. I didn't consider myself to be the least bit religious. I was at a loss to formulate the questions that tumbled around in my head.

"Gentry, your view of me is intriguing; it's not without its charm, but it's pretty intimidating, as well. To tell the truth, it scares hell out of me. I'm not even sure that I understand what you're talking about when you refer to a direct encounter with God."

"For right now, just let it be, Kathleen. All of it will unfold in its own time. Eventually, you'll understand. I'm just sort of preparing the way."

I stared at him.

"Where did you learn all of these things? How do you know so much? I guess what I'm really asking is, how did you become the person you are?"

Gentry threw back his head and laughed. "There's no simple answer to that. But since you asked: I am the ever-changing product of the daily life I live, as is every person alive. Everyone we meet, every experience we have, every thought we think shapes us into what we are in this present moment, and at the same time it gives a glimpse of what we may become. I've had almost forty years of experiencing life. Not one part is inconsequential. This is the result. This is who I've become. I've had several teachers along the way, good teachers–and I honor them. There's an old saying: 'When the student is ready, the teacher will appear.' I think you're ready."

"And you're my teacher?"

"Everyone is your teacher, Kathleen. You need to understand that. You learn from everyone and everything. I can only help you along the way. I think that's why I became a part of your life at this particular time."

"A very welcome part, Gentry, but right now I feel as if the ground is shifting under my feet so fast that I can't quite grab a foot hold."

"Don't dwell on it. Just let go for the time being. Those who are ready to awaken *will* awaken. You can count on that."

He stood up from the table and smiled as he helped me from my chair.

As we headed for the door, he added, "One more thing–just remember, God's timing is impeccable."

Chapter 6

"Come on, Kathleen. Say you'll go."

My friend Anne called, begging me to consider joining her and her long-time companion, Mark, for an evening of dinner and dancing. She thought I should get acquainted with Mark's friend, a new teacher at City College.

Annie and Mark had been going steady, as we used to term it, for several years. Anne once told me that she wasn't ready for a life-long commitment, that maybe she never would be. I found this a bit surprising, given the strong social impetus to marry, but Annie enjoyed being a rebel.

I groped for an excuse. "I don't know–I really don't like the idea of dates, particularly blind dates."

Matthew had been my steady beau from high school all the way to marriage. I had had little experience with dating. To me, going out with an unknown man was as foolhardy as stepping into a field of land mines. I rarely enjoyed myself those times that I gave in to well-meaning friends' blandishments that I meet George or Jimmy or Jerry, the lawyer or Bill, the doctor.

"I'm not sure I want to," I finally said.

"It'll do you good. You need to meet people, get out more. Russ is an interesting guy–good looking, too. He teaches geology. I know you'll like him," Anne cajoled.

With considerable reluctance, I finally agreed.

Annie turned out to be right. I did like him. I liked him a lot. He was charming and affable and he was exceptionally smooth on the dance floor. I studied his face as we twirled around the crowded, dimly lit room. Russell had rather long, light brown hair that kept falling over his forehead, and he had a disarming cleft in his chin, giving him an almost rakish look. The admiration that glowed in his dark brown eyes as he looked down at me was surprisingly erotic. It had been a very long time since I had seen that look in masculine eyes. *Let's keep it light here,* I admonished myself. *You don't know this man and you certainly don't need any problems in your life. Just go slow.*

It felt dangerously alluring to have strong arms hold me close. Inwardly, I fought against the realization that I might well be smitten. As women have always been able to sense since time immemorial, I knew that he was as attracted to me as I to him.

The next day, he called to thank me and to tell me how much he had enjoyed our evening together.

"Could I interest you in going with me to Santa Monica on Saturday afternoon–just sit and watch the sunset, and then go somewhere for dinner, somewhere casual?" he asked.

"That sounds great. I haven't done anything like that in a very long time."

"Good. I'll pick you up at about 3:30. I'm looking forward to it."

"Me, too," I said, smiling as I hung up the phone.

I admonished myself again to let this relationship develop slowly. I knew nothing at all about Russell. I needed to proceed with some semblance of intelligence. I didn't need hormonal exigency to rush me into actions I might later regret.

Russell Reed turned out to be an intelligent, interesting companion. As we watched the sun glistening on the diamante sea, we chatted easily about many things. Hired by various oil companies, he had traveled extensively over the years. As a change of pace, he had decided to teach for a year, filling in for a professor who was taking a sabbatical.

"I'm kind of a wanderer," he informed me. "I like to see new things, go to places I've never been. The more exotic they are, the better I like them." He brushed his hair off his forehead, a gesture I was to find habitual to him. "I think that's why I got into geology. An uncle of mine was a geologist. He was able to travel all over the world and get paid for it. That really got my attention. I guess I'm not your typical rock hound. I'm more interested in traveling to new places than I am in geological formations. Do you like to travel, Kathleen?" He leaned back on the blanket he had thoughtfully provided.

"Mmm–I don't really know. I've not had much opportunity. I've never been off this continent. I've been in Mexico, and my parents and I took a trip through western Canada when I was young; that's about it. One year we drove across the country to the east coast–a long, long trip to a child. Oh, I've had to travel some in my work–New York, Chicago, Washington D.C.–but I resist leaving Dylan for any length of time." I looked thoughtfully out at the dazzling sky, awash with watercolor hues of pink and lavender and apricot. "It would be fun to see Paris and Rome, the English countryside, London. I think I'm something of an Anglophile."

"Ah, then you'd love visiting there; Ireland, too. Aren't your roots there?" I nodded in assent. "I'd love to be able to show you."

I sighed. "That would be nice. Maybe someday I'll have a chance to go abroad. I'd like to see first hand all that magnificent art–and the architecture, too. Right now though, I have my hands full raising Dylan and making a living."

I again silently reminded myself to be cautious. I didn't need complications in my full and satisfying life. Dylan was my main responsibility; her welfare must come first for many years to come. And I was content, wasn't I?

As the horizon slowly swallowed the sun, we sat huddled together against the suddenly cold wind coming off the ocean. Silently we watched the ever-deepening kaleidoscope of colors in the rapidly darkening sky.

"Every time I'm out at this time of evening," I murmured, "Wordsworth's lines come to me:

It is a beauteous evening, calm and free,
The holy time is quiet as a Nun
Breathless with adoration; the broad sun
Is sinking down in its tranquility;
The gentleness of heaven broods o'er the Sea...

I paused. "It really is a very holy time, isn't it?"

"It's certainly beautiful." Russ turned toward me. "As you are, Kathleen–particularly with that radiant look you have right now."

Suddenly he jumped up, pulling me up with him. "It's getting cold out here. Let's go find something to eat."

That was the beginning of many such times. Russell liked to be active. He loved to dance, hike, ride bikes. I rediscovered the joy of many of the things I had done when I was young. Somehow, I hadn't kept them up after Matthew's death. It felt good to get out and use my body vigorously once again.

Before long, I was rediscovering the joys of physical intimacy as well. As our friendship deepened, I thought long and hard about what I wanted from this very enjoyable relationship.

I finally decided that a discreet affair would be the best road to follow. I knew Russell was thinking in those terms. He hadn't asked me to marry him and probably wouldn't. His wanderlust restrained him, I felt, from making any long-term, serious commitment. I could live with that. I didn't want to upset the even tenor of Dylan's life–nor my own, for that matter.

I liked the life I had created for myself. I liked my independence, my being able to provide for my child and myself, my being able to come and go without the constraints that a marriage would bring. And yet, I discovered that, more than I had realized, I needed intimacy. I needed passion. I needed the simple comfort of body against body, skin against skin. It took meeting Russell to realize how parched and dry and incomplete I had become without any avenue for sexual expression.

I knew that our relationship must move inevitably toward increased intimacy or that it would certainly flounder; I knew that it could not remain static. Our increasingly urgent attraction for each other couldn't be indefinitely ignored. Russell would never be content with a platonic relationship, nor for that matter would I. I made a very conscious decision, probably not a typical decision for a widow in mid 1950, to have an affair rather than to aim for marriage. This was well before the sexual revolution of the sixties, so we took great effort to be discreet. We had no desire to put our livelihoods or our reputations at risk.

Russell was a skilled and considerate lover, and we both were reasonably content with the limited times we had together. Occasionally we managed a weekend trip to Santa Barbara or to Laguna Beach, always deliciously satisfying.

I was wary though of stealing time from Dylan's weekends. Now that she was ten years old, she had many after-school activities. Her free time was limited too; as much as possible, when she was home I wanted to be there for her.

During that period, I was seldom without some writing project. Fortunately, I had developed a considerable network of editors who liked my work. I was pretty much able to pick and choose those subjects that were of particular interest to me.

I continued, too, with my painting. I was developing more confidence in my work, buoyed by Gentry's generous help and gentle criticisms. He was such a delight to me. He never intruded; he was always accessible, ever ready to help in any way. I deeply valued his friendship.

He knew that I was involved with Russell. He had met him. Typically, he had offered nothing but support concerning our relationship. I knew, though, that Gentry did not admire him. We never discussed it, but I felt that he considered him to be something of a lightweight, perhaps a bit shallow and superficial. I had sensed this myself, but Russell was an interesting and fun-loving companion and a passionate bed partner. For now, at least, we nourished each other.

* * *

"Mama–Mama." Dylan burst into my small studio where I had stolen a little time to work on a half finished portrait of her.

Cheeks flushed, she announced breathlessly, "I got into trouble at school today."

Her auburn hair was pulled up in a topknot ponytail. Clutching her ginger cat Sunny in her arms, in her pale apricot dress she looked like a delicious, dewy peach.

Indignation flashed in her eyes. "I didn't deserve it. That mean old Benjie Schmidt got me into trouble."

"Uh-oh! What happened?"

"Well–first he pulled my ponytail–hard–then when I hit him in the stomach, weird old Mr. Crawford benched me for all of recess. He's not even my teacher," she announced scornfully.

I tried not to laugh. "It was probably Mr. Crawford's job to supervise you kids. It sounds to me like you can expect to be benched if you're going to go around hitting people. That seems mild enough punishment, don't you think?"

"Yeah, but he didn't do a thing to Benjie. That's not fair," she wailed.

"Well–that's the breaks, honey. He probably didn't see that Benjie started it."

Dylan considered. "Why does Benjie act so mean? I hate him."

Looking at her troubled face, I searched for words to help her understand.

"You need to calm down a little" I temporized. "There are some grapes and cookies and milk over there on the table. Go have your snack while we talk about it."

She gulped her milk. "I don't see why he always picks on me. He doesn't tease the other girls that way. Mmm–cookies are good. Thanks, Mama."

"You're welcome. You don't like Benjie at all? What's he like?"

"Well–he's really kind of cute. He's the best speller in the class and he's awfully good at arithmetic." She munched her last cookie. "I'd like him fine if he'd leave me alone."

"You know, maybe he likes you–wants to get your attention," I said. "Do you think that's possible?"

Tipping her head to the side, she considered. "Maybe–I guess he does try to get me to notice him. That's a really dumb way to show me he likes me, if that's what he's doing–but then, boys are dumb." Her face brightened. "Do you think that might be why he acts so dopey?"

"Could be. You know, your daddy and I were the best of friends when I was your age. He never needed to do anything like that; he already had my attention. I remember that some of the other boys would shove and tease girls. I guess they didn't know what else to do. You know, their pals teased them if they weren't careful. They weren't supposed to be interested in girls."

"Yeah–that's so dumb–dumb boys."

"Dumb, but cute, huh?"

"Yeah," she laughed.

"Why don't you try to make it easier for him. Do you ever talk to him? Smile at him?"

"Naa. I thought he didn't like me. So who needed him?"

She tossed her auburn topknot.

"Well–I think I'd try smiling and saying 'hi' and maybe asking him to help you with your arithmetic when you don't understand it. You say he's really good at it–and it's not your best subject."

"Okay, I'll try it. Hey–could we ask Gentry to dinner on Saturday? I want to show him the pictures I took with my new camera. He's neat, and he makes me laugh. I haven't seen him in a long time."

"Okay. We'll see if he can come."

Satisfied, she raced from the room, ponytail flying behind her.

We had a lovely Saturday night dinner. Gentry, Aunt Peg, her new friend Richard, Dylan and I sat around our old oak table. Peggy had gotten her degree and was into her first year of teaching kindergarten. She had met Richard Saradon, a school psychologist when he had come to evaluate a disturbed youngster in her class. Though Peg had gone out with him a few times and seemed to enjoy his company, I had not had an opportunity to meet him. I thoughtfully considered him. I liked his strong rather blunt features and his honest face. He wore black-framed glasses; his hazel eyes were bright with intelligence. Peggy had told me that she thought he was about forty-five.

"Dylan, would you clear the plates off the table and bring in the trifle that Aunt Peggy made?" I asked. " If it tastes as good as it looks, it's going to be a real treat. I'll bring the coffee."

No, you sit still, Kathleen. Dylan and I can handle this." Gentry got up and started stacking plates. "I have to earn my keep some way; besides, Dylan and I are a team. After you, Madame." He bowed in courtly fashion to Dylan, making her giggle as they headed for the kitchen.

"You should have plenty of time to make it to the concert, Richard." I glanced at my watch. "It's only 6:30. What are you going to hear?"

"There's a violin duo playing. I didn't recognize the performers' names, but the program looks interesting. They're playing Bach–a double violin concerto."

"I don't think I know any of his violin concertos–I didn't know he had written any, but I love his music, don't you, Kathleen?" Peg asked. She looked especially pretty in her burgundy dress. Her face was animated and lively.

"Indeed I do. I'm not familiar with Bach's violin concertos either–at least

I don't think I am though I'm constantly surprising myself by recognizing various musical themes. Things I've heard on the radio, I suppose."

"Hmm–I do that, too." Richard remarked. "Do you play that beautiful grand piano in the living room, Kathleen?"

"Yes, my dad insisted I bring it with me when I moved out of our family home. It was an important part of my childhood and I'm delighted to have it. How about you? Do you play an instrument?"

"No–I sure wish I did, though. I never had the opportunity to study as a kid, but I love music and I love to sing. I was in my high school choir when I was a kid and I'm in a church choir now."

"That must be fun. Choirs are great. Years ago, I played the piano for my high school choir. In my estimation, singing religious and liturgical music feeds the soul."

Dylan and Gentry brought in the trifle and coffee then, and soon Peggy and Richard were on their way.

Later, when Dylan was in bed, Gentry looked at my unfinished portrait of her. I was now used to his long, silent appraisal of my work. His eyes narrowed as he studied it.

"You've really caught the essence of Dylan. I like the colors that you've used to surround her. I see you have them reflected in her face, too. Nice. How did you come to choose those particular colors?"

"I'm not sure. I guess I chose them intuitively. They just felt right. Why do you ask?"

"I think perhaps you're doing something you aren't consciously aware of. If I'm right, it's a direction that might be worth exploring."

"What do you mean? I don't follow you."

"I think you're choosing colors that you sense are representative of your subjects' souls. These greens and pinks are quite different from the colors you used on your last portrait. Each time they're quite individual. I've been noticing."

"Golly, Gentry. If I'm doing that, I don't know I'm doing it."

I studied the portrait, thinking to myself that it was probably the best work I had done so far.

"That's why I'm pointing it out to you. It will make your work uniquely your own if you can develop that technique consciously."

"Hmm–I'll think about it."

As usual, I wasn't sure I understood Gentry's comments. They always seemed to hint at more than the surface words revealed.

"By the way, Kathleen, I think its time we get some other opinions about your work. May I take your paintings to some of my gallery pals–see if they agree with me that you have a unique and marketable style?"

"Gosh, I'd be really thrilled, Gentry. Take whatever you like. You are such an angel." I threw my arms around him and hugged him tightly. "I never dreamed that anyone else would ever be interested in my work."

"Well–let's see how it's received before you get too excited." He smiled as he patted my shoulder.

After Gentry had chosen a few pieces, including my almost finished portrait of Dylan, and had gone on his way, I looked over some of my earlier work. I had really improved a lot, no doubt about that; it was scary to think of anyone other than Gentry or Aunt Peg and Dad looking at my stuff though. If someone actually liked my work and wanted to show it, I knew I would be dreadfully nervous, but, oh, how wonderful!

* * *

I cautiously set down my wet paintbrush and ran to answer the phone.

"Hi, Kathleen–will you come and play with me?" Light hearted Russell, his voice brimming with laughter. His infectious enthusiasm was one of his greatest charms. A small boy excited by his next adventure.

"Play with you? That sounds like an offer that would be hard to resist. What do you have in mind, Russ?"

"I feel like taking a run up the coast this weekend–maybe Santa Barbara. Can you make it?"

"I'd sure like to. You know, I was going to call you. I'm in the middle of researching an article about the Santa Barbara Art Museum and they have a neat show there right now. I think you'd enjoy it. And lucky me, Dylan's been invited on a day trip Saturday complete with sleepover. This would be a great time to get away."

"I thought maybe we could leave early Friday afternoon. My last class is over at eleven."

I quickly made calculations in my head. "I need to check with Peg about Friday night, see if she's free to supervise Dylan. Do you think we could be back home by noon Sunday? That would give me the afternoon and evening to spend with her."

"I don't see why not. See you Friday then unless I hear differently from you."

The ride up the coast was perfection. A cerulean blue sky dazzlingly laced with low white clouds gave a sharp definition to the hills on one side of the road and shadowed the crevices and chasms on the other side, reflecting a jeweled glitter on the ever-moving sea. Paradise, indeed.

After settling in at our hotel we made leisurely love, luxuriating in the rare stretch of time at our disposal. Languidly we rested, saying little. We sipped wine and chatted desultorily. I felt deliciously complete, my body satisfied, my spirit soothed.

Russ, settling on one elbow, looked down at me. "What's the show about that we're seeing tomorrow?" He brushed back his hair from his forehead and leaned over to give me a quiet kiss.

"It's official title is *Royal Persian Painting: The Qajar Epoch.* I think the period covered is something like 1785 to 1925. If nothing else, it certainly should be exotic. The paintings are supposed to be incredibly ornate. You know the detail that the Persians gave to their work, the mosaic effects and the patterns? We're used to seeing miniatures or book illustrations, but these are life-size paintings of public figures, just as ornate and detailed as the smaller stuff. I think you'll enjoy the show."

"I'm sure I will, too. I spent some time in Iran years ago when I was working for an oil company. It's an interesting and mysterious land. I don't think I ever saw any life-size paintings there, though."

"They were meant primarily for public buildings–but what kind of buildings I have no idea. I'm going to want to take some notes. I'll include a description of the paintings in my article about the museum. You know, 'a recent show–etc. etc.'"

"Sounds fascinating." He again brushed his hair from his forehead. "What do you want to do tonight? I noticed that there's a rodeo at the Show Grounds. Want to go?

"I don't think so. I really don't like rodeos. You go, if you want. I won't mind. I have lots that I ought to read about the museum."

"I don't want to go without you, Kathleen. That wouldn't be any fun. What do you have against rodeos?"

"I don't know. I really don't know that much about them. I've only been to one. I'm well aware that some of the events reflect activities that are necessary for ranching, but bull riding, for instance, certainly isn't one of them. The whole thing seems cruel and exploitative to me," I said mildly.

"For Christ's sake, Kathleen," Russ' voice suddenly began to rise with indignation. "These are animals we're talking about. Why shouldn't people enjoy seeing a competition like that? It's a sport."

I seemed to have hit a sore spot.

"I guess there's no reason, if you like such things, but I don't. The whole atmosphere makes me genuinely uncomfortable. The animals have to feel threatened. The one time I went, I could almost smell their fear." I paused. "You know, Gentry thinks that animals have souls too–not like ours–maybe

65

more like group souls. "

"Oh, Gentry–he's such a pansy." Russell's voice carried a disgusted tone that infuriated me.

"How can you make a statement like that? You've only seen him once or twice. Surely you aren't jealous of him?"

"No, I just don't like him. Furthermore, you spend too much time with him. I don't think he's a good influence on you." His voice had changed from disgust to accusation.

"Not a good influence?" By now, my voice was rising too. "What business is it of yours? What gives you the right even to offer an opinion?" I sputtered. "Gentry is one of my dearest friends and I don't take kindly what you said about him. Furthermore, I certainly don't like your presumption. I don't need or want your advice about how I live my life."

Russell could see that I was genuinely upset and hastened to back down.

"I'm sorry, Kathleen. I guess I was out of line. I apologize. I really don't understand your feeling about rodeos though. It seems overly sentimental to me. As I see it, animals are animals. What's the big deal?" He reached over and hugged me to him. "Let's forget about it–it's not worth arguing over."

By mutual consent, we dropped the subject. We had a quiet dinner at Maison de Françoise and went early to bed.

Later, as I thought over our conversation, I was aware of a mild disappointment in Russell. Not because of the rodeo, everyone to his own tastes, but I didn't at all like his intolerant view of Gentry–his unwarranted and belittling attack. And the really bothersome thing was the proprietary assumption he had expressed, as if it were his business to control my life. Somehow the glow had gone from the day.

* * *

Sitting quietly in my living room, Gentry and I were enjoying the warmth of a roaring fire. The evening had turned surprisingly cold and a light rain was falling.

"Kathleen, one of my gallery friends was quite encouraging about the paintings I showed him." His silvery eyes sparkled as he grinned at me. "How long has it been–how long since I accosted you at the Van Gogh Exhibition? Three years? Four?"

My thoughts went back to our first meeting. "It's probably more like five years. Why do you ask?"

"Oh, just curious. For the short time you've been painting, you're making excellent progress." Dressed in his old cord trousers and fisherman sweater, he slouched low in his chair by the fire.

"I really work hard at it, Gentry. If I'm going to paint, I want to do it well. I know I need to practice drawing more, but painting's so much more fun for me that I tend to neglect the tedious stuff. I really get a thrill out of putting paint on canvas. You never know quite what will evolve–at least I don't. I enjoy the fluidity and brilliance of the colors, the subtle effects that often take me by surprise. I think *'how did I do that? Can I do it again?'* I've become increasingly aware that you have to be willing to take risks."

"That you do. Creativity demands a lot–risks and then some. It takes physical and psychic energy, as well." He paused to sip his wine. "It takes real courage to face that blank white canvas and then to lay on the first decisive stroke. Anyone who hasn't tried it simply doesn't understand."

I stared into the fire thoughtfully. Its crackle and sweetly smoky smells were pleasantly hypnotizing. I was vaguely aware of the rain rhythmically plopping on the shake roof.

"I hadn't thought about it quite that way, but it does take courage. In a sense you're putting yourself on the line every time you start a new piece. And it certainly takes courage to show your work to others. It's like putting your soul on display."

"I agree; it's not easy and it's perilously revealing. Well," he roused himself. "I had better start for home."

In typical Gentry fashion, he waited until he was headed out the door to remark, "Oh, by the way, Marshall at The Marshall Anderson Gallery wants to hang one of your pieces. I told him you'd drop by soon to discuss it with him."

With a grin and a wave, he was gone.

I walked into the Anderson Gallery, a few days later, with some trepidation. It was a very small Gallery on La Brea Drive. I looked around curiously. Subtly textured very pale gray walls were hung with paintings. The light was soft but well focused. Rectangular black pedestals holding sculptures and iridescent ceramics were strategically placed around the room. Little arched niches held smaller objects. It was a fairly typical gallery with a very lovely ambiance.

"Good morning. Can I help you?" A man, perhaps sixty years old, approached me. He was impeccably dressed in light gray flannel trousers and a double-breasted dark gray coat. He wore a pale gray shirt, clearly tailor-made, with a silver gray tie. He was very tan–a good foil for his thick silver hair. Not a handsome man, I thought, but very soignée.

"Hello. I'm Kathleen Parrish." I held out my hand. "Gentry told me you were interested in some of my work."

"I'm glad you came in." He shook my offered hand. "I'm Marshall Anderson. My assistant isn't here right now, so I may have to interrupt to take care of customers. Come back to my office and we'll chat."

I followed him to the back of the gallery to his office. It offered a sharp contrast to the display rooms. His desk was old and scarred. It was piled high with papers and catalogues and books. He waved me to a chair, at the same time removing a pile of books from it.

Settling into his chair, he sighed. "Call me Andy. Forgive the office–it's a mess, but I like it that way. I get really tired of the image I have to project for my clientele. It's a relief to come back here and slouch a little. La Brea breeds certain expectations, I'm afraid. And I do aim to make a living."

I was slightly taken aback by his frankness, but his casual approach put me very much at ease. "I suppose a certain formality is required," I ventured. "Jeans and a sweatshirt wouldn't make it, I guess."

"Hardly. If I had some talent–beyond having a good eye for what will sell–I could be my slovenly, slouched-down self." He smiled deprecatingly.

"You mean like some artists?" I grinned; it was impossible to translate his elegant image to casual, let alone sloppy.

"Exactly. They can be as outrageous as they like in dress and manners and get away with it."

"If they're any good," I countered.

"Well, yes, it helps to have talent. You know, I really liked that unfinished portrait of your daughter that Gentry brought in. I'd like to show that piece–if it's as good when it's finished."

"I understand what you're saying. It's perilously easy to overwork a painting." I paused to consider. "I hate to tell you this, but that's the one piece I really don't want to sell–at least, not right now." Dylan's portrait was infinitely precious to me. I knew that down the years it would become even more so. I doubted if I would ever want to part with it.

"Hmm–I really don't think I can afford to give space to something that's not for sale. I thought that painting had a little different quality than your other work." He leaned back in his chair and studied the ceiling. "How about if you bring in any of your new work as you finish it? I'd be glad to look at it."

"I'd appreciate that. It would be helpful to get your opinion even if, in the end, you don't feel it's marketable. So far Gentry and whoever else he's shown it to are the only outsiders who have seen any of it. I could use some knowledgeable criticism. I find it really difficult to be objective."

In truth, it was all too easy to fall in love with one's work, rendering objectivity impossible. I knew all too well the seductive power of a certain line, a certain cast of features, almost accidentally fallen upon, that needed to be ruthlessly expunged for the higher good of the whole canvas. Sometimes it seemed more than I could bear to paint out areas that were clearly not working well in the over-all scheme of things. My reluctance probably stemmed, to a degree, from my lack of trust in my ability to re-create the same effect a second time. In truth, though, re-creation was not true creation anyway; it was copying. Each brush stroke demanded a fresh beginning; no prior expectations dared be allowed.

"Feel free to bring anything in," Andy told me. "I'm always willing to give an opinion." He paused. "Gentry's something, isn't he?"

"Yes. He's special. He has a quality that's hard to define. He seems to see more–see farther than most of us can."

"How right you are. Are you aware that he's psychic?"

"Gentry? Psychic?"

"I think so. He underplays it, but several years ago, he told me that I should go to a doctor and have a check up. I don't much like going to doctors, so I procrastinated. The next time I saw him, he gave me holy hell for not going. And you know Gentry; he never gets upset. 'Tell your doctor to check your left leg carefully,' he said. Well, I figured maybe he knew something I didn't, so I went. And sure enough, I had a blood clot behind my knee. The doctor said it could have killed me if it had pulled loose and traveled to my heart."

"Interesting," I murmured somewhat diffidently.

I wasn't sure I was prepared for a psychic Gentry. Somehow the whole idea smacked of charlatans and turbaned gypsies dripping with bracelets and reaching out bangled arms to read one's palm for a dollar.

"There was another strange incident, too." Andy continued. "One day close to closing time, Gentry came in. He said he was in the area and just dropped by. He walked with me to my car–I used to park in the alley behind the gallery–and a young punk took off running when he saw that there were two of us. He had an iron bar in his hand, and I feel certain he was waiting for me so that he could rob me. I always take the day's cash to the bank on the way home and he had probably been following my moves. I hate to think what might have happened had I been alone."

"Maybe it was coincidence–Gentry coming in, I mean."

"I don't think so. Gentry never comes in late like that. And he never before walked me to my car. He just shrugged it off when I tried to question him about it afterwards. Clearly, he doesn't like to talk about it."

"Thank you for sharing this with me. I count Gentry as my closest friend."

I stood up to go. I felt that I had taken up enough of his time. "And thank you for talking with me, Andy. I've enjoyed it immensely."

"I have too, Kathleen. Drop in any time."

As I drove home, I pondered this new insight about Gentry. Should I ask him about it? Just see what he would say? *I don't think so*, I thought, *at least not just now. After all, he hasn't chosen to tell me anything about this. He's never used his psychic ability on me–or has he? Maybe that's why he struck up that conversation at the Museum. Hmm–that's an interesting thought. I think I'll leave the whole subject alone–it will be soon enough if and when something of relevance comes up.*

Chapter 7

Waiting for my friend Anne, I sipped my wine and thought about the generosity and dependability of her friendship and her love. Always I looked forward with anticipation to our semimonthly luncheons. They provided me a chance to catch up with Annie's latest ventures and her sometimes rather outrageous opinions. She was a fiercely independent, diminutive fashion plate with regal bearing and vast enthusiasms.

As she hurried through the door, a little late as usual, she spotted me. "Hi. Sorry to be late. I got stuck in traffic and then couldn't find any place to park. I had to walk a mile."

I interpreted this to mean that she probably had to walk half a block.

"Hi, Annie." I rose to hug her. "And aren't you looking terrific?" She had on a beautiful cream suit with a deliciously pale peach blouse, perfect foil for her vivid coloring.

"Aren't you looking splendid yourself?" She sat down and looked at me with interest. "And isn't that a new dress?"

"'Tis," I laughed. " I have good news to relate. Andy has hung two of my paintings–not one, but two. So I decided to treat myself to a new dress in celebration."

"He didn't?" Annie exclaimed. New dress forgotten, she leaned over and hugged me again. "Grand! What're the paintings like?"

"Let's order and then I'll tell you all about everything."

As we ate, I told her how thrilled I was that the Marshall Anderson Gallery had seen fit to hang my work, a first for me. Andy had chosen a study I had done of Aunt Peg. I had painted her looking out a window, her garden beyond alive with spring colors. The interior background was heavily maroon with hints of celadon and turquoise. Peg held a sheaf of calla lilies in her hand. Her eyes were fastened on the horizon, as if waiting for some unknown splendor to arrive.

"I remember that one. I like it," Anne said. "I didn't see it after you completed it, though. What's the other one?"

"It's a very simple painting of an old neighbor woman of mine. I don't think you've seen this one at all. She's sitting at a table with her Bible open, her hand resting on a cup of tea. I tried to get the feeling that she's ready to cross over, maybe a little excited and yet a little afraid. I used lots of lavender and pale blue on her skin."

"Hmm, I'm going to have to drop in at the gallery soon. I can't wait to see your work framed and hanging. This is so exciting!"

"Yes, it is. Now, tell me about what you're working on."

Anne was the author of some very popular children's books, the *Amazing Amanda* series. Her heroine was a ten-year-old girl who could time-travel. Amanda's travels ranged from Rome, 44 B.C. to Mars, 2050 A.D.

"Well, right now I'm just about finished with *Amanda Goes To Atlantis*. She's desperately trying to save an eleven year old boy, Gaius, and his family."

"From what?"

"From continental devastation. Don't you know about Atlantis? I read all the stuff of Edgar Cayce that I could find about that lost continent."

"Sorry. I've heard the name. That's the extent of my knowledge."

"Well, according to Cayce, Atlantis was super-sophisticated technologically. Maybe more so than we are. They had an immense crystal that powered their whole civilization. With misuse, they blew their country out of existence. Amanda's trying to get Gaius and his family to Egypt. Plato supposedly mentioned Atlantis, you know."

"No, I don't know. I'm abysmally ignorant about Greek philosophy. Somehow I never had to study it. You know how it is, if you don't have to read for a class, you just don't get around to it. I know only the most basic stuff about Plato. But go on, tell me more."

"Not much more to tell. Cayce says that the continent suffered huge earthquakes, volcanic eruptions and Noah-like flooding several times and that those who survived fled to Egypt and to Mexico and South America, even supposedly to New Mexico and Colorado. There seem to be some similarities in their early cultures. Interesting to contemplate anyway, don't you think?"

"Yes, it is and I can see that you have another blockbuster success on your hands. I want to read it."

As we finished eating, Anne turned serious. "I have some news to impart, too." She paused. "Mark and I are finally getting married."

"But that's wonderful. Congratulations! What makes the self-reliant Miss Wilder decide suddenly to give up her much-valued independence?"

Mark's patience in allowing Anne to go her own way had always amazed me. Most men of our generation would have insisted on matrimony long before, given their mutual love.

"Kathleen," Annie leaned forward. "I want to have children. I'm almost thirty-five years old. I envy you Dylan. All of a sudden, I'm aware that I don't have forever to make the decision to have kids. I can literally hear my biological clock ticking away." She tapped her fingers on the table impatiently. "I'm already ten years behind most of my friends."

"You've talked this over with Mark?" I asked.

"Sure. He's all for it. Had it been up to him, we would have done this six or seven years ago. He's been so dear. Patience personified. We're going to go look for a ring this evening–an emerald, he says."

"Terrific! And when will the ceremony be?"

"As soon as possible. I don't want a big wedding. Just you and a few of my other closest friends–and both of our parents, of course." She paused, considering. "I don't know quite why I stalled for so long. I guess I needed to prove to myself that I could make it on my own."

"Well, you've certainly done that. You've gone from success to success with astonishing speed." I considered a moment. "You know I couldn't be happier for you–your being engaged. Why don't we all go out to dinner this weekend to celebrate? Mark, you, Russell and I. My treat."

"I'd like that. How about Saturday night? I'm pretty sure Mark is free."

"Great."

As we got up to leave, I promised to call with the particulars of our evening out.

Getting in touch with Russell proved to be an elusive business. I tried and tried. Each time I called, he was out. I finally reached him near the end of the week.

"Gosh, I'm sorry, Kathleen. I can't make it on Saturday." He seemed vague and curiously indifferent. After a long, awkward pause, he added, "It's really great that Mark and Anne are getting married. They're nice folk."

"Don't you want to celebrate with them, Russ?" I was more than a little perplexed by his atypical lack of enthusiasm.

"Sure. I just can't go on Saturday." He offered no explanation.

"When would be good for you?"

"Well, I guess I could make it on Sunday night. How about that?"

After agreeing to dinner at Andre's on Sunday–not the best time for a celebratory dinner in my estimation–I hung up thoughtfully. As I thought back a bit, it seemed to me that Russell, normally the most enthusiastic of beings, had seemed reluctant lately about a myriad of little things. He was increasingly hard to contact; nothing I could quite identify. I wondered if I was only imagining a touch of ambivalence in his manner toward me.

When I called Anne to discuss the change of plans with her, I mentioned my surprise that Russell wasn't available for Saturday night. That had been, from the beginning, our accustomed and unspoken evening together.

"I'm a bit confused, Annie," I confessed somewhat diffidently. I was not in the habit of discussing personal relationships with anyone. My inclination was to work things out in my own mind and to keep my own counsel. "Russell seems to be uncharacteristically inaccessible recently. I don't quite understand what's going on."

After a long pause, Annie answered. "I've been bothered for awhile about something, Kathleen. I've been reluctant to say anything, but I guess I'd better tell you."

"About Russell?" I asked in surprise.

"Yes, about Russell. A couple of weeks ago, I happened to see him at The Samovar–you know, that new expensive Russian restaurant? Mark and I went there to try it out. Russell was sitting in a curtained booth with a pretty blond young lady–a very young lady. My guess would be that she's a student. He was so absorbed in this girl that I don't think he saw us. They were holding hands and seemed, to my casual glance, to be on intimate terms. I knew that he wouldn't appreciate being seen by us, so I hurried past without speaking to him. It was a strange feeling."

My heart sank. "Did Mark see him, too?"

"Yes, he did. We discussed it and decided that we'd say nothing about it to you. It's none of our business and, you know, it's no fun to tell tales. I haven't been able to dismiss it from my mind though. Since you're questioning his behavior, I thought I should tell you. Am I right to let you know?" she asked anxiously.

"Oh, absolutely, Annie. But I have to admit it's quite a shock." I tried to pull myself together. "I have nothing to complain about really. Russell and I have never promised anything to each other."

"Still–," Annie's voice drifted off.

"Yes, exactly–still. I expected better of him. It hurts me–hah, actually it infuriates me–that he hasn't been more honest about our relationship. If he's lost interest, he should be up front about it. I'm not into dishonesty nor into promiscuous sex."

"No, of course not. I think you're completely justified in expecting some loyalty from him."

"Right. Well, what are we going to do about Sunday night? I don't know that I could pull off an evening with him right now."

"Are you going to confront him?"

"I think I have to. It's only fair to give him a chance to explain. Maybe there's an easy answer, though I doubt it. I'm not about to continue a relationship with him if he's sleeping with someone else; good grief, especially a student."

"I'm sure I'd feel the same way, Kathleen. Let's put the dinner on hold for a bit. It's okay. Mark will understand."

And so we hung up, leaving me the task of confronting Russell about this shabby fiasco. In my heart, though, I already assumed that our affair was over.

I hardly knew how to approach him. Finally, I called and told him that Anne and I had postponed our dinner date, suggesting that we go to a quiet, casual dinner by ourselves.

"Sure, Kathleen. But why is the party being postponed?"

"Sunday didn't seem like a very good night," I temporized. "Besides, there's something I want to discuss with you. How about my meeting you at Taylor's Café? Say 7 o'clock?"

At dinner, we chatted lightly about inconsequential subjects and toyed with our food. Neither of us had much to say. Finally, I put down my fork and confronted him.

"Russell, I get the feeling that all's not well in our relationship. Is there something wrong?"

"Something wrong, Kathleen? What makes you think that?" He dropped his eyes to his plate. "I've been pretty busy the last couple of weeks." Brushing his hair back from his forehead, he pushed his food around on his plate. "Do you feel that I've been neglecting you?"

"Maybe a little, Russ, but it's more than that. Actually, I feel that you've been really distant lately, as if you'd just as soon be somewhere else." I stared at him. "Would you? Would you rather be somewhere else–or with someone else?"

"Gosh, I don't know where you got that idea." He flushed and dropped his eyes. Finally, hesitantly, he looked at me.

"Someone told me that you've been seeing another woman." I watched him carefully. "I want the truth, Russell. Is there someone else?"

"Oh, I get it. Anne saw me with Susie that night; I thought I caught a glimpse of her." He sounded defensive and nervous. "Leave it to her to run tattling to you."

"Never mind where I heard it. The point is, is it true? Who's Susie?"

Russ shrugged. "She's just a girl I know. She doesn't mean anything to me. Really, Kathleen, she doesn't mean a thing to me."

"Is she a student of yours, Russ?"

"Well–yes, she is. But really–I can explain."

I interrupted. "You don't owe me an explanation, Russell. You don't owe me anything except honesty. *That* I expect from you. Are you bedding her?"

Looking down, he moved restlessly. "Well–uh–yeah–a couple of times."

"I guess that's it then," I said firmly.

I had known for some time that Russell relied on his considerable charm when under duress. This evening was no exception. He did his best, in his captivating way, to convince me that I should forgive and forget, that I should overlook his indiscretion. He found it almost impossible to accept that the end had come.

"Gosh, Kathleen, give me another chance. I really care about you."

He tried again to convince me, reaching out for my hand. " I won't see her again–I promise."

Stonily, I looked at him. "Russell, I'm not asking you to choose between us. You've already made your choice. It's over."

Even though I had always known that our arrangement couldn't be permanent, I was hurt and shaken. With as much dignity as I could muster, I said goodbye and, without a backward glance, I left the restaurant.

I missed Russell even more than I had expected to. It was difficult to adapt to life without his congenial charm and panache. To distract myself, I threw myself into my work, taking on more assignments then were easy to handle. I spent hours painting in my studio. I played the piano more frequently, a pleasure I had neglected for many months. I also spent more time with my daughter and with Gentry. Nonetheless, I missed the easy give and take of my former pleasant liaison.

I suppose it was naïve of me to expect honesty and loyalty in a relationship based on expediency and congeniality rather than on love, a relationship that demanded no true commitment from either of us. I had come to realize, too, that Russell's values were not my values. I had refused to consider these obvious truths. Whose fault then, this debacle? I was at least as responsible for it as was Russell. Still, I missed him greatly.

In the aftermath of this unhappy ending, I felt drawn to a more contemplative way of being. I thrashed around pointlessly for some time, trying to find a direction that would satisfy my soul. Aunt Peg had, some years before, found her way back to the Catholic Church, a return to the religion of our Irish forefathers. I tried going to Sunday Mass with her. After all, the Catholic Church had given birth to most of the saints that I had read about so many years before. At one time, it had clearly been a fertile breeding ground for spiritual growth.

I found the Cathedral magnificent, the music divine, the ritual soothing to the spirit. Yet I was uncomfortable with the currents of guilt and punishment that swirled below the surface of that majestic panoply. I preferred the more lenient theology of the church of my childhood, but that no longer sustained my spirit either.

On my own, I seriously began to study some of the less formalized teachings of spirituality. I discovered Gerald Heard and Evelyn Underhill and that spiritual giant, Thomas Kelley, the Quaker professor from Haverford College. They all shared the conviction that God was in essence Love. Their chosen path to the Ultimate seemed brighter, lighter, more expansive than most. My spirit resonated to their joy-filled theology.

Gentry, dear man, supported my faltering search. We talked endlessly. He was ever ready to answer a question, to discuss any issue without imposing his own views on mine. His innate wisdom precluded his giving me his answers. He knew that a spiritual edifice took years in the building; that it had to be constructed piece-by-piece, plank-by-plank, structured by the experiences, the innate soul-stirrings of the individual. No mass consensus would suffice if the structure were to endure.

Now that my spiritual needs were taking precedence in my life, Gentry, wise Gentry, directed me into various avenues of exploration. We went to lectures; we sought out books, both in bookstores and in libraries. As I read and mused and meditated, slowly I reached beyond Christianity into Buddhism, Hinduism, and, in time, even into such esoteric literature as we were able to find. The dimensions of my consciousness were rapidly expanding and, to my surprise, I found that I was content.

Chapter 8

All Soul's Day 1961; a day that I will never forget. I was awakened early in the morning by a frantic call from Elizabeth.

"Kathleen, it's your father," she gasped. "Please come as soon as you can. I don't know what's wrong."

Her words stumbled over each other, making it difficult to understand her.

"Slow down, Elizabeth." I fought off the panic that threatened to overtake me as well.

"Tell me what happened."

"I don't have time. Just come–I think he's had a heart attack. I've sent for an ambulance. I have to get back to him." She broke off the connection.

I hurried to Dylan's room to rouse her. "Dylan, wake up." I softly shook her.

"Wake up, Dylan. Granda's ill and I have to go to him at once."

She opened sleepy eyes and stared at me. "Granda's sick?" she asked, disoriented by her sudden awakening.

"Yes. I have to hurry and get dressed. I need you to get up and fix your breakfast and get ready for school."

"School? I'm not going to school. I'm coming with you."

"I don't think you should, Dylan. It would be better if you just got yourself to school. I know it will be difficult, but you can handle it."

She was adamant. "No, I want to come." Her eyes filled with tears. "I'm not a little girl anymore. I should be there. Maybe he's really sick and I'll never see him again. I've got to come."

I made a quick assessment of the situation. At sixteen, she was a mature and thoughtful girl. She was almost as old as I had been when my mother had so suddenly died. I remembered clearly my feeling of anguish at not having had any warning of Mother's death.

"All right. But hurry."

I ran to get dressed. We scrambled into the car and drove to my father's house just a few short blocks away.

Elizabeth, deathly pale, was waiting for us.

"The ambulance left just a couple of minutes ago," she murmured. Clutching her keys in her hand, she looked completely distraught.

"Come on, hop in. You don't look like you're in any condition to drive."

Without further comment, she replaced Dylan in the front seat. As we raced to Valley Presbyterian Hospital, I tried to get a clearer picture of what had happened.

"Stephen woke me with his groaning. His forehead was beaded in sweat, and he was obviously in great pain. I asked him what was wrong, but he couldn't answer. His face was contorted and he clutched at his chest." Tears filled her eyes. "It was terrible. He looked so pale, so ill. I ran to call an ambulance and then you. When it came, they immediately gave him some oxygen and bundled him into the ambulance. Oh, God, he looked so bad."

I reached over and put my hand on hers for a moment as we careened down the road.

"Let's just pray that he makes it."

Dylan leaned forward and put her hand on Elizabeth's shoulder and we drove in silence the rest of the way.

Dad had had a serious heart attack. His doctor was optimistic, though, about his recovery.

"He has a strong constitution. You know, his last physical showed no signs of any heart problem. Unfortunately, that's quite often the case." Dr. Parker sighed. "Our diagnostic techniques aren't foolproof by any means. We'll monitor him carefully and then, with rest and care, he should be back on his feet in no time."

Dr. Parker had been our family physician since our arrival in California. He had then been a young doctor just starting his practice. Now, his hair was gray, and his eyes were pouched and tired.

"I've called for a cardiologist," he said. "We want to be sure he gets the best care possible. You can go in and see him, but don't say anything or disturb him. I gave him something to put him to sleep. He needs to rest quietly now that we have his heart stabilized."

We crept into his room and stood at his side. He seemed barely to breathe and his face had a greenish cast. He was so pale, so drawn looking that I had to fight back tears. His tremendous vitality had simply leaked away, leaving him looking fragile and old, years older than he had seemed just a day or two before.

We were hard put not to touch him. Elizabeth began to reach for his hand and then abruptly pulled back. I longed to smooth his hair, to make some kind of contact.

"I guess we'd better go," I said finally. "We'll find a place close by to get some breakfast. We won't be any help if we don't take care of ourselves. I need to call Aunt Peggy, too."

I glanced at my watch. "Hmm, she'll be in class by now. I don't think we should interrupt, do you?"

Elizabeth thought a minute. "Why don't you call Richard? He may know better how to handle it than we do."

"Good idea." Dylan agreed.

And so I called Richard, who had married my Aunt Peg the previous spring, and left him the grim task of telling Peggy that her older brother was seriously ill.

Forcing ourselves to pick at a hurried breakfast, we wasted no time in getting back to the hospital. We wanted to be there when Dad woke up. The staff was not disposed to allow people to visit indiscriminately, but Dr. Parker had gotten special permission for us so that we could be with him when he stirred.

We quietly stood around his bed and watched him. He still slept but his color seemed much improved. His breathing appeared to be more normal to my inexperienced eye, as well. I pulled up the only chair for Elizabeth, and we silently waited.

A small movement after what seemed a very long time, then his eyelids fluttered and he opened his eyes and looked around in a confused, disoriented way. Slowly he focused on us. I could see that he was beginning to remember what had happened to him.

Elizabeth took his hand. "Hello, dear."

With Dylan at my side, I stood and quietly watched him.

"Hi, girls." He grinned feebly. "I guess I caused some trouble for all of you today." His voice sounded tired and flat.

"Oh, Granda," Dylan interjected with relief, "it's so good to hear your voice."

"How are you feeling, Dad?" I asked.

He paused as if to intuit his condition before answering. "Too good to die," he finally said.

"Thank God for that." Elizabeth kissed his forehead. "You had us pretty worried."

"Dad, I know you're completely exhausted. We'll leave you alone for a while and be back in a few hours. All right?" I smoothed his covers.

He half-smiled and nodded before his eyes fell shut again. Quietly, we tiptoed out.

That afternoon during visiting hours, we gathered around his bed again. His color seemed even better than when last we had seen him. We kissed him and held his hand, not saying very much. Obviously, his energy level was still very low.

Suddenly, my father sat up in bed, reaching out with one hand. "Mom! It's my mother!" Astonishment played across his face. "And, look, she's brought Catherine with her!" A radiant smile lighted up his face. "Look,

Kathleen, your mother is here."

Then, abruptly, his hand dropped and he fell back heavily on his pillow, seemingly unconscious. I frantically rang the bell for the nurse. The next few minutes were pandemonium. We were shooed from the room as doctors and nurses and equipment descended on it. We huddled together in the waiting room, fearful of the news that was awaiting us.

"Did you see anything, Kathleen?" Elizabeth finally asked. "Did you see anything at all where your father was staring so fixedly?"

"No, I didn't. I've read about deathbed visions though. I'm afraid it doesn't bode well for his survival."

Dylan's eyes glazed with tears. "I think Grandmother and Granda's mother came to get him, to help him cross over. It's wonderful and it's terrible all at the same time."

I hugged her to me.

Just then, the resident doctor came out and confirmed our worst fears. In spite of their best efforts, they could not resuscitate him. At sixty-four, my father was dead.

For several weeks, I moved through time in a frozen, muffled way, a somber reprise of my reaction after Matthew's death. Life had a sense of unreality. I wondered why people bothered to get involved in the many daily tasks and concerns that cluttered their lives. All of the time and effort we habitually expend on trivialities seemed strangely banal. In the face of the Great Imperative, to me they were meaningless and shallow.

I understand now that I was suffering from depression. For some time, I was unable truly to grieve for my father. Dylan though, self-sufficient child that she was, openly grieved and then firmly turned her attention elsewhere. She had loved her Granda dearly; he was as close to a father as she had ever known, but she resolutely put her sorrow behind her. I believe that she found untold comfort and peace in the scene we had witnessed at Dad's death.

At that time, I understood intellectually that death was not an ending but a new beginning. I understood that Dad had simply stepped through an open door into another dimension, but it took several years before I could put those intellectual beliefs into any real perspective, before I could appreciate that my father's death was in fact a gift to me, a gift that propelled me to a deeper and more urgent questioning of spiritual realities.

My need to understand intensified markedly. I was eventually able to translate some of my sorrow and newfound awareness into meaningful expression. In my journal I wrote a poem in his memory:

My father's final gift was graced and strong,
shaped by failing breath,
by heart's bright blood,
carved from harsh realities of flesh and bone.

Shattered cage,
white bird free.

Ablaze against illumined void
past molten Gates of Grace,
rise triumphant, Soul, on radiant wing.

Sing the final song,
Holy, silent song,
piping, siren song:
gift of Grace.

Deep in my being's loam
something awakes.
A nameless secret stirs:
small, green seed dropped from radiant wing.
Small, green, green seed
Frail
and tenuous
and raw
Green potent seed
awakes and bids me dance my soul's pavane,
The sacred, ancient dance
that has no end.

Faltering footsteps, timid of the Light,
turn and turn again the circled climb,
struggling, slipping,
fearful to be free.
"Beloved one, come dance with Me."

Clarifying my feelings regarding Dad's dying finally released the dull depression that had constrained me. Freed at last from its somber cloud, I longed desperately to be renewed. I yearned, with re-kindled zeal, to travel the ever-upward spiral path that, with God's grace, could bring me to the clear crystal cathedral of my inner Self.

Having finally come to terms with my grief, I worked diligently to develop a new artistic vision, as well. I struggled to find symbols that would suggest, with discrimination and grace, the implicate, unfolding nature of the unseen universe, that which was hidden from our casual eyes, that which kept the stars moving in their shining orderly orbit. I experimented with abstractions, with swirling colors and textures, but my efforts yielded only the palest suggestion of the vivid scenery of my imagination. *How can I give my work more depth without being obvious and trite?* I thought. *Maybe I'm just not ready for such an ambitious task. Maybe I never will be. Then, again, maybe I'm striving for the impossible. Maybe what I envision simply can't be done.*

With some disgust, I gave up trying to capture my inner world on canvas and turned again to painting the human face and form. I had sold a few pieces in the last years. Andy at the Marshall Gallery had been very supportive of me. I contented myself with enhancing my paintings, both subject and background, with some of the techniques I had worked at earlier. Slowly, I developed a vibrant, mystical quality that pleased me.

I showed a few pieces to Gentry. I could always count on him for an unsparing and uncompromising evaluation. Typically, he studied them at length without comment. Though I was used to his silent, meditative scrutiny, I was, as usual, a bit unnerved.

Finally, he turned to me.

"Good, Kathleen. Very good. I especially like this one." He picked up a study of a seated woman. Her head was turned away toward a large mirror behind her in which she saw another world, another dimension of being, bright with swirls and color and motion, atoms dancing in the light. Her reflection had been transformed. In sharp contrast, the room and she, herself, were ephemeral and diffuse.

"As your spirit matures," Gentry said, "so does your work. I see implicit depths and dimensions that were barely hinted at before."

"Hmm, thank you, Gentry. They fall short of my vision, though, deplorably short."

"That's the burden of the artist, Kathleen: striving to mold the unmoldable, struggling to delineate the matrix of life. An impossible task that will not let you go."

He grinned his leprechaun smile. "Take them to Andy. He'll love them."

Andy hung three of my paintings. He called me several days later.

"Kathleen, those new paintings of yours are really catching attention. They're very good, you know. I sold one, and my most discriminating clientele are really taking note of them. Uh, would you consider doing a portrait for a valued customer of mine?"

"Goodness, Andy," I stammered, "that's a scary idea. I've never done anything on demand before. It really puts me on the spot. What if I can't do it? Or what if he doesn't like it?"

"He's a she–and she'll like it. I know she will. And I know you can do it. How about it?"

"Well, I guess I could at least meet her and then see what I think."

"Good. I'll have her call you. Her name's Charlotte Dermot."

"Andy, wait a minute. Even if I decide to do it, I have no idea how to handle the business end of it."

"Hey, trust me, Kathleen. You do the work and I'll handle the rest, just as I've done with your other pieces. Maybe it would be a good idea if we worked out a contract for selling your work. Drop by soon and we'll talk about it."

That was the first of my commissioned paintings. I signed a contract with Andy that gave him the sole right to sell my work. I trusted him, and it freed me from business considerations. I was not so much interested in making money–Dylan and I were comfortably enough off–as I was in having an audience for my particular voice. It seemed to me that the uniqueness of each artist's vision added something of value to society, hopefully something redeeming and uplifting. I sensed that artistic revelation had a renewing influence and that it was a very necessary antidote against cultural stagnation.

With interest, I sized up my new subject. She was a wisp of a woman, tiny and fragile looking. Her lustrous black hair was fastened in a chignon and her rather chiseled features were curiously expressionless. I was surprised that she would value the kind of work I had been doing. She seemed too bound, too restricted both emotionally and physically to take the risk of exposing herself to my objective scrutiny.

"Are you sure you'll be comfortable doing this?" I asked. "I'm committed to painting what I sense about a person as much as what I see. I'm never quite sure what the results will be."

She leaned toward me. "That's what I'm counting on." She waved a delicate hand. "I guess I want someone else to plumb my nature. I don't seem to know who I am."

I studied her for a moment. Her candor eased my mind somewhat. I decided that I could trust her to accept, without agitation or rancor, my vision of her.

"I'd like to see you in something loose and flowing–maybe with your hair down. How does that strike you?"

"I'm in your hands," she said. "Whatever you want will be fine with me. I promise I won't second-guess the results."

I finally decided on a long canvas, placed horizontally, and I painted only her upper torso and head. I used an electric fan to blow her beautiful, abundant hair far out behind her. Positioning her face well to the left of the canvas, I allowed her luxurious hair to flow freely across the entire painting. I dressed her in a gauzy white blouse and turned her so that her delicate features were in semi-profile, painting the background in an unrelieved vibrant copper. The effect was exotic and liberating.

The final work pleased me. Thankfully, Charlotte, too, approved of my version of who she was, or possibly who she could be.

Because of that painting, I was soon as busy with commissions as I cared to be. I had, much to my surprise, made something of a name for myself in the Los Angeles art scene. I still made my living by writing, but I could be increasingly selective in what I chose to do.

One evening, I paused in the doorway of our family room and took in the scene before me with my painter's eye. Dylan, sitting cross-legged on the floor, her back against the couch, held Sunny, our aging orange cat in her lap. Auburn hair pulled back with a green ribbon and dressed in jeans and a green sweater, she was intent on a television program. She made a charming picture. *Maybe*, I thought, *I should get my sketchbook and try to capture this moment. She changes so rapidly.*

"I was hungry for some popcorn." I handed her a bowl. "Here, have some. What are you watching?"

"*World View*. My history teacher says we ought to see it regularly. This week it's about Vietnam and some of the historical background of Indochina." She picked up a handful of popcorn and munched it. "Thanks, Mum. The program's pretty interesting. Why don't you watch it with me?"

So I sat with her, letting my mind drift to her coming graduation from high school in June. She was a serious student. We needed to make some decisions about college very soon. I dreaded the thought of her leaving home, but I knew that she needed the chance to try her wings on her own.

I was musing and paying scant attention to the program, thinking I should rouse myself and get my sketchbook, when the voice on TV interrupted my reverie: "I've asked Douglas Cameron, international correspondent for BBC who has just returned from Vietnam, to join us this evening."

Startled, I looked up. I was stunned to see him there on the small screen in our home. How wonderful he looked! Memories flooded into my mind. Even on our black and white set, I could see the well-remembered intensity of his eyes. He wasn't the slim young man I remembered. His face was fuller, his forehead higher; yet, he had changed little. I would have had no trouble recognizing him anywhere. A sweet delight flooded my being.

"I know Douglas, Dylan," I gasped. "I met him long ago, when I was younger than you."

"Really, Mum. He sounds awfully intelligent."

"He is. He's very special. Or at least I thought so when I was young."

I lapsed into silence and turned my attention to him.

"The United States should be very wary of involvement in that difficult and highly volatile land" he was saying.

I was so carried away by the sound of his beautiful, deliberate voice and the improbability of his presence in my family room that I hardly comprehended the rest of his words. I was unnervingly dazed and dazzled by the impact of seeing him again.

I had lost all contact with Douglas after his marriage. What little I knew, I had gleaned from an occasional reference in the newspapers. I was aware that he had joined the BBC shortly after World War II, and that he had eventually gone into television, covering tension spots around the globe. I had not dreamed I'd ever see him on TV here in America.

Bemused, I stared at the screen until the program came to a close. It was clear to me that he still had the power to disturb my emotional equilibrium. I hugged Dylan goodnight and retired to my room. I desperately needed to be alone to sort through the avalanche of feelings that swept through me.

A few days later, Dylan, dumping her books on the dining room table, came to find me in the kitchen where I was preparing dinner. She had gone directly from school to her weekly dance lesson. She had been taking ballet from the time she was seven years old. In the beginning, my dad had subsidized her lessons. He had very much liked the idea of a ballerina granddaughter.

It turned out to be an excellent choice for her. She had a narrow, fluid body and long, slender dancer bones. Also, she had the natural elegance and grace of my mother, Catherine. In many ways she reminded me of Mother though her vivid coloring was directly attributable to Matthew.

"Hi, dear. How did everything go today?" I asked. Her teacher, Madame Irena, I well knew, could be a difficult and demanding taskmistress.

"Oh, great." She fairly sparkled with suppressed excitement. "Guess what?"

"Can't. You'll have to tell me." I continued cutting carrots, intent on my task.

"Madame Irena took me aside after class and told me that she had selected *me* to go to New York for a summer semester at the Martha Graham School of Contemporary Dance! Can you believe it?" She twirled around the room excitedly. "I can go, can't I?"

I dropped my knife and smiled at her. "But that's wonderful, Dylan. Of course; you must go. We'll work it out."

She ran to me and boisterously hugged me.

"Do you know how long the semester lasts?"

"I think it's eight weeks. I'm not sure. Madame Irena will give me all the information next week" The smile left her face. "Gosh, it'll be awfully expensive, won't it?"

"I'm sure it will cost a bit. New York City is an expensive place. But you'll love it, and I think it would be a fair use of some of the money that your grandfather left you. After all, he's the one who insisted you learn to dance."

My dad had set aside a trust fund for her. Until such time as Dylan was twenty-one, it was up to me to decide how she spent it. I was sure this use of the funds would meet with his approval.

We poured over the literature that Madame Irena had sent home with her and immediately sent in the required recommendation, registration forms and money. Dylan would live in a dorm with three other girls to a room. The classes were four hours a day, with two Master Classes conducted by Graham, herself. A high-powered program by the sound of it. Apparently Madame Irena's reputation was sufficient to assure acceptance. Dylan was ecstatic.

"Dylan," I said a few days later, "I've been thinking–how would you feel about my flying to New York with you this summer? I've been giving serious thought to doing a series of interviews with influential people. Several I'm interested in are on the east coast–New York City and Washington, D.C. I could help you get settled in and then go on and do my work. What do you think?"

"Gosh, I'd like that, Mum. In such a big city; I won't know my way around. To tell the truth, I've been feeling a little nervous about going all alone."

"Actually, once you get the hang of it, it's not too bad. You'll get used to it very quickly. June will be a good time for me to go, before it gets so hot that everyone will want to leave the city. I'll start making calls tomorrow. Famous people have hectic schedules; I have to give them lots of advance notice."

A few weeks later, I came upon her sitting at the kitchen table staring off into space. She looked troubled. I had noticed that she had been unusually quiet the last few days.

"I feel like a cup of tea and some cookies, dear. Do you want some?"

She roused herself. "Sure, Mum. Sounds good."

As I waited for the water to boil, I tried to figure out how to get to the source of her disturbance without barging into her private thoughts and feelings. I knew that teenagers needed their space.

"How are things going, dear?" I asked as we sipped our tea. "Is everything O.K.?"

"Sure, Mum. Everything's fine." She hesitated and then looked at me. "Uh, I saw my school counselor a few days ago–to talk about college."

"Oh, good. I know it's time we make some decisions. Did she help you make up your mind?"

I had been pushing for a school in California–preferably one not too far from home. I thought the University of Southern California would be a good choice. Since I had not fulfilled my father's dreams regarding that school, maybe Dylan could. We had already agreed that she would live on campus, wherever she chose to go.

"Uh–" she fiddled with her cookie. "Uh–Mum, I'd like to stay in New York after my summer dance school." She rushed on without looking at me. "My counselor says I could probably get a scholarship for Columbia. That's a really good school." She looked up hesitantly "Would you mind terribly, Mum? I sort of feel like I'd be deserting you."

I understood at once what had been bothering her. She was afraid I'd be hurt if she chose a school so far from home.

"I'll miss you terribly, sweetheart, but that doesn't mean you should stay here." I stood up and put my arms around her. "You'd be leaving home some time before long anyway. But are you sure that's what you want?"

"I want to be a professional dancer, Mum. That means New York City. I'd really like to try out for Julliard. It's my dream to go there. They have a terrific dance program, you know." Her young face fell. "I'm probably not good enough though."

"Julliard. Well, it's certainly the best. If you don't try, you'll never know whether or not you're good enough. Hmm–you'll need to have an audition, I'm sure."

"Yeah. I asked Madame Irena about it. I have to apply and then they set up an audition. I thought I'd try for Julliard and apply to Columbia, too, to be on the safe side. I'm almost certain to be accepted there. Are you sure it's O.K. with you, Mum?"

"Positive. You've obviously given it a lot of thought. If this is what you really want, follow your heart, Dylan." I smoothed back her hair and dropped a kiss on her forehead. "Don't worry about me, dear; I'll manage all right. And Dylan–I'm exceedingly proud of you."

Later that night, I considered the realities of life without my daughter. She had been the focus of my attention for eighteen years. I was keenly aware that once she boarded that plane for New York, nothing would be quite the same ever again. I wasn't hurt by her decision, but I knew that I was in for a tough adjustment to life alone.

Chapter 9

The flight to New York was uneventful and I soon had Dylan settled in her new domain. The room she was sharing with three other girls was in an old brownstone not far from the dance school on East 63rd Street. The room was a bare bones affair with four bunks and minimal floor space and furniture. Apparently, another quartet of would-be dancers was housed on the same floor.

Only one of her dorm mates was there when we arrived. She was a striking-looking dark-haired girl from Tucson, Arizona, Maria Redfern. We chatted together for a few minutes and then I took my leave, promising to call the next few evenings to see how they were getting along. Maria, I sensed, would be a reliable companion for Dylan. Together, they could learn the ins and outs of both the dance world and of bustling, bursting, frenetic New York City.

I had two interviews set up for the next day. I was fortunate to have won an hour with Yehudi Menuhin, premiere concert violinist, who was renowned and loved the whole world over.

He was in New York to give a concert at Avery Fisher Hall in Lincoln Center. Then that afternoon, I had an appointment with William S. Paley, chairman of CBS. He was the first to have seen the enormous possibilities inherent in television. His was the vision that propelled that medium into the reality it had become. I knew both men were witty, cosmopolitan and urbane. I looked forward to meeting them.

I found Yehudi Menuhin to be the most gracious of men. I had done my homework and knew that he was a child prodigy who, by twelve, was a virtuoso. I had discovered that in 1960 he had been awarded the Nehru Peace Prize for International Understanding. I knew, too, that he was a teacher, a conductor and a humanitarian. I was struck at once by his immense enthusiasm for life. It fairly shone out of him. He spoke with animation about his new school for promising young musicians that had just opened in Surrey, England, a school modeled after the Central School of Moscow where music and scholastics were both taught to the aspiring youngsters enrolled. He talked at length about his love for all music, from Ravi Shankar to Beethoven, a particular favorite of his. He insisted on showing me some yoga postures that were part of his daily routine. He spoke of his interest in Oriental philosophy. All in all, it was a delightful hour that I spent with him, an hour that flew by. I knew I would always remember the force and vitality of his personality.

After a quick lunch, I headed for CBS. I was a little early, so I asked the taxi driver to let me out a few blocks from the building. I remember the day well. It was a soft, shimmery day in June. A mild breeze gently caressed the skirt of my cerulean linen sheath, evoking a feeling of intense aliveness. Car horns honking, whistles blowing, trucks rumbling by; teeming energy surrounded me. The world seemed preternaturally conscious, as if every atom were aware. It was one of those rare moments when the earth seemed perfect. The liveliness of the day seemed to imprint itself on my mind, bringing forth an answering surge of vitality through every cell of my body.

As I waited at the desk for the receptionist to clear my visit to Mr. Paley, the elevator door opened, spilling out a large group of people. To my surprise, I saw Douglas Cameron was among them. Without stopping to think or to consider, I called out to him. It didn't occur to me that he might not recognize me.

Hearing his name, he turned and looked at me. He hesitated and then, frowning slightly, headed toward me. His cream linen suit looked faintly British; his silk tie was the color of his eyes. As he neared, I could see that he was struggling to place me.

I put out my hand. "Kathleen Parrish–formerly Curran, Douglas."

Delight lit up his face as he reached for my hand. "Kathleen. Kathleen Curran. What a surprise! How are you? What brings you to New York?"

"I'm here to do a series of interviews and I have an appointment with William Paley in a few minutes." As I spoke, I noticed that he looked haggard and tired. "How are you?" I asked.

He waved his hand dismissively. "Oh, I'm fine. Kathleen. When can we get together? I want to catch up with your life. I know you can't keep the great man waiting–but could I buy you a drink later?"

"I'd love to meet you somewhere. I won't be longer than an hour."

"I have several things to take care of, so let's meet in the bar at the Algonquin at 4 o'clock. Is that convenient?"

"Sounds good. I'll look forward to it."

He turned and strode away, leaving me hoping that I could shed my bemused state sufficiently to do a creditable interview with William Paley.

I was pleased to be meeting Douglas at the Algonquin, home of the prestigious Round Table of the 20's and 30's, hangout of Dorothy Parker, Heywood Broun, Alexander Woolcott, Robert Benchley. Surely a place of ghostly voices, I thought.

Douglas had been watching for me. He rose in greeting as I stepped into the dark bar. He had chosen a small corner table a bit apart from the other larger tables and banquettes. He was nursing a glass of wine.

"Kathleen, it's a real treat to run into you like this." His smile erased ten years from his tired looking face. "What will you have?"

"Oh, I think a glass of white wine."

"I'm drinking a Sauvignon Blanc–very good. Shall I order the same for you?"

"Yes, that will be fine."

We were silent as the waiter brought my wine. I had so many questions swirling around in my head that I didn't know where to begin. I wanted to know everything about him: why he was here in America, what he was presently involved in, what his next project was, whether he was still married, whether he had children.

He broke into my chaotic thoughts with a toast. He raised his glass. "To our renewed friendship."

As I raised my glass to his, our eyes met–casually at first, then with galvanic imperative. Without warning, I was suddenly engulfed in the shoreless ocean of his eyes. Without design, our gazes locked together in timeless wonder. We found ourselves catapulted into a vast, boundless, moment–a place of no place, a place of no sound, a place of no time. Where there had been, only a heart beat before, a bar, rattling glasses, people talking–the world around us vanished completely. The two of us were an island in a warm, interior universe, cradled in an enfolding, loving web of knowing. Recognition flooded through us. Without touching, we merged. Completeness. Ecstasy. Homecoming. Joy.

As the ordinary world slowly returned, we sat in stunned silence. I reached out toward him, desperately wanting to make some sort of physical contact. "Douglas?"

He covered my hand with his and shook his head slightly, as if uncertain what had really transpired. "My God, Kathleen." He slumped back in his chair and studied me. "What in hell happened just then? I feel as if I've been pole axed." He shook his head again. "I can't seem to scrape together one coherent thought."

"Nor can I." I picked up my glass and sipped some wine as if the doing of something mundane and physical would clear my head.

"I was charmed by you when you were fourteen, Kathleen. Now, God help me, I'm overwhelmed. I feel as if I'm in a dream and can't wake up."

Suddenly the bar seemed impossibly constricting. "Maybe, if we got some air?"

"Yes, let's get out of here and walk a bit."

We walked the streets of New York City for several hours, oblivious of the crowded sidewalks, the noisy streets, the pulsing humanity that surged around us. Douglas tucked my hand in the crook of his arm, and we walked, talking desultorily about inconsequential things. It was sufficient that we were close to each other, our spirits touching. We recognized that we had been, for mindless years, only half-whole. Together, we blended into a synergistic unity, a complete, perfect harmony. And so we walked, content to push aside, for this short while, all obligations and requirements. We refused to allow any consideration of the future to spoil this glorious now.

Eventually, fatigue asserted itself. We found a small restaurant, quiet and homey. As Douglas ordered wine for us, I made a quick phone call to Dylan to see that all was well on that front. She was excited and enthusiastic: Maria was wonderful; they had gone out and acquainted themselves with their new neighborhood; they had stopped in at the school to get their schedules; class was to start the next morning. I said goodnight and promised to call again the next evening.

Douglas stood as I approached the table and seated me with the same courtly grace that I remembered from years before. The fatigue and strain that I had observed in him earlier had vanished. It seemed as if he had momentarily tapped into some inner source that was lacking before, a connection that infused him with vitality and élan. I noted again the mole just above his finely modeled mouth, and I longed to reach out and touch him, to stroke his face, to feel the crispness of his brown hair. A part of me still walked in a dream.

As we ate, we related, briefly, the histories of our pasts. Douglas knew nothing of my marriage to Matthew, of his courageous death in the war, of my lovely Dylan–the history of all the years before this charmed meeting.

"Dylan is here in New York City right now," I told him. "That's one of the reasons I'm here." I paused. It occurred to me as I spoke that perhaps some benign synchronicity had placed me in this particular place at this particular time, but I said nothing of this to Douglas.

"I helped her settle in for a summer course in modern dance. She's pretty young to be on her own; just eighteen, and I thought she could use a little moral support."

"She's just a little younger than Craig. He turned twenty this spring."

As we detailed our lives, I learned that Douglas was still married to Rosalind and that Craig, their only child, had just completed his second year at Oxford. Douglas recalled for me some of his experiences in the world's hot spots and talked easily of his interviews with senators and statesmen, with prime ministers and presidents.

Exchanging factual, commonplace doings, we were all the while achingly aware of each other. Our prosaic conversation helped to ground us, to give a semblance of normality to our charged emotions. Neither of us ate much; we were too filled with the miracle of finding each other, too internally aroused to care for bland bodily sustenance. Constrained by prudence, awash with desire, we hesitated, uncertain of the next measure, even as our bodies cried out for physical union.

Douglas pushed his plate aside, leaned back and lit a cigarette. He looked again as haggard and tired as when I had first seen him. "Kathleen," he considered me seriously. "I'm a battered, burned out wreck of a reporter. I've seen too much; I've experienced too much horror; I've pushed myself beyond reason. I've done some things I'm proud of and others that I deeply regret, and right now I'm mentally and physically exhausted."

I started to interrupt. "Douglas—"

He held up his hand. "Please hear me out. I'm married; I'm too old for you; I've become cynical and hard. I'm too shopworn and jaded to act spontaneously now, though God knows I want you desperately. I'm so afraid that I'll hurt you." His eyes darkened in misery. "That would be more than I could bear."

"Douglas, it would hurt me if we turned our backs on this miracle, this grace given to us; it would hurt me beyond repair. I would happily trade a king's ransom for just one hour with you." I reached my hand out to him. "I love you. I think I've always loved you. I want to be with you, no matter how short the time." I smiled and looked into his eyes. "Douglas—be my love."

His smile transformed him. If you're sure, dearest. I should give you time to think about it."

I shook my head. "I need no time."

Very deliberately, he placed his hand, palm to palm, against mine in a courtly, silent pavane. "I love you, Kathleen. It's incredible, but true. For now, that's all that matters."

In the bar at the Algonquin Hotel, just brief hours before, the inner citadel of my being had been breached. It seemed a most ironic setting for the impregnation of spirit. Now spiritual unity compelled completion, a sacred, holy marriage of flesh.

By the time we got to my room, we had reached the very edge of forbearance, and as we silently embraced, we simply flew away. Together, that night, we scaled Olympian heights, Adonis and Aphrodite born again. We shouted down the wind and up the spires of radiant steeples. Breathless, we flung our sound against the hills like tumbling, scattered stars sown in the dawn.

We gamboled, hand in hand, across Elysian meadows. Latter-day Adam and Eve, we feasted on the honeyed apples of paradise.

Together, as one, we plumbed the heights and depths of the sweet pas de deux of love.

Chapter 10

I awoke the next morning to find Douglas propped against the headboard watching me. His hair was rumpled, he smelled faintly of tobacco, and he needed a shave. To me, he was incredibly beautiful.

"Good morning, love." I levered myself up to curl against his chest. "Have you been awake long?"

"A little while. I've just been sitting here savoring everything about you." He held me close to him and stroked my hair. "Kathleen, just think, we might have missed each other completely yesterday. What divine intervention brought us to the lobby at CBS at the same time, do you suppose? If I hadn't stopped to visit with my friend Eric, I'd not have even known you were in the city."

"So you thought of that, too." I curled up closer to him. "I could so easily have been given an appointment with Mr. Paley another day or another time. Dylan and I might have come to New York a different week, or not at all. Instead, I turned around and there you were, leaving me breathless. It took all my will power to talk to you sensibly. I've idolized you for years, Douglas. I didn't think I'd ever see you again. My dear–" I traced my fingers over his beautiful mouth, "my friend Gentry would say that what is meant to be, will be."

"There *does* seem to be a kind of inevitability about our meeting. Ah," he sighed, "there's so damned much I don't know about you, Kathleen. Gentry, for instance, who's he? He sounds to be someone of worth." He nuzzled my hair. "You told me about your free-lance work; I know that you paint; I know that your dad died; but there are vast holes rattling around that need to be filled."

"Umm, for me, too, Douglas. How much time do we have to catch up with each other? Do you have plans for the day? I don't even know how long you'll be in America."

"Do you mind if I smoke?"

At my nodding assent, he fumbled for a cigarette and lit it. I absorbed the way he looked, the way he moved, his eyes soft with love, his unique smell. I wanted to store away every detail, every richness, every sweetness so that I could replay each in my mind when he was no longer by my side.

"I'm on leave from BBC right now, Kathleen. I made a quick trip to Indochina a couple of months ago. It was my last assignment–for awhile at least."

"I saw you on television right after that trip. Seeing you again, looking so much the same, aroused all my old memories of you. I never, never dreamed I'd shortly be with you here in New York City." I sighed, contentedly. "It's unbelievable."

"Unbelievable and wonderful. Thank you, God, for divine intervention, if that's what it is." He kissed my forehead. "I told you last night that I was burned out? I am, totally. The world has gone insane and I need to distance myself from it for awhile."

I shifted around until I could cradle him in my arms. "When you say you're burned out, that you're battered and bruised, as you told me yesterday, it breaks my heart." I gathered him close as a mother would a child. "Dear, let me help to heal your spirit."

"You are, Kathleen; you are doing that." He smiled and leaned to kiss me. "I feel reborn this morning." He kissed me again lingeringly, and soon, once again, we stormed the gates of paradise.

Later, over a late breakfast, I again asked Douglas about his plans for the day. His eyes crinkled with amusement as he lit his cigarette. "We never did get around to discussing that, did we? Well, I've got an appointment with a publisher this afternoon. As I told you, I'm on a leave of sorts. I thought I'd try my hand at writing a book. I'm a bit uncertain about it," he said diffidently. "It will be a new experience. You see, I've never written anything professionally before. It will be altogether different than writing a script."

"You speak so easily in front of a camera, Douglas. I'm sure this will come to you just as readily. You, yourself, told me many, many years ago that I could do anything if I really believed I could, and I trusted what you said."

"I did? I must have been a pompous young ass to tell you that!"

"No, you weren't. You were sweet and kind and interested in a gawky kid. I was enthralled, and your words kept me going many times when things were tough. What are you going to write about?"

"I'm not sure how it will work out, but I thought I'd do profiles of some of the influential personalities of recent years, political, artistic and intellectual figures–those who have significantly shaped our world. I've had a ringside seat for observing the lives of the great. I think I have a unique point of view to offer."

"That sounds fascinating, Douglas." I was delighted to see his enthusiasm increasing as he talked.

"I hope so. I've interviewed the major players in almost every country on the globe. I want to start each profile with a full-page portrait and then continue with either a new interview or a recap of an old one from my files–I'd have to edit them a bit, maybe update each one, too–along with personal vignettes and observations. I've kept a journal from the beginning and I've talked with so many people that I certainly wouldn't lack for material: Nehru, Robert Kennedy, Lillian Hellman, Picasso, Dame Judith Anderson–I could go on and on. I've given myself a year to see how it goes."

"That's a wonderful concept. You've clearly thought about it a lot. It would be great if it could be an over-sized book." I thought a minute. "How about Yehudi Menuhin? I just talked to him–was it only yesterday? –and found him to be purely delightful."

"Hmm, he'd be a good addition. I interviewed him very briefly many years ago. I'd need to arrange an update, but I think I could swing it without too much trouble. He's fairly accessible."

"He's a lovely, lovely human being." I reached out to cover his hand with mine. "So are you, Douglas. How long will you be in New York?"

"My schedule's pretty flexible. I'm planning to stay in the United States for a month or so. I need to re-establish some ties with people and update some interviews before I go home." He frowned slightly as he regarded me. "*If* I go home." He paused and shook his head in disbelief. "Yesterday, I just wanted to finish my work here, pack my bags, and leave. Now, I don't want to go at all." With a sardonic expression, he sighed, "So quickly do our fortunes turn."

Caressing me with his eyes, he went on. "I can't bear the thought of leaving you, Kathleen." His face softened as he raised my hand to his lips and kissed it. "I love you more than I can fathom. From where does such instant knowing spring?" he puzzled. "It seems to me that I recognize and adore you from some distant past, that I've always known and loved you. How can that be?"

"I don't know, Douglas. I don't understand either. You've been in my heart all these years, but I've never really understood the why of it. I loved Matthew dearly and sincerely; I loved him with all my heart and I treasure his memory, but even then, beneath the surface of my life, there bubbled this spring of love and longing that had no name."

He looked at me wonderingly. "It's as if our souls have been united for endless eons across the corridors of time. What an awesome concept! Dare we trust this, Kathleen? Are we truly graced, or are we just a foolish man and woman wildly attracted to each other?"

I considered his question. Finally, I answered. "I've learned over the years, partly with Gentry's help, that joy is always to be trusted. And when I'm with you, I'm filled with joy almost beyond containment. That's the only answer I can find."

He smiled his wondrous smile. "Well, right now, my enchanting sweet, I suggest we move you to my rooms at the Waldorf. Best we take this one day at a time."

His suite at the hotel consisted of a beautiful sitting room, bedroom and bath, elegantly and expensively furnished. Flowers were on the coffee table and bureau. Choice paintings decorated the walls. Crystal ashtrays, Waterford glasses on the small bar. To me, it looked worthy of royalty. As I looked around, I realized that he had become accustomed to this grand style of living, and I suspected that his home in Great Britain was just as sumptuous and magnificent.

A new picture of him was beginning to form in my mind. It was clear that he inhabited a sophisticated and highly cultivated world, a very expensive world. I shouldn't have been surprised. I had noted that his clothing and his manner were cosmopolitan and urbane. My beloved was a polished man of the world, undoubtedly a man accustomed to British upper-class society.

I could hardly integrate this new picture of him with the young man who had inhabited my dreams for so many years or the man who, as a foreign correspondent, must have lived in primitive conditions for weeks on end. I wondered that he should love me, this man who had dined with presidents and princes and who must have many times held glamorous, bejeweled beauties in his arms at formal balls.

I sank down on the coach. "Douglas–this is beautiful. Somehow I didn't expect anything quite this elegant. Is your home in England like this, too?"

He looked around as if he had never seen his rooms before. "Well, yes–I guess so. When Rosalind's father died, she inherited his estate. She has no brothers or sisters, so someday it will all belong to Craig." He paused to light a cigarette. "I don't have much interest in it, to tell the truth, though it's beautiful. I leave the running of it completely to Rosalind." He sat down beside me and put his arm around me. "Fortunately, Craig will be a fine custodian of the place. He loves the land and when he's home, he's very involved in helping his mother."

He stretched his legs out in front of him and sighed thoughtfully. "I've worked hard since I was a youngster to make a place for myself in my profession; my success is greater than I ever expected. I've had a pretty good marriage, considering how much I've been away from home. Rosalind has been a fine mother, raising Craig almost single-handed, and, thank God, he and I are close in spite of my frequent absences. It's more than I deserve. And yet, right now, none of it matters to me. You are my only reality." He pulled me close to him and buried his face in my hair. "I just don't understand how everything could change so quickly. I thought I knew pretty well who I was, but now my image of myself has been completely blasted apart. I love you so, Kathleen."

We held each other close without speaking.

"Do you know what I'd like to do tonight?" Douglas asked.

"No–tell me."

"I want to take you to dinner, I want to wine you and dine you and then to dance with you 'til dawn."

"Umm," I kissed him lightly. "That sounds like a good plan to me." The thought filled me with delight.

He got up and straightened his tie. "Well, I'd better be off to my appointment. Will you be okay here?"

"Of course. I'll call Dylan and tell her I've moved." I grinned. "I'll tell her I found accommodations that suited me better. She'll want to tell me all about her first day at school. Then, I have some work I need to catch up on. I'll be fine."

I dressed carefully for our dinner, more conscious of my appearance than was usual for me. I had packed my crimson silk dress in case I had need of it, and the last minute had added my mother's diamond bracelet and earrings. Thank God! Now that I had a better sense of Douglas' life, I knew we would be dining in elegant surroundings and I wanted to do him proud.

I studied myself in the mirror. My scarlet dress, with narrow straps over the shoulders, clung close to my upper body, the skirt ending in a flirty flare. I twirled around and liked what I saw. In an abandoned mood, I brushed my hair straight back from my forehead, a leonine mane. As I put on my diamond earrings, I thought, *You look radiant. It's Douglas; his love is transforming your appearance.*

As I came into the living room, Douglas, cigarette in hand, looked up from the paper he was reading. He stood up, papers spilling to the floor, and stared at me. "My God, Kathleen. You're magnificent. You're like a Celtic goddess, incandescent, burning bright."

"Thank you, Douglas. You look splendid yourself." He held me to him for a moment, kissing my forehead. We walked to the elevator, arm in arm.

We dined and danced wrapped in a cocoon of love. Sometimes tenderness, sometimes devotion played across his face as we sipped wine and looked into each other's eyes. And as we danced in exquisite harmony, again our spirits blended. I felt curiously expanded–as if my ego had dissolved, as if the 'I' I normally considered to be Kathleen had transmuted into something finer and more beautiful. I was of 'no mind.' I was immutable, complete. Douglas, holding me with courtly grace, was translated, to my eyes, into a lapis-eyed Apollo. We danced in reverent, sacred ceremony, paying homage to our devotion and love.

Our days passed in halcyon bliss. I called Dylan every evening to reassure myself that she was adapting well to her new life. Douglas and I walked and talked, worked and made love, radiant in our oneness. We both had commitments that we assiduously honored, but we each hurried back to the enchantment of the other as quickly as we could.

Douglas signed a contract for his book, tentatively titled *Voices of Destiny*. He worked desultorily at reading through his journal, jotting down ideas and suggestions to himself. I spent much of my time with sketchbook in hand. I wanted to capture each fleeting expression that played across his intelligent face.

I lingered in New York longer than I had planned. We drifted in a euphoric haze through the days and nights, but I knew that our time together was running out.

"Douglas," I put my head on his chest. "I'm going to have to go back to California soon. I really have to go. I have obligations at home." I could hardly bear to say the words.

He sighed, as he stroked my hair. "Ah, Kathleen, love—I know." He sat up against the headboard. "I've been thinking—" he looked down at me. "I could fly back with you—stay for awhile. What do you think?"

"Douglas! Do you mean it? " I was elated. "Oh, darling, could you do that?"

He hugged me close. "I have people to see out there, and I can work on my book anywhere. I need to be with you, Kathleen. You fill my soul."

The last morning of our stay in New York, I awakened to find him propped against his pillow, intently staring into space. "Good morning, love." I kissed his cheek. "You're looking serious this morning."

His face softened momentarily as he raised my hand and kissed it. "Morning, dearest." He sighed. "I've been thinking about what we're going to do about all this." He waved his hand vaguely.

"Whether you will return home or stay here?" I asked uncertainly.

"Yes." For a moment, he seemed to withdraw. His eyes darkened and furrows deepened across his brow.

I watched him in silence, though I longed to smooth away the corrugating lines on his forehead. My emotions were a chaotic roller-coaster ride.

Finally, he looked up and spoke as if the words he had been thinking could be contained no longer. "I want to be completely open with you, Kathleen. I've been so filled with joy, so content to be sharing this cherished time with you, that it's been distressingly easy to overlook the reality of my other life. I've conned myself into believing it doesn't matter. I'm so torn between my overwhelming love for you and the responsibility I owe my family. Yes, and my love for Roz and Craig; I don't see how I can deny them. Both love me deeply; they don't deserve to be hurt because of my frailties–and, God knows, I have plenty of those." He fumbled for a cigarette. "I've done things that I deeply regret. I don't want to add to that burden. It's a tangled web, a dilemma I don't know how to resolve." He frowned. "I didn't expect this to happen, dearest, and I'm ill-equipped to sort it out." He looked almost physically ill, pale and distraught.

Dear God, I thought, *I feel his disquiet and his moral uncertainty as if they were my own. I need your help, God. I long to ease his pain, but I don't know how. I'm not a saint; I'm not strong enough. I can't say, 'go'.*

"Of course you love Rosalind," I finally managed. "You've shared memories and years together, days that will forever be lost to me. And there's your son. How could you not love the mother of your son, being the person you are?" I smoothed his hair back. "And I know that you love me, too."

"That's almost too pale a word to describe what I feel for you, Kathleen. I didn't know that it was possible to love this deeply."

"Experience has taught me that the heart is as deep as we allow love to stretch it, as wide as the sky. It can accommodate an infinity of loving, an infinity of caring, an infinity of devotion. There can be room for both Rosalind and me in your heart." I took his hand. "There are endless degrees and shades and colors of love. The more of that precious nectar we can contain, the larger our souls will become."

"Ah, wise Kathleen. Your words touch my heart and I know you're right, but the moral issue still tears at my gut. Either I stay here with you–God knows that's what I want more than anything in this world–or I honor my commitment to Rosalind. And Craig–a look of pain crossed his face. "If I abandon his mother, in a sense, I'll be abandoning him."

"I understand, Douglas. If I were in your situation, Dylan would be my primary concern."

"I just don't know–" He sighed. "My love for you is beyond volition; beyond my control." He reached for a cigarette. "I'm sorry to dump all this on you, darling, but I no longer know who the hell I am."

"Douglas, could you, for a while, put your decision on hold? Could we just be together for a time–accept this grace unquestioningly–until your heart tells you the path you should take? I promise I won't make demands on you. I want, above all, for you to decide freely."

He searched my eyes. "Can we handle that? Can we be happy together for whatever time we have without second-guessing ourselves? Without thinking of the future?"

"Without a firm commitment, without a guarantee about our life together?" I considered. "Given the alternative, yes, I think we can. We can live in the present, appreciating to the full each day as it comes. For me, every day, every hour with you is a gift, a treasure without price. My allegiance will be to you forever, no matter what the surface circumstances of my life may become. In time, you'll be clear about your decision."

We flew to Los Angeles two days later. We agreed that Douglas would spend a couple of days with me and then look for accommodations elsewhere. He was well known in broadcasting circles, and we wanted to take no risk that we might hurt Rosalind or Craig unnecessarily. We were achingly aware that we were betraying their trust; we desperately hoped we could spare them the humiliation of rumor and idle talk.

Douglas looked around my house–modest by his standards, I'm sure–with interest. He had taken our bags to my bedroom while I went to the kitchen to feed Sunny. He leaned against the door frame and watched with amusement as I fed the outraged cat, who, after being petted and cajoled, finally settled down to eat.

"This opinionated fellow is Sunny. He doesn't think much of being deserted for so long."

"I can see that. Who took care of him while you were gone?"

"Oh, Aunt Peg came in twice a day to feed him. He's just lonesome. He's Dylan's cat–she's had him since she's four–so he's full of years."

"He'll miss her then?"

"He certainly will. I can't believe Dylan's really gone–that she won't come dashing in any minute, hair flying, eager to tell me about her day. You know, I've never lived alone before in my life. It's going to take some getting used to." I lifted my shoulders in resignation. "I know I'll miss her dreadfully."

Douglas came over and put his arms around me. "Dearest, I know you will. I hope it helps that I'm staying in the house with you for a few days."

"It does, Douglas–more than I can say." I smiled. "Ah, I see you've become a Californian already." He had taken off his tie and his coat and had his sleeves rolled up to his elbows. "Make yourself at home, dear. I'd better call Peg and tell her I got in on time; otherwise she'll worry. She and Richard are leaving for Europe day after tomorrow for a month's stay. That's one of the reasons I had to come home–to look after Sunny. I'll want to drop in and say good-bye to them sometime tomorrow. It's their first trip to the continent. They're so excited."

"Go ahead and make your call. Is it okay if I look around?"

"Of course. I won't be long."

I found Douglas in the family room studying the painting of Dylan that I had done some years before. He turned to me. "A young Dylan?" he asked.

"Um–huh."

"She looks very much like I remember your mother looking, except for her coloring."

He had met Dylan in New York. The three of us had had a late lunch together just before we left. Douglas had treated her with the same courtesy and charming attention that he had bestowed on me when I was young. He had an easy manner with young people, accessible and interested, and Dylan had been clearly thrilled. Watching him with her, I knew that his son must adore him.

Now I went over and stood beside him, trying to see the painting objectively.

"It's very good, Kathleen; I like it." He drew me close to him. "Dylan's a lovely girl. Finely, but vividly, made."

"She is that–and she has my mother's elegant bearing, as well."

"Do you have other work you've done?" I nodded. "I'd be honored if you'd show it to me."

I took him into my workroom where I had several partially finished canvases. I often worked on two or three at a time.

After studying them a bit, he turned and regarded me. "You gave the impression that this was a hobby, Kathleen. I can see that you're a very accomplished artist. Have you sold some of your work?"

"Yes, I have a contract with The Marshall Anderson Gallery. Andy, the owner, has been wonderfully helpful to me. I have several commissions in the offing–another reason I needed to get home."

"But that's wonderful, dear." He took my hand. "You're work shows your keen perception."

"I'd like to do a painting of you, Douglas–just for me. Would you mind?"

He grinned. "Certainly not; I'd be honored."

"Tell me about your self," I said as we lazed away the day by the pool. "I know nothing about your background–your family."

"I was raised in upstate New York. My father had a feed store there. Actually, he eventually owned several in other states as well. He came from very humble beginnings, and he was determined to do well financially. He worked to put himself through college. Why he chose to go to the University of Chicago I'm not sure; that's where he and your father met. You know, they kept up a life-long correspondence; that's how I happened to visit your family in '39. My dad was a quiet man who loved books. He died in 1941."

"I'm sorry, Douglas. Do you have brothers and sisters?"

"I have two sisters, both younger. Jeannie is, oh, I guess forty-five, and Margaret's about your age. They're both married. Jean lives in Ohio and Margaret, in Buffalo, New York. We don't get to see each other too often, but I spent some time with both of them this trip, before I went to New York City."

"Tell me about your mother. I remember the dream you told us–the one where she directed you to television. She must have been special."

"She was, Kathleen, she really was. We were raised Presbyterian, and as long as I can remember, mother played the organ for the church services. I can still see her sitting perched on the organ bench, reaching for the pedals. She was just a little thing, small but mighty. Her word was law at our house, but I never knew her to be unfair nor to say an unkind word about anyone. When I was a kid, I worked at the feed store after school, and my mother told me, 'Douglas, after you've weighed the feed, always put in an extra scoop.' That was the heart and soul of my mother–generous, caring, kind."

"She must have been wonderful. I wish I could have known her. Which of your parents do you look most like?"

"Hard to say. I guess I favor my father more, but I have my mother's eyes."

"And her character, Douglas."

And so we passed the day, rambling about in our memories, sharing our past years with each other.

"You'd really appreciate Gentry, Douglas. Not every one does. He's too different; something of a solitary, an outsider. He cares little for what other people think. Gentry's the one who got me started with painting."

"I'd like very much to meet him. He sounds fascinating. I wish I could meet all your friends–and Peggy and Richard, too–but it's better right now that I stay in the background, don't you think?"

I sighed. "Yes, for now it's best."

The next day, Douglas rented a dark blue Austin-Healey and we spent a lovely day wandering around several beach communities. In Malibu, we found a small bungalow on the ocean's edge that could be rented by the month. Douglas liked it immediately. It was wood frame with a large deck cantilevered out over the sand. Indeed, there seemed to be almost as much deck as living space inside the modest house. The furniture was plain but in good condition, and the living room boasted a small fireplace. "Perfect," he exclaimed.

I looked around dubiously. "There's not much choice in restaurants around here," I observed. "Can you cook?"

"Well enough to get by. I certainly can fix something for breakfast and lunch. I'm looking forward to hanging my hat here for a while. It reminds me of a lake cabin my family owned when I was a kid." He gathered me into his arms. " Dear love, I plan to be with you a good part of the time, anyway."

Douglas settled in the next day. We laughed and fooled around, and with frequent hugs and kisses we stocked his pantry and his refrigerator. Together, we rummaged around, getting acquainted with his new home.

"Ah, I like my new digs," he exclaimed as, later, we sat on the deck, sipping wine and watching the blood red sun slip silently into the sea. Smoke curling up from his cigarette, his face relaxed and peaceful, Douglas stretched his long legs out and sighed. "Paradise."

"*Earth has not anything to show more fair,*" I murmured.

Douglas finished with the last lines:

Dear God, the very houses seem asleep;
And all that mighty heart is lying still![2]

He took my hand. "It's paradise only because you're here to share it with me, Kathleen."

In the gathering gloaming, joy from the most inner core of my being flooded, sweetly and without volition, through my whole body. I was blissfully content.

The days passed in joyful abandon. We tried to keep some semblance of order in our lives, separating unwillingly from each other for brief periods. Douglas worked on his book, interviewing a few people and renewing important contacts. I made arrangements to do a portrait of a young man, pushing the first sitting off for a few weeks. I checked in with Gentry and with Anne, who was expecting her first child. I talked frequently with an ecstatic Dylan; she loved her training and adored the city. I minimally maintained my house and checked Peg and Richard's place every few days. But my heart flew always to the little beach house in Malibu, and I rushed back to it at every opportunity.

Douglas and I took long, slow walks in the sand, barefoot, letting the water lap at our toes, sometimes splashing and playing with the abandon of children, coming home wet and happy. In Douglas' blue sports car, we explored the coast from Laguna Beach to Santa Barbara, stopping for lunch in quiet, unobtrusive little places. We walked and talked about our past histories and about our beliefs. We shared our innermost thoughts with each

---

[2] William Wordsworth: *Composed Upon Westminster Bridge*

other in a joyful intimacy of body, mind and spirit.

Douglas told me of some of his experiences as a correspondent. He talked eloquently. At times, with deep distress clouding his eyes, he recounted some of the harrowing scenes he had witnessed in the terrible conflicts he had covered.

"You know, Kathleen, if this book I'm working on works out well, I think I'd like to do another about some of the stories common foot soldiers and pilots have told me over the years. Some are heroic beyond belief; some show a touching faith in God; many, of course, are horror stories of death and destruction.

"One particular story comes to mind. It impressed me greatly when I first heard it; it still does. A sergeant told this to me during the Korean conflict. He and his platoon were defending a position close to Hawanggan. Several of his buddies were hit by artillery shells, as was he. One was killed; the others were badly stunned by the concussion of the shells. They all insisted—when they compared notes later—that they literally saw the body of their dead comrade pull itself together and stand erect. Then they all distinctly heard a voice say, 'I will die, but you will be saved.' The body then seemed to return to its disintegrated condition. They were in an isolated position and realized they were unlikely to be rescued. Suddenly a helicopter appeared from seemingly nowhere and, dropping down, picked them up. Later the pilot told them that he heard in his ear, 'There are three wounded men in that dugout. Pick them up.' No one had radioed the pilot; no one could explain how this could be.[3] The sergeant had tears in his eyes as he related the story to me."

"Incredible. We don't begin to understand the web of interrelationship that binds us all. How else can such an incident be explained?"

"How indeed? I certainly can't explain it. But I have no doubt that the story the sergeant told me really happened."

Another time, with misty eyes, Douglas told me that his mother's intervention once saved his life in a harrowing situation. He had been on a tour of the Pakistani, India border, doing an in–depth report on the entangling problems besetting that troubled area.

"One night, before setting out into rough, mountainous countryside the next day, I had a dream. I was driving a jeep on a steep mountain slope.

---

[3] As told in *Unknown But Known*, Arthur Ford, 1968. This incident took place in the Vietnamese Conflict. For the purpose of this story, it was changed to the Korean War

Suddenly, huge boulders tumbled, with a terrible roaring sound, down onto the road. The jeep was completely buried under a massive landslide. I woke up sweating and shaken.

"Two days later, I was driving along a rough, bumpy road, intent on my destination, when I very clearly heard my mother's voice. 'Douglas! Douglas! Stop!' I was so taken by surprise that I slammed on my brakes. Seconds later, a few yards ahead, a rockslide came roaring down the mountainside. It was exactly like my dream, except that this time I stared in open-mouthed astonishment at the terrible destruction ahead of me. The road had been completely blocked, much of it tumbling down to the canyon below."

Douglas' face was serious. "After sitting there stunned for a few minutes, I said aloud, 'Thank you, Mother. Thank you, God.'" With awe, he added, "There's no doubt her voice saved my life."

I wrapped my arms around him and leaned my head on his chest. "How wonderful to know that your mother still watches over you, dearest. You are blessed, richly blessed."

I knew that he must have been in the path of danger times without number, given his insistence that news should be immediate and firsthand, but this was the only close call he ever shared with me. I quietly breathed a prayer that his guardian angel mother might be with him always in times of need.

Our days began to fall into a pattern. We did our best to get our disparate obligations completed in a day or two each week, leaving the rest for us. After a few trips home to feed Dylan's long-suffering cat, I brought him back to the beach cottage with me to share our board and bread. He acclimated well, and Douglas enjoyed his feline presence.

I was eager to start painting Douglas. I had thrashed around in my mind, trying to decide how I wanted to present him on canvas. I knew that I wanted the informal Douglas, not the well-buttoned up professional or the sophisticated man of the world. I wanted *my* Douglas.

Finally, I chose to paint him sitting in his accustomed spot on the deck where we spent so much of our time together. I liked to work in the morning, usually a time of unusually luminous clarity. Douglas had no objection to posing for me; in fact, he seemed to relish it.

"I can meditate while you paint," he said.

"I didn't know that you meditate, Douglas," I remarked in surprise. He had not mentioned it when we had earlier discussed various theologies.

"I've spent considerable time in India and China, Kathleen. It was there that I got interested in Oriental religions. I ran into an old saddhu who taught me. I don't pretend to be particularly spiritual, and I don't meditate on an ongoing basis, but I've come to rely on it in times of turmoil. It settles me down and brings me back to my self."

"I know a little about meditation, thanks to Gentry. You two would like each other so much–you'd have an instant rapport." I paused. "He's encouraged me to read a wealth of spiritual literature–some fairly esoteric–so I know a little about it, but Gentry never pushes his beliefs on me. He says it's important that I find my own way."

"Wise man. Maybe someday we can meet."

When I began painting Douglas, I posed him with his elbow on the arm of an old wooden slat chair, his chin resting on his loosely curled hand, a typical posture that he often assumed when he was lost in thought. An open-collared white shirt, white duck pants. I added, on the deck floor, a few bits of the flotsam and jetsam of the sea: a sand dollar, some broken shells, a few pieces of sea glass. In the foreground, the bubbling curls of the ocean made lacy inroads on the wet sand. I had chosen to make all around him very subdued in color: tans, creams, the palest of blues–and then, in sharp contrast, the vivid intensity of his lapis eyes.

We spent happy hours on the deck, painting, resting, talking, painting again. We had gotten into the habit of turning the small radio that had come with the cottage furnishings to the classical music station in Los Angeles. As I worked, we listened to Chopin, to Brahms, to symphonies, to string quartets. I treasured these moments together, soaring music in the background, my mind focused on my work. As I painted, I sensed a flowing out to Douglas and, at the same time, a drawing in from him to me, as though in an invisible embrace.

My original intent had been to paint him with the soft look of love in his eyes, a look that was so familiar and dear to me, but as our summer of love dwindled toward September, I saw that it would be false to present him in such a personal way, for that was not the expression he wore when he stared, often unseeingly, at the constantly thrusting and drawing sea. He was a complex, stirring, multi-dimensional man; I had to strive to capture that on canvas if it was to be true to the essence of him and if it was to bring me joy in the days ahead.

By the time I had finished the painting, it had changed. Now his expression was fathomless, listening, lost in a universe of his own being. I painted each brush stroke with infinite and enduring love.

One morning, as I worked at his portrait, Douglas broke his pose to cock his head and turn toward the cottage door. "Kathleen, listen to that. It's the *Enigma Variations.* Do you know it?"

110

"It sounds very familiar, but, no, I wouldn't say I know it." I put down my brush and listened. "It's breathtakingly beautiful. Who's the composer?"

"Sir Edward Elgar. It's one of my favorite pieces of music. I have a wonderful recording of it at home." He stared off into the churning sea, lost in the music's haunting, glorious themes.

As the last strains faded away, I could see that, for a moment, he was filled with longing for his home in England, certainly, for Craig, his son. That may have been the beginning of his growing awareness that he could no longer put off a resolution of his dilemma–that he had to do the unthinkable–make a choice between his former life and me.

Douglas spoiled me outrageously. He had gotten into the habit of returning from his appointments in the city with a bunch of flowers, a small thoughtful gift, a book. One time he brought me a smooth soapstone rabbit, pale green and lucent, that fit into the palm of my hand with sweet satisfaction. I loved to hold the small stone creature and admire its compact carving.

He brought calla lilies–sheaves of calla lilies–elegant and pristine. Another time, a small wooden paneled Russian icon of St. Michael, exquisitely executed in jeweled tones of red and gold; once, a huge bunch of yellow freesias in bloom. Buried beneath the camouflage of my sophisticated, world-weary foreign correspondent there lived a complete romantic, alive and well.

One translucent morning in August, we made our way down the coast to the Wayfarer's Chapel on the verdant Palos Verdes Peninsula. That glorious little chapel stood, a faceted glass and redwood pinnacle, on a bluff above the pounding ocean. No one else was there, and we silently made our way up the several broad steps that led to a simple stone altar. Douglas put his arm around me and drew me close.

"I want to give you, something, mavourneen"–a new name he had taken to calling me. He opened his hand. In it, were two intricately carved silver rings. He silently placed one on my middle finger. I took the other and placed it on his. He leaned down and kissed me gently.

I looked at my ring more closely. "It's beautiful, darling. It has a very Celtic look about it."

"It is–it's a Celtic love knot. It's inscribed with our initials. Wear it as a symbol of my enduring love for you, dearest."

"Thank you, Douglas. I'll treasure this always." I kissed him again with passionate love. Soon, we left that enchanting place and drove back to the cottage in silent communion.

Shortly after our trip to Palos Verdes, he returned from the city one afternoon with a package. "Look, Kathleen, at what I found." He was visibly excited.

He handed it to me. "You open it "

I tore off the wrapping to uncover the simple, beautifully made sculpture of an angel. It appeared to be carved in alabaster. The figure was kneeling, arms folded over its breast in devotion, head bent. It was a lovely piece, maybe ten inches high.

"Look at the face, Kathleen. It looks like you." He smiled with delight at his find.

I examined the figure more closely. The simply carved wings were curved slightly forward, giving a sense of reverence and awe. I could see some resemblance between my own face and that of the beautiful little sculpture. Broad forehead, firm chin, an abundance of sweptback hair. Possibly a similar profile.

"It's exquisite, Douglas. Where did you find it?"

"I was just walking by an art gallery and it was displayed in a small lighted shadow box. I just had to have it."

"I guess it looks a bit like me. But angels are androgynous, aren't they?"

"That's what our mythology tells us; nevertheless this one reminds me of you. Anyway, I love it."

"I wonder if there really are such things as guardian angels–or any angels for that matter." I said longingly. "I've read that, apart from the well-known stories in the various scriptures of the world, a few people have actually seen them. I remember reading about a professor from Smith College and his wife who saw a group of them. As I recall, he and his wife were walking in a wooded area, when they heard the murmur of voices. Looking up, they saw, floating past them, six angels. They described them as young, beautiful women dressed in flowing white garments, radiant and glowing."[4]

Douglas tipped my chin up and kissed me lightly. "It makes me happy to believe that they exist. Maybe there are many kinds of spiritual beings who tend to our welfare. I'm convinced that my mother looks over me–and I suspect that your mother and father do the same for you."

I smiled and traced my finger across his mouth. "I hope so, darling, and I thank, with all my heart, whatever benign force propelled us into each other's arms across endless space and time."

---

[4] Sophy Burnham describes this incident in detail in *A Book of Angels*, 1990. The professor mentioned was S. Ralph Harlow of Smith College.

Chapter 11

Each season has its own quality, its own texture, and with each comes a change in the psyches of us humans who walk the earth. The departing days of August bespoke another year's rapid dénouement and issued a silent command to cease the levity of summer and prepare for the sobriety of winter. Reality, on hold for a few magical weeks, called for resolution. Both of us felt it keenly.

With the rapidly approaching days of September, Douglas realized with awful clarity that we could not go on indefinitely, drifting along without direction. He was unusually quiet. His face often wore a somber expression. I would frequently come upon him sitting on the deck, staring unseeingly at the capricious sea. When I saw that he was lost in his thoughts, I would slip away, leaving him to his musings. I knew that I could offer him no help in his *cris de coeur* and that my physical presence was a distraction to him. I knew, too, that in time he would unravel the tangled strands of his disparate relationships and arrive at a firm decision. I was desperately afraid I knew what that would be. I knew Douglas better than he knew himself.

One balmy night, full moon overhead, we sat on the deck listening to music on our small radio. Douglas was withdrawn and silent. He suddenly got up and, fiddling with the dial, searched until he found a station playing songs of the forties. As the orchestra began to play *Dancing in the Dark*, he came over and took my hand. "Dance with me, mavourneen."

I heard with my whole being the sadness of his voice and I knew that he had decided, that this could well be our last dance.

We held each other close, absorbing the other, body and soul. Our psyches were woven together into one indivisible being. Every cell of blood and nerve and spirit were irrevocably intertwined. The wrenching apart that I knew was inevitable would be cataclysmically painful for both of us.

After awhile, he drew me down beside him on a small bench. "Kathleen, love–" He stroked my hair. "I have to go. I can't stay with you, much as I want to. I love you more than life, itself–but I must go."

I had been dreadfully sure for some time what his decision would be. I had tried to steel myself to this outcome, but my heart clenched within me in a spasm of pain. I hugged him to me fiercely. My voice caught in my throat; I couldn't speak.

"Ah, mavourneen. I know, I know." His eyes darkened with grief. "It's so painful. Do you understand, love, why I have to go?"

"I think so, Douglas." I managed to get the words out.

"If I stayed, Kathleen–if I stayed, I'd become a different person, not the man you love and respect. My guilt wouldn't let go of me. I'd begin to despise myself, and, before long, I'd become someone other than who I am. God, if I'm not the person my heart tells me to be, then all will be a sham. To lose the love you hold for me–and it would happen, love–would be more than I could endure."

"Douglas–"

"Shh, sweet–" he hugged me tighter to him. "My love for Rosalind is woven into the fabric of my life, too. I can't tear that apart. There are too many years, too many memories, and too much love to overcome. Rosalind is a strong, lovely woman who has given me constant support–and she loves me. I respect her completely." He paused and tipped my face up so that he could look into my eyes. "You know, darling, I'm not against divorce; often it's the best option–but not for us." He sighed. "I don't know how I know, but I do."

"I understand what you're saying, Douglas. I'm bleeding inside, but I respect your decision. I think each of us walks a different path, and only our spirits can guide us to proper choices. I firmly believe that our souls have their own agendas." I sighed. "Sometimes I think that God is a trickster, that He draws us with enigmatic lines as He shapes us to His purpose." I looked into his eyes. "I'll always love you, darling–always."

"I know, Kathleen. And I, you. Somehow, by the grace of God, we'll survive."

A few days later, as we packed up our few possessions, the meager remnants of our time together, Douglas asked if he could take the little angel sculpture.

"Of course, Douglas."

"There's one other thing I would dearly love to have, mavourneen."

I looked at him questioningly.

"When we were in your workroom, I saw a painting that I'd like, if you'd part with it."

"Which one?"

His smile lit up his eyes. "The one of you."

"Oh–I didn't realize that you had noticed it."

"I did–and I liked it immensely. I'd like to hang it in my study at home. That's my favorite room, where I can relax and just be. I'll find a place for this little angel there, too."

I went back home and retrieved the painting. It had been an experiment in a somewhat pre-Raphaelite style. In it, I was holding a round-backed mandolin that my aunt Peg had once played. My face was in profile and I had painted my chin and lips a bit fuller than they actually were. My hair was brushed back and bound with white ribbon, my dress long and white. Several calla lilies were carelessly strewn on a table by my side under *de rigueur* casement windows. Rich, deep red draperies formed the background. It was a slightly sentimental piece, unabashedly romantic, but it comforted me to think of it hanging in Douglas' study, sweet company for him.

We had decided that a clean break was necessary if we were to survive. No letters, no calls, no visits–just one searing mutilation. We could not bear more.

Our last night together was a bittersweet offering of ourselves in quiet harmony muted with deep despair. Grief and love were intermingled in our every touch, our every word. Exquisite torture; exquisite delight. Pulsing bliss and fractured hearts.

Douglas had been firmly adamant that I should not drive him to the airport. "No, mavourneen. I want to remember you here in this cottage, standing in this doorway–as if in greeting though we both well know it's in farewell."

The next morning, we parted. Before he drove off in his little Austin-Healey, he handed me an envelope. "Please don't open it, Kathleen, until you get home. It's going to be hard enough as it is."

We stood silently, one last embrace, one last kiss, one last farewell.

Douglas pressed his face to my hair. "I'll always love you, Kathleen–always."

I traced my fingers for the last time over his lovely, mobile mouth. "I know, sweet. You will always be in my heart."

His last view was of me standing in the doorway as he had wished. I had picked up Sunny and held him tightly to me as if to stanch the wound that pierced my breast. Then I, too, left the enchanted little bungalow in Malibu and drove home, the envelope he had given me clutched in my hand. No tears fell from my eyes, but I could feel the silent weeping, weeping, weeping of my heart.

How I got home safely, I don't know. I was bruised and agonized; a part of my being had been torn asunder. My psyche screamed with pain and grief.

I sank into a chair in the family room and opened Douglas' message. A small silver pin fell out, enameled blue forget-me-nots fashioned on a delicately curving stem. There was a card inside. Douglas, in his own hand, had copied the first verse of an old-fashioned song that I had known as a child, a song unbearably poignant to my lacerated heart.

Mavourneen–

How can I leave thee!
How can I from thee part!
Thou only hast my heart
Dear one, believe.
Thou hast this heart of mine
So closely bound to thine,
None other can I love
Save thee alone.

Douglas

The tears came then, racking, scalding tears. My beloved had known that I would need one last loving touch across space to open the floodgates of my soul so that healing could begin.

Chapter 12

My grief, as do all deep sorrows, needed time to heal. My world seemed fractured, as if, in a moment of monumental anger, some crazily petulant god had hurled it to the ground in a fit of rage and smashed it beyond repair. I felt disjointed, disoriented. The numbers of my life refused to add up to a single sum. I, who had read spiritual literature widely and prayed faithfully, who had built an edifice of belief that had satisfied my soul, suddenly found myself plunged into a dark abyss of doubt.

When my mother had died, I felt abandoned and lost. When first Matthew, and later, my father had died, I had been depressed. This grief wore a different face. It manifested itself in a sharply focused pain in the region of my heart and in an inexorable existential questioning. I couldn't sleep. I couldn't concentrate. I couldn't paint. All I could do was question. I had to understand.

Often, I walked long hours along the bluffs of Santa Monica, questioning, questioning.

The churning sea below seemed an apt metaphor for the ebb and flow of uncertainties that threatened my worldview. In happier days, I had established a foundation. Now I could find purchase nowhere. I had been centered and secure in my knowing. Now I struggled for equilibrium. I was obsessed with ultimate meaning, with finding answers where, since ancient days, minds much wiser than mine had faltered. My former speculation about angelic verity seemed specious fantasy in light of my shattered *Weltanschauung*.

Endlessly I brooded: was there a God who knew our comings and our goings–who cared what happened to us insignificant beings who walked this green land? If so, why had Douglas and I been thrown together only to be so ruthlessly wrenched apart? To what purpose this love that usurped our volition and yet demanded our fealty? Did God indeed note the sparrow's fall, or had He, as some philosophies asserted, created us and then, totally indifferent to our fate, tossed us away as so much flotsam to manage on our own?

Maybe we lived in an uncompromisingly materialistic universe, void of Deity, that cared naught for us creatures who had, willy-nilly, been spawned on its shores. If so, why did we sacrifice for others? Why did we not all live for the moment without concern for right and wrong, for decency, for compassion? Why did we not reach out and take what we wanted as spoiled children do? Did it matter? Was there order in the universe–or was it, finally, a roll of the dice?

I floundered in doubt, sometimes convincing myself momentarily that there was indeed meaning, a *raison d'etre,* the next moment turning with weary skepticism against my previous conviction. I was consumed by a crisis of faith. I tried to pray, but the doors of Heaven were barred to me.

Along with my spiritual malaise, the pain of separation from Douglas was awful and relentless. I reeled from existential brooding to insatiable yearning for my beloved and back again to brooding. Anguish tore at my heart. Sometimes, my confused mind wasn't sure if my yearnings were for Douglas or for God.

As much as possible, I avoided contact with friends. I was too raw, too disordered to be fit company, and I wondered if Douglas was going through the same dislocation that I suffered. I knew that Peggy, Anne and Gentry were concerned for me; it was impossible to escape altogether their loving scrutiny.

Finally, Aunt Peg accosted me one morning as I was making a desultory attempt at cleaning my house, my conflicted mind circling endlessly.

"Good morning, Kathleen. I haven't seen you for a while. Do you have time for a cup of tea?" She hugged me to her.

"Of course, Peg. Come on; let's sit in the kitchen. The sun's shining in there."

We settled at the table with tea. With Dylan gone, I seldom had cookies or biscuits in the house. It mattered little to me what I ate.

"Would you like some toast, Peg? That's about all I can offer you."

Peggy sighed. "No, dear. I might as well just come right out with it. I'm worried about you. So is Richard. You don't call, you don't come around–and you're losing weight at an alarming rate." She shifted uneasily in her chair. "Can I help, Kathleen? Is there anything I can do?"

Dear, good Peggy who had been so generous with her love after my mother died. Her palpable concern deserved some kind of honesty.

"I guess I'm trying to figure out what life's all about, Peggy." I looked at her with anguish. "Is there any meaning, Peg? I want *so* to believe there is, but somehow the structures that sustained me before have splintered apart. They don't hold together for me now."

My aunt studied me silently for a moment. "It's not just Dylan going away to school, is it? I don't mean to pry, but Richard and I couldn't help but speculate, after we returned from Europe, that you were in love. Your joyful radiance was evident." She smiled. "Besides, you were never home."

"Yes, you're right of course. I had three wonderful months with a man I will always cherish. It had to end. Forgive me if I don't say more about it."

"I think there must be something beyond ordinary disappointment in your distress, dear. I won't ask questions, but I will pray for you. I think you should talk honestly with Gentry. He may be able to help you to regain your footing."

"Ah, Peg," I sighed. "I know I should. I'll give it serious consideration. He's my court of last resort, so to speak. I guess I'm afraid that even he won't be able to set me straight again."

I had entertained the thought of asking Gentry for help. He was infinitely wiser than I, well established in spiritual verities. If anyone could help me to cut through my troubled brooding, it was he. Pride, I think, kept me from immediately seeking him out. Imprudent spiritual pride tempered with an inchoate dread. I was ashamed to admit to my mentor the extent of my terrible malaise.

I had stringently avoided seeing Gentry though I had talked frequently with him on the phone. Each time he had mildly suggested that we get together for dinner I had put him off. I have no doubt that he was patiently waiting for me to realize the desperate extent of my psychic upheaval. With his far-seeing vision, Gentry knew that in time I would seek him out.

A few nights after Peggy's visit, I had a dream that woke me with a start. Sensing that it had something important to say to me, I tried to focus on the rapidly ebbing image still lingering faintly in my mind. I was in a painting class with a few other students; a master teacher made his way from easel to easel with suggestions and comments. My canvas was a ruin and I was in despair. The variously colored paints refused to stay in place. They dripped and rained onto the floor, the images blurred and streaked. The teacher came to my work and studied it quietly. Finally, he turned to me. "It can't come together until you let go of your sorrow," he said.

The message was clear; it needed no interpretation. I knew at once that the master painter was Gentry, and I knew that I must honor the dream's intent.

The next morning, I called him.

"Can you come to dinner Gentry? Tonight?" Having taken a tentative step toward help, I was restless for resolution.

"Yes, Kathleen, of course. Fix something simple and I'll bring the wine."

When he arrived, attired as usual in brown corduroy pants and fisherman sweater, clutching a bottle of Cabernet Sauvignon in his hand, he held me back and studied my eyes. Then, saying nothing, he hugged me to him and held me as a father would a child. His understanding presence was simple comfort, cool water on a desolate, withered landscape. I wondered why I had waited so long to reach out for his compassionate hand.

Gentry had always been completely comfortable with silence. He felt no need to make meaningless conversation, and so we ate quietly, saying very little. He asked about Dylan, who, to her joy, had been accepted for the dance program at Julliard. I told him how proud I was of her poise and grace, of her dedicated discipline. What I didn't say was that she was the only relief I could find in my turbulent spiritual maelstrom.

When we had finished eating, he pushed his plate back, and leaned forward, elbows on the table. "Tell me," he said simply.

"Oh, Gentry–" the empathy in his eyes destroyed my self-control. "I'm such a mess. I can't stand it anymore. I feel like I'm in a dark cavern where God does not exist; and if God doesn't exist, I don't know–" To my horror and dismay, I broke down completely, sobbing convulsively.

He put his hand on mine and waited until my tears had subsided. Then he said once again, "Tell me."

It was hard to find a place to begin. Always reticent about personal matters, I was reluctant to discuss even with Gentry my love for Douglas; but I knew, as the dream had plainly told me, that my sorrow had to be addressed if I were ever to take joy in life again.

"Gentry, something unbelievably incredible and yet unbearably difficult has happened to me." I wiped at my eyes, struggling for control. "I deeply love someone who loves me as much in return–and yet, we feel that we can't be together, that it would be wrong for us. I'm in such a muddle; I simply don't understand. Both Douglas and I sense that something beyond our understanding drew us together, that some invisible force is shaping our destinies. But to what purpose, Gentry? To what purpose if we can't be together? I, like Milton, struggle to justify God's ways to man." I paused to get my scattered emotions under control.

Gentry didn't answer. He quietly waited.

"When I was with Douglas, I talked as if I understood his decision–and I did at that point. But then after we parted, all my fine words became a mockery. I believed then that each soul has its own agenda, its own constraints, its own frailties to overcome in order to grow. But I don't know what I believe anymore; I'm not at all sure I can trust my judgment. If there's a design, it eludes me. I just keep circling around, over and over." I sighed. "What does it all mean?"

Gentry gently asked a few questions about Douglas and about his decision to return to England. He probed delicately, quickly understanding the depth of my psyche's disorganization.

"Kathleen, let me explain something to you. Often, violent psychic dislocation is the precursor to spiritual transformation. Sometimes, our being's center needs to fly apart, almost to disintegration, before it can reassemble itself to a greater, grander design. I think that's what's happening to you. Your world view has crumbled apart so that you can refashion one more resilient, more deeply centered–indeed, so that you can become something greater, something closer to the glorious pattern of who you really are."

"The words sound fine, Gentry–but how do I know I'll be able to pull myself back to a stable self, let alone a glorious one? I have no faith in my ability to do that. I don't know how."

"I've often told you that you must find your own way, right?" I nodded. "Well, for the time being, forget that." He grinned his leprechaun grin. "Since you can't trust yourself at this point, I'm asking you to let me trust for you." His face sobered. "You are going through what mystics call the Night of God. It will come right, Kathleen. It really will."

I began to feel marginally better. "But, Gentry–is there nothing I can do to help the process along?" I was bewildered by the possibility that any kind of transformation could take place without my doing anything to further it.

"Ah, Kathleen–the spirit knows what it's doing. It never sleeps, it never dreams, it never doubts. Our confusions all stem from the insecurities of our egos. Trust me that the seed for rebirth has been planted; in time, it will bear fruit. There *is* one thing though that you should do faithfully; it will speed your recovery."

"Tell me."

"You must ask–every day you must ask–sincerely, yearningly. Even if you have no faith, you must ask. Storm heaven, so to speak, even if you feel that you're battering your head against an unbreachable wall."

I thought his words over. "I do trust you, Gentry. You give me hope. I'll do my best."

After a moment, I said, "Can you help me to understand about Douglas? Why I feel so closely bound, so interwoven with him that I hardly know at what point we become separate persons? When he smiled, a smile unbidden rose from deep within me, slow and sweet. When he was sad, my heart twisted in pain. Without him, half of me is missing; I'm split apart at my core."

Gentry leaned his elbow on the table, chin in hand, reflecting on what to say. Finally, he looked up and asked, "How much do you know about reincarnation?"

I was startled. "Not much. I've never paid much attention to it."

"I hesitate to bring it up because it's a subject that's shrouded in mistaken

121

notions; it's badly misunderstood. The media–and, of course, all Occidental religions systematically trivialize the theory by ignoring it totally or by dismissing it as inconsequential nonsense even though a huge percentage of the world believes it to be a fundamental law of the Universe. Western minds find it much easier to discount its merit than seriously to study the issue even though a substantial number of our most astute thinkers subscribed to it."

"Really?"

"Oh, yes–Emerson, Thoreau, Walt Whitman, Benjamin Franklin–to name a few."

"I vaguely remember from my college days that the Transcendentalists and Yeats and other English poets were interested in reincarnation, but the text books mentioned it in passing and the professors skipped over it entirely. No one discussed it seriously."

"I know; that's the problem."

"I'm aware that Eastern religions without exception accept it."

"As a matter of fact, it was an accepted part of our church doctrine, too, until 553 AD." Gentry thought a minute. "Mark Twain was another who wrote about it. Mahler, Rudyard Kipling, Tolstoy, Jack London, Rilke–oh, Thomas Edison and Henry Ford, as well. A few scientists and many philosophers have entertained the idea in every century. Some of the greatest minds of Western civilization have embraced it, and yet the majority of people in our culture have no idea that this is a viable way of looking at life."

He laughed. "I didn't mean to go off on a lecture, but it's a complex subject. I'll give you a few books to read. For now, just let me explain that one of the tenets of reincarnation is that souls come together again and again over millennia to work out their problems, to support each other, to love each other. In some cases two souls will return again and again in loving reunion. Douglas and you fit that pattern, Kathleen."

"I resonate to what you say; it feels right. Douglas once said that he felt that we had been together from time immemorial. But Gentry, why would we set ourselves up for such pain if we've loved each other over stretches of time? What are we to gain from it? Again, I'm in a quandary. If life has a design, what's the purpose of this painful separation?"

"Our souls are seeking perfection, Kathleen; that's why we return again and again. Perhaps there's unfinished business in Douglas' life that must be completed if he's to honor his soul's deepest intent. Perhaps the two of you have become so intertwined over time that this lifetime you must distance yourselves from each other so that you can become independently whole. I can think of several scenarios that would not only explain, but could give meaning to your sacrifice."

"Ah, Gentry, that's the crux of it, isn't it? To understand my sorrow so that I can let it go. You give me a good deal to think about. I thank you from the bottom of my heart, dear friend."

He got up to leave. "I'll drop some books off tomorrow."

I had said nothing to him about my ambivalent yearnings, but he knew. "You're right, Kathleen; your fundamental longing is not for Douglas; it's for God."

I avidly read the books that Gentry brought me. In the early sixties, reincarnation was not the household word it is today. Even now, though the terms *reincarnation* and *karma* are a part of our cultural vocabulary, few people entertain the hypothesis seriously. Gentry's books opened a new world to me–a world where there is no selective salvation, where there is no need for a punishing God, a world where every relationship has hidden dimensions of meaning and purpose. Slowly I wove threads of understanding into the design I had been seeking.

I mounted an assault on heaven with all the fervor I could muster. My ideas of God were vague and unfocused, but I was determined to break through to clarity and to an abiding interrelationship with Spirit.

Each day I grew in strength and in faith. I was slowly finding increments of happiness and joy. My dreams took an unexpected turn. I had seldom remembered them clearly, if at all. Now when I awoke, I retained clear images of my nighttime journeys. I had read enough Jungian psychology to know that dreams can be messages from the soul, so I paid scrupulous attention to them, ferreting out what meaning I could from their sometimes-chaotic scenarios.

One that came early to me still remains vividly in my mind. I was presented with a death procession in a large, dim cathedral with high vaulted ceilings. There were no mourners. In silence, a solemn cortege of priests dressed in formal vestments slowly carried a coffin, shoulder high, down the narrow aisle to an alter ablaze with candles. I knew that it was my death that I witnessed. When I awoke, I understood that this was a symbolic death–a death in order that new life might begin. I took it as a sign of healing and regeneration.

Gradually, I moved into the new beginning foretold in my dream. I began to paint again and to take new writing assignments. I changed the guest bedroom into a study, a private place for me alone. I lovingly hung the painting I had done of Douglas and found a home there for the small gifts he had given me. In this sanctuary of the spirit, I wrote and studied and meditated. Douglas' mention of that discipline had awakened an interest in me. I eagerly read what meager information I could find and successfully taught myself.

Gentry continued to be of invaluable help to me as I rebuilt and redefined my edifice of belief. We had long walks, long dinners, long discussions as he answered my questions and gently stimulated my growing desire to become whole. I told him about my teeming dream life and sometimes shared one or two dreams with him. His insights were invaluable.

In one such dream, I was sitting under a tree. The sky was gloriously blue; the grass preternaturally green, each blade shining in ecstasy. A white bird, a red rose in its beak, silently glided down toward me. It dropped the rose in my lap and then soared away into the azure sky. As I sat there, little white flowers sprang up all around me. It was a lovely dream.

Gentry smiled. "The seeds of your sorrow have taken root, Kathleen; your suffering has been transformed into something of value."

* * *

One early December evening, Dylan called to tell me that she planned to fly home for Christmas. I was, of course, delighted.

"Is it OK, Mum, if I bring Maria with me?" Maria, Dylan's first friend in New York, had successfully auditioned for Julliard as well; the two were inseparable.

"Of course, dear. I'll look forward to getting to know her better. Has she no family that will want her to come home for Christmas?"

"Her mom's remarried and she can't stand her stepfather. She says she doesn't trust him, so she tries to avoid going home. She feels bad about it, really bad."

"How sad. We'll try to give her a happy time here then, darling."

I picked the girls up at the airport Christmas week. My heart leapt with joy as I watched long-legged, graceful Dylan come bounding toward me, Maria in tow. Such vitality, such vividness of coloring. I realized that over the few months she had been gone, my image of my daughter had become dimmed. I silently thanked God for my lovely girl and for my regained equilibrium. We would have a beautiful, joyful Christmas.

Even the house was cheered to have Dylan back for a time. Sunny, her orange tabby, patiently followed her from room to room, curling up in her lap in bliss whenever she finally settled somewhere. The magic of the season, the bright and glowing tree, the candles, the sweet music of Christmas were a quiet benediction on our home.

One morning, Dylan came to my study to tell me she and Maria were going shopping. As she looked around, she noticed the painting of Douglas.

She went closer to study it.

"That's a wonderful interpretation of Mr. Cameron." She turned to me. "You love him, don't you, Mum?"

"Yes, Dylan, I do." I was surprised at her perception and I knew that I must answer honestly. "Is it because of the painting that you think that?"

"Oh, no. When we went out in New York, I could tell. The way you looked at each other, the way you touched each other in passing. It was obvious; I could feel it in the air."

"Does it bother you, dear?"

"Mercy no, Mum. I'm happy for you."

"There's nothing to be happy about, sweetheart. It's all over." I thought Dylan should understand. "Douglas went back to England; he isn't coming back."

"But why? You both were so happy. You were just radiant. I know he's married, but can't he get a divorce?"

"Yes, he could, Dylan–but we've decided that, for us, it would be a mistake." I saw the disappointment on her face. "It's all right, dear. I've made peace with our decision. I know it's the way it was meant to be."

She came and put her arms around me. "Oh, Mum–I'm so sorry. I was hoping you'd marry him; I like him so much. Maybe you'll find someone else. I wouldn't mind–I really wouldn't."

"Thank you for your concern, sweetheart. But no, I'll never marry anyone else. I'm fine. Don't worry about me. I'm really fine."

She looked into my eyes, and satisfied that all was well, she hugged me and left me alone. Thank God, I had gotten myself patched back together before I had to face her penetrating gaze. I pondered our conversation. She must have wondered why I had never mentioned Douglas to her. It was good that we had talked about it, gotten it out into the open. It was good, too, that she could see that life did not always work out in storybook fashion.

On Christmas Day, Gentry joined the girls and me for dinner at Peggy and Richard's house. Because he seldom could be persuaded to take part in holiday festivities, I was surprised that this year he had accepted Peg's invitation. After we had surfeited ourselves on her excellent dinner, we settled comfortably by the fire and listened to Gentry read Dylan Thomas' *A Child's Christmas in Wales*. My father traditionally had read it to us each year when he was alive. I offered a silent prayer for my dad, and acknowledging that I was deeply blessed, I prayed that Douglas, too, was enjoying a beautiful Christmas day.

Chapter 13

My greatest pleasure was to sit in my study, Douglas' portrait keeping watch over me. I often imagined him sitting in his, with my likeness looking down on him in quiet companionship. Perhaps the little angel sculpture stood close to him where he could reach out and touch it. I thought of him constantly, but the pain had, for the most part, subsided. Only occasionally did my wayward heart twist with yearning. As I had told Dylan, I was fine; I had made peace with our separation.

Now that I had returned to some semblance of normalcy, friends showered me with invitations to join them–to go to the movies, a concert, dinner. I soon learned, though, that I needed to be careful in my acceptance.

Gentry took me one spring evening to an orchestral performance. The program included Gustav Mahler's tender and romantic *Adagietto*, the love letter he had sent to Alma Schindler to declare his love. As the music soared in plangent beauty, I found myself in tears, my heart writhing with yearning for Douglas. He had particularly loved this piece. I struggled to control myself. Gentry leaned over and put his hand on mine in silent support. I couldn't bear it; I fled precipitously to the ladies room until the exquisite little composition was finished.

I found it best, too, to avoid drama, whether book or play. I soon learned to read only nonfiction, to go only to light-hearted films. Though I had come to terms for the most part with my grief, my heart still splintered unexpectedly when it was faced with poignant emotion. I fared better if I avoided anything that might agitate that capricious yearning in my soul.

In May, I again had a cluster of meaningful dreams.

I was diving down, down in a clear, dark sea. A shaft of light from the surface lit my way. I could see my pale greenish form, my hair floating behind like undulating seaweed, as I followed a luminous path downward. On the ocean floor an ancient cask had broken open. Pearls and rubies and gold stuff spilled out on the sandy bottom. All of it was mine for the taking. Then I awoke.

Several nights later, I dreamed that an unseen ancient hand held out an ornate silver chalice. I accepted it, and then the same bodiless hand poured bubbling, effervescent life-giving water into the cup until it rained down over the sides. The hand kept pouring–and still it poured until I awoke.

There were two more dreams that I remember vividly; at the time I carefully detailed them in my journal. I was in a fair, gently rolling land. It looked to me like some of the pictures I had seen of English countryside–a counterpane of greens and browns and russets. I wandered along a path where weeping willows dipped down to a clear running brook. Birds sang. The sky was cloudless. An enchanted and enchanting place. As I walked, I came upon a barrier in the stream. It had been split partially open, as if by a tremendous force. I was appalled to see brown, slimy dross come spouting through the fissure. Dark waters and black waste material spewed out. Clots of mud were ejected. As I watched, the waters gradually cleared, first to lighter brown, then to a dusty gray hue. I stood rooted to the spot. Suddenly, the whole barrier splintered and collapsed and fresh, bubbling clear water roared down, carrying bits and pieces of the destroyed planks with it. When all the debris had been carried away, I went to the edge, and kneeling down I drank my fill from the crystal stream.

As I reflected on my dream, I interpreted the viscous masses of dross and slime to be knots of suffering, of self-pity, and of doubt that had lodged deep within my psyche. I understood that something clear and lucent within had broken through the wall of my sorrow and desolation. I knew that a massive burden had been carried away by the loving benevolence of God's grace.

The last dream of the series came a few nights later. A woman, dressed in a loose white dress, was walking along a high bluff overlooking the ocean. Large boulders and rock formations at the edge had broken off precipitously, the sides of the canyon dropping away sharply to the sea far below. As she ventured very close to the edge, I noticed that she had a long red scarf wrapped around her. Suddenly, as if catapulted by some unseen force, she spread her arms out and flew out over the canyon, her long scarf trailing behind her in the downdraft of her flight. I awoke, my heart pounding. I knew that I was that woman. As I lay there in bed trying to decipher the dream, I recalled a poem I had read several years before. It reminded me vividly of the scene I had just witnessed in my dream. The next morning, I looked through my various papers and found it.

> *"Come to the edge," he said.*
> *They said: "We are afraid."*
> *"Come to the edge," he said.*
> *They came.*
> *He pushed them.*
> *And they flew.*[5]

---

[5] "Come to the Edge" by Guillaume Apollinaire

The other dreams I had understood with little trouble. This one, however, was mysterious and a little frightening. I talked with Gentry about it and told him of my association of it with the poem. I had memorized the few lines and I quoted them to him.

"Yes, I'm familiar with the poem," he said. "I can tell you nothing about your dream that will be helpful to you beyond the fact that you have nothing to fear. In time, you'll understand."

I knew he would say no more about it.

The next few days, I occasionally thought about my flying dream, trying to figure out its meaning. At odd moments I would find myself repeating the last three lines of the poem to myself:

"They came... He pushed them...And they flew."

* * *

I had vague, unformed glimpses of my dream's meaning, but nothing coalesced to give me a sense of completion. I would have to wait and see if time would clarify its significance for me.

Dylan called often. She had had a minor lead in a dance performance at school that thrilled her, a solid achievement for a first year student; she thought she would go to another dance workshop in the summer if it was all right with me. Annie had her baby, a fair-faced little girl whose name was Allison; I was appointed godmother. Peg and Richard insisted frequently that I come to dinner. And Gentry–dear Gentry–chose to give up large portions of his precious solitude to keep me caring company. With the solicitude of family and friends and with my renewed interest in work, I became aware with surprise that a year had come and gone since that day when Douglas' and my paths had converged in New York City.

I had formed the habit of driving, about once a week, over the mountains from my home to the coast. I loved to walk along the bluff in Santa Monica where a grassy area extended along its length. As far as the eye could see were sand and ocean and light–sometimes naked sunlight, sometimes hazy, diffused light, occasionally sullen light–but always a profusion of light, spilling over, pouring abundantly down from the heavens. I reveled in it.

Sometimes I read, sometimes I walked, sometimes I simply sat on the grass without thought and lost myself in the ever-moving sea. I usually made my odyssey just before sunset and each time, hardly aware of rushing traffic counterpointed by the ocean's ebb and flow, I watched the earth momentarily pause in benediction as the sun settled in ritual descent into the welcoming sea. I loved this holy, sacred time.

One mid-September afternoon, I took my weekly ride to the coast, thinking to have a bowl of chowder at the little café on the Santa Monica Pier once dusk had fallen. I sat on the grass, arms wrapped around my knees, and gave myself to the lapis sea. Silently I watched the accustomed drama unfold. Slowly the great celestial sun sank toward the horizon as the hush of the world wrapped its splendor around me.

As I watched that glorious sunset, almost more beautiful than I could endure, a high- pitched, piercing sound suddenly resonated through my head, penetrating throughout my whole being. I thought, *My God, am I having some kind of epileptic attack? A cranial aneurysm?*

I shook my head in disbelief, trying to clear it, but the pitch only got higher and oscillated with even greater intensity. It was a thin, electronic frequency that made my whole body tremble in synchronous entrainment. I uttered a silent prayer–*My God, help me*–. Then, with a sudden rush, I was devoured in flame. I was purged in the raw white light of God's Eternal Eye. I stood defenseless from that All-absorbing Light, that Radiance, that one Nuclear Being.

Linear thought processes falter and accustomed words pale in describing what happened next. I vaguely recall an answering 'yes' within me to some divine Imperative. I can't describe the order of events; much is fragmented or forgotten. But this I remember clearly: completely aware, indeed, more gloriously aware and conscious than ever before in my life, I found myself flung far out over the ocean, into the darkening sky, dancing and soaring joyously through the heavens. Great swirling lights blossomed on every side of me amid streaming constellations. Flaming meteors streaked by.

In abandonment, I loosed myself completely to God's shining splendor. Immediately I was transported to the farthest reaches of the Universe. Angelic choirs, intermingling in exquisite harmony, sang in shimmering antiphonal exaltation.

Drunk with ecstasy, I soared through celestial heavens. I danced down grids of dazzling light. I danced through galaxies of stars. I danced on oceans of luminous, quivering gold. In exultation, I danced a pavane of reverence. I danced in praise: *Praise to God, Praise to All That Is, Praise to Adonai, to the Atman, Praise to every living thing.* I danced and soared and spun with rapturous delight across the radiant, infinite star-seeded fields of God

Somehow I was given to understand that every created thing was irrevocably alive, cradled in God's loving hands. I understood that every stone, every blade of grass, every drop of water were humming units of the universal, all-encompassing One. I understood that all–humans, beasts, fields, flowers–were inter-connected by shining strands of light, each individual unit linked to every other in an endless web of support and love, enclosed in God's living Presence.

I was shown that, in truth, His love was the glue that held the universe together, that tracked the planets in their spheres and maintained the nebulae in the heavens, that contained and sustained each atom, each minutia of living matter. I was shown that in essence we all are surrounded, interpenetrated, and literally contained within His mighty Being forever, and, astonishingly, that we are His beloveds. I knew that were He to withdraw that love, all would fall into destruction.

Suddenly, I was slammed back into my body. I found myself still sitting on the grass, my cheeks wet with tears. I had no idea how long I had gamboled among the stars. I looked around in a daze. It was now dark, a slender moon suspended in space. A cool breeze had sprung up, and suddenly cold, I started to stand up. As I moved my hand, I saw luminous light streaming from my fingers. At first, I thought this must be some trick of moonlight falling on my body. I closed my eyes and opened them again. Still, numinous light seemed to pour from my hands, and, as I looked down in bewilderment, I saw that my arms and legs were aglow, too, with some ethereal radiance. I sat stunned, unable to comprehend; then slowly I got up and drove home.

I couldn't sleep that night. I felt exhilarated, electrically charged; my whole body was magnetized and glowing. Every cell vibrated at a frequency that was almost impossible to contain. I lay on the lounge by my swimming pool all night long, wide-awake, searching the heavens as if to gain understanding from the skies. As the dawn came, I knew, with humble joy, that I had been touched by God's hand. I was a totally different woman from the one who had casually driven over the mountains to enjoy the setting sun so short a time before. In some undefined way, I had been transformed.

In the clear light of a new day, I tried to evaluate my ecstatic experience. I knew I had been awake; this had been no dream. I knew I had not imagined the light flaring from my fingers because I could still see a luminous patina on my hands and arms. It was clear to me that I could tell no one but Gentry about this cataclysmic event; I didn't question my sanity but anyone else would surely think me mad.

I slowly got up and went into the house. I needed to write down all I could remember of my night of joy. I had to catch hold of the ephemeral and elusive images lest in time I forget. To capture its essence would be daunting, I knew, for I had brought back only snatches of the knowing that had been mine. What words could portray with any sort of verisimilitude that cosmic interlude?

For several days, the humming vibrations continued within me, making it difficult to concentrate or to sleep. An overwhelming love for creation flowed through me. Every creature blazed with an inner illumination; people were exquisite in their unconscious splendor. Every leaf and every tree hummed with vitality, and the earth's colors were magnificent in their brilliance.

The beauty around me time and again brought tears to my eyes: Sunny lying in the sun, his orange coat a bonfire of ecstasy; a spider web–delicate, quivering molten luminosity; an unknown old woman passing by, wrinkled as an ancient peach, light pouring off her withered face. Everywhere I looked, golden motes glittered in radiant light. My foray into celestial dimensions had stripped a layer of insulation from me, leaving me vulnerable and exposed. My heart had been wrenched open; Brahmic Splendor overwhelmed me.

Gradually, the aftermath of that night faded and I returned to a more normal state. I had no idea why I had been the chosen recipient of God's ineffable grace, but I was filled with gratitude. I felt a deep humility and an abiding sense of the symbiotic unity of all life. I knew that life was eternal for all. I knew beyond a doubt that all was indeed well, as I had read so many years before in the book Douglas had given me.

A few months later, I drove into Los Angeles to interview a man who made handcrafted lutes. I had heard of him through Annie; I thought his vocation unusual and interesting. He would be an excellent subject for an article. I had no trouble finding his small frame house bordered with a well-tended lawn. I rang the bell. No one answered. I rang again and wondered if somehow I had gotten the time of my appointment wrong.

I rang once more and was turning to leave when the door opened and an older man, his hand wrapped in a towel, peered out. He looked to be close to eighty, with a gray beard and sparse hair neatly combed. I noticed lively brown eyes behind thick glasses.

"Mr. Vittorio? I'm Kathleen Parrish."

"Oh, yes. Come in; come in. I'm sorry I kept you waiting, but I've had an accident." He ruefully held up his hand. "I was carving the neck of a lute and my knife slipped. I grabbed a towel to stop the bleeding."

"Let me see how bad it is." He looked dreadfully pale and shaken. "Maybe I can drive you to the doctor."

He held his hand out and I gingerly pulled back the bloodied towel. It was a deep cut between his thumb and forefinger; I was appalled at the extent of his injury.

"I really can't see much with all this blood. Shall we try to wash it?"

He nodded, his face white with shock. "This way." He led me into a small immaculate kitchen.

"Now, let's see how bad it is." I put his hand in a bowl of water, then, drying it gently, I took it in mine and, with the other, I tried to assess the damage. As I cradled his injured hand in both of mine, I was amazed to see the blood suddenly stop flowing. I pressed my fingers around the edges of the wound. I could see a little oozing, but it seemed almost to have stopped. It looked clean but fairly deep.

"Maybe you should see a doctor. You might have a damaged tendon." I was concerned that he could lose the use of his thumb and finger, a necessity for his occupation.

He looked at it. "You know, since you held it, it doesn't hurt like it did. And, see, it's not bleeding anymore." He cautiously moved his thumb and finger apart and then back together. "I don't think I could do that if the tendon were cut, do you? See, I can bend my thumb, too."

"Um–maybe not. But I don't know much about such things. Why don't we go have it checked just in case? There's an emergency room close by. I'll go with you."

"You know, I have a feeling it'll be all right with a little time." He flexed his thumb and finger again. " I'll go tomorrow if it doesn't look right to me, Mrs. Parrish. Thanks for offering, though."

"I'm Kathleen. Do you live alone?"

He nodded. "Yes, my wife died a few years ago."

"I'm sorry." I studied him. "You look dreadfully pale. Let me at least bandage this for you and make you some tea."

After I had cleaned up his hand, we sat at the kitchen table and I gave him well-sugared tea with packaged cookies that I had found in a cupboard. I watched him carefully; his color was returning and he looked comfortable, but I didn't want to tire him.

"Look, I can come back another time. You've had a real shock."

"Nah. I'm feeling better all the time. We can talk now." He set his cup aside. "Come on–I'll show you my workroom." I followed him, noticing that he had a slight limp, probably rheumatic. He led me into a room off the kitchen crammed with woodworking equipment: saws, files, varnishes, brushes, fine woods, all in meticulous order. Lutes were hanging from the ceiling in various states of completion and design. There must have been six or seven of them. On his workbench, a partially carved instrument laid, a bloody knife in a pool of blood close by. Blood, by now dark and ugly, had spattered on the unfinished lute as well.

I helped him clean up the mess and he then showed me, step by step, the process of lute making. He had learned the craft from his grandfather who had learned it from his father in Italy. He talked knowledgeably about the supreme importance of the finish for superior sound and the grain of the wood for beauty. His eyes were alight with enthusiasm. It was a good interview

"And you sell these without trouble?" I asked.

"Oh, yes. I have more orders than I can easily fill. My lutes have a lovely, rich tone. And see," he showed me the back of a completed one. "Look at the grain of this wood. Isn't it beautiful?" Mr. Vittorio ran his hand lovingly over the exquisitely finished instrument.

"It is, indeed. And the wood inlay is remarkable. It's incredibly beautiful. It makes me wish I could play one." I took pleasure in his pride, amazed that this old gentleman should still have such passion for his work.

"Do you do this all alone?" I asked. It seemed to me more than even a younger man could handle.

"Mostly. A young high school boy comes in a couple of hours after school. He helps me clean up the place and do some of the basic work. I'm trying to pass on what I know to him. You know, lute making is becoming a lost art. There aren't many left who know how to hand-craft an instrument like this from start to finish. I'd like to see it continue into the next generation."

"It would be a shame if that knowledge were lost." I rose and held out my hand. "Thank you, Mr. Vittorio. I'm honored that you shared your knowledge with me. I'm going to call you tomorrow to be sure your hand is okay."

"I thank you for helping me out of a mess, Kathleen. Come back any time." He looked down at his hand. "It doesn't hurt at all anymore," he said in surprise.

He showed me to the door, and impulsively, I reached up and hugged him. His bright eyes glowed with this simple show of affection. I knew he must be deeply lonely.

The next day I called to check on his injury.

"How's your hand, Mr. Vittorio? And how are *you?*" I was concerned for the old gentleman who lived alone.

"Ah, Kathleen, I'm fine. You wouldn't believe it. It looks almost healed. It doesn't even need a real bandage anymore. I put a large band-aid over it to keep it clean."

"Are you sure you shouldn't have it checked, sir? That was a nasty cut." I hoped he wasn't being too cavalier about a very real injury.

"It looks good, Kathleen–it really does. I know it'll be fine."

"Well, look–don't try to use it for awhile. Give those fingers plenty of time to heal. Maybe I'll stop by and see you in a day or two, if that's all right with you." He was too proud to ask, but I knew he hoped I'd visit him again.

"I'd be delighted, Kathleen. Please come any time. I enjoyed our little talk–and I can't thank you enough for helping me out."

What a dear man. We said our good-byes with the promise that I'd call soon.

I waited for a week before visiting Mr. Vittorio again. He was a truly old-fashioned gentleman, and I liked him immensely. I fixed a picnic lunch of deviled eggs, potato salad, crusty bread, and ham. I added a bottle of Chianti, along with some little apple tarts and cheese.

He was waiting for me, dressed up in old-fashioned looking brown wool trousers and a white shirt. His eyes tearing slightly, he hugged me and led me to the kitchen. That room and his workroom seemed to be the center of his life, though I doubt he cooked any but the most simple of meals in his small kitchen.

I set the basket on the table and turned to him. "Okay–let me see your thumb."

He held it out eagerly, showing me that he could easily move all of his fingers. I took his hand in mine. The smallest faint white line was all that remained of his injury. I looked up at him, puzzled. "This has certainly healed well–and fast. I can hardly believe it."

"Kathleen–," he looked uncertain about how to begin. "When you held my hand in both of yours the other day, I felt something. Your hands were really hot–like they were on fire. I didn't say anything at the time, but remember how the bleeding suddenly stopped?"

"Yes, I remember. It did seem to stop."

"This might sound strange, but I think you have some kind of energy that healed me."

"Oh, I don't think so, Mr. Vittorio. Maybe it wasn't as bad as it looked–or maybe you're just a fast healer." I felt vaguely upset at his suggestion. I started to unpack the picnic basket, eager to change the subject. "Come on, let's eat."

He ate with relish, looking up now and again to grin at me. Obviously he found the attention and the food equally enjoyable. I cleared up the table, and we settled down with the remains of the Chianti.

"Kathleen, listen to me." He thought a minute. "I had an aunt back in Italy who had the gift of healing. There *is* such a thing, you know. I visited there when I was a small boy, and I came down with a terrible case of pneumonia while I was there. My parents were afraid they'd lose me." He laughed. "They didn't have antibiotics in those days, you know. Anyway, after the doctor had all but given up on me, my parents allowed my aunt, who claimed she could help me, to do whatever she could for me. You see, my parents prided themselves on being above superstition. They were both well-educated, urbane people and their faith was strictly in medicine. I had a raging fever, so I don't remember much of this. It's just what I've been told. My aunt came and sat by me, and put her hands, one on my forehead, and the other on my chest. My parents told me with tears in their eyes that after about ten minutes, I opened my eyes for the first time in several days and asked for water. The fever had broken and I recovered very quickly from my illness. Really, Kathleen–you *know* there's no other reasonable explanation for my hand healing like this."

This was a new idea to me and one I was not sure I wanted to consider. "There *must* be some other explanation," I said, fiddling with my wine glass.

"Like what? I'm telling you, your hands were like fire." Mr. Vittorio studied me. "Since it makes you uncomfortable, I won't say more about it except to thank you. I'm convinced that because of you, I can continue to use my hand to carve lutes. I'm in your debt, Kathleen."

I left soon, promising to come another time. On the drive home, I thought about his certainty that I had been instrumental in restoring his hand. I had never seen a wound of that severity heal so rapidly, but still...

I thought back. Was there anything else to suggest that my hands were channels for healing energy? I thought of Sunny. He had taken to leaping into my lap anytime I settled myself for any length of time. Strange behavior for him. I knew he greatly missed Dylan, but this aberrant behavior had not started until the last few months. Now he was unmistakably drawn to me while before he had squirmed away anytime I attempted to hold him. My plants and my yard were flourishing with unusually surprising vigor, too. Even Peg, master gardener, had mentioned that. But surely that proved nothing at all.

Suddenly, my mind flashed back to an evening when I had been visiting Annie. She had called and asked me to spend the evening with her. Mark had gone to a conference in San Francisco and she thought it would be nice just to sit and talk. Allison, an unsteady toddler, had been bringing me toys, one by one, laying them gravely in my lap. Each time, I'd say, "Thank you, Allison"; then she would beam and trot off for another offering, a game she was enjoying immensely.

On one precarious foray, she stumbled and fell, cracking her head against the edge of the coffee table. She howled in pain. Annie was in the kitchen making coffee, so I snatched her up and cradled her in my arms as her mother came running. In tears, she went to Anne, but as soon as she had calmed down a bit, she came and snuggled into my lap.

She had a nasty bruise that had already swelled into a sizable knot on her forehead. I rocked her and kissed her, and stroked her hair. Then–why, I'm not sure–I put my hand over the bruise. She fell asleep in my arms, sucking her thumb. I carried her to her crib, noticing when I put her down that there was no sign at all of her nasty fall. At the time, I was mildly surprised but thought little of it.

Now, I was discomfited by my memory of that evening. Could it be? Could I have been given the gift of healing?

Back in September, after I had shared my adventure in the stars with Gentry, he had told me that mystical encounters often brought unusual abilities in their wake. He had given me a copy of *Cosmic Consiousness* by Richard Bucke, who had been a medical doctor. Gentry suggested that I might find it useful to read of others' experiences of illumination. That little classic, published first in 1901, was still in print, readily available to a new generation. I discovered that Bucke believed that cosmic consciousness was an evolutionary process toward which humanity slowly but surely was growing; that, in time, it would be a natural attribute of mankind.

If humanity were to evolve in the direction of Bucke's theory, certainly all of our social systems would be radically transformed. Nothing could remain the same. I considered his theory with interest, but, much as I might have liked, I could feel little resemblance to that august group Bucke had identified as prototypes of illumination. And I was wary, indeed, of implementing this gift of healing if it was truly mine.

Chapter 14

Gentry and I were enjoying a late lunch in a small café close to my home. We frequently met there to eat and to hash over the many questions I invariably had, whether about painting or about things of the spirit. It was a pleasant, homey place, reasonably quiet, and Mary, the owner, was accommodating about our frequent lingering conversations.

Gentry interrupted his eating to lean forward and put his hand on mine.

"Kathleen, what are you afraid of?" His eyes were filled with compassion.

"Everything, Gentry–everything that has to do with this business of healing." He had convinced me that some kind of power was being channeled through my hands, as Mr. Vittorio had tried to tell me.

"I foresee only trouble," I said. There was little general acceptance of psychic phenomena or of alternative healing methods in 1965, though a blossoming interest emerged in the 70's and '80's.

"I'll be setting myself up for endless ridicule and misunderstanding if I pursue this."

"What makes you so sure you'd be misunderstood?" Gentry's quiet question did little to assuage my concern.

"I've read enough to know that the average person would see me as a fraud, or worse, as a spawn of the devil. I want no part of it."

"Hey, Kathleen, relax. It's not that bad," Gentry said mildly, pausing to take a sip of coffee. "I'm not suggesting that you hold a tent meeting or take out a full page ad. Has it occurred to you that in effect you're throwing God's gift to you back in His face?"

I sank back in my seat. "Oh, Gentry–" I mulled over his statement. "I guess you're right. I'm being horribly ungrateful–and after the transcendent grace that was given me–but I'm still scared about all of this. I can see myself being accused of witchcraft, complete with Sunny as my familiar. It all seems more a burden than a blessing."

"Are you just going to turn your back on this power given you? *Can* you ignore it?" His eyes held mine.

After a moment, I shook my head, still dismayed, but beginning to grasp the implication of his comment. "You're right. If I'm to honor my inner being, I have to respect this, whatever it is. I don't like to call it a gift–and 'power' is even worse. To me, to claim either one is arrogant and presumptuous."

"Think of it as an attribute or an ability, Kathleen. Just as you have a talent for art, you now, by the grace of God, have a talent for healing."

"Umm, that feels better to me."

"As for presumption, isn't it arrogant to decide that you know more about what's appropriate than God does? You've been singled out, dear. Not Anne, not Dylan, not me. *You*." He was uncustomarily intent.

"That's the problem, Gentry. That's what I have trouble accepting. *Why* me instead of you? Why *not* my loving, sensitive Dylan? Both of you are much more compassionate by nature than I am. It's a huge, scary responsibility."

"Yes, I can understand why you feel that way. But it *is* your responsibility, isn't it?"

I nodded numbly.

Mary wandered over and refilled our cups. After she left, Gentry continued his argument.

"Look, Kathleen. There's no need to be overt about this. You don't need to proclaim yourself a healer. Go slowly—very slowly—and see what develops. As in all things, you have to learn your craft; that takes time. I think you'll know when it's appropriate to use this new talent and when it's not."

I smiled, feeling marginally better. "Thanks, Gentry. You always help me to put things in the proper perspective. What would I do without you?"

"Umm—I just speed the process along a little. You'd eventually come to the same conclusions by yourself."

"Maybe, but bless you for being here for me, dear friend," I said as we got up to leave.

In April, Douglas' book, *Voices of Destiny* came out in the United States. I had received a package from England in late March. I knew before I opened it that it was his book. I understood that he wanted me to be the first to see it. It was the only contact from him since he had gone. He had autographed it simply: *To Kathleen with love, Douglas.* I sensed the unspoken language of words left unsaid.

His photograph was on the inside cover. To see it was infinitely precious to me. My thirsty heart absorbed each nuance of his dearly remembered face. He appeared older to me, and his features seemed more sharply defined, etched with new lines around his mouth—that beautiful mouth that had always fascinated me so. I could hardly tear my eyes away. My heart was full.

I knew that he wouldn't expect to be thanked for this gift. To write a restrained note would be unthinkable, a charade, but I treasured his offering. I took joy in reading the words he had written, in seeing the notable personalities he had presented from his unique point of view.

Voices of Destiny was extremely well received both in England and

America; it was a handsome and well-written volume. My heart sang for Douglas. I knew how much he would treasure this achievement; I knew also that the conflict in Vietnam was escalating alarmingly and I prayed that he would choose to stay at home, that he would make a peaceful transition from foreign correspondent to successful author. The brief biography on the book cover told me little of his life. I searched newspapers and news magazines but could find no further information about his current plans. All I could do was to commit him daily to God's care and pray that hosts of angels might attend his way.

I had decided, shortly after that magical night of transcendent revelation in September that I would give up both free-lance writing and painting portraits on consignment. I wanted the luxury of time to explore new avenues of painting and to nurture my soul. Fortunately, I had an adequate nest egg, thanks to good investments and a substantial fund from my father's estate. Providing for my simple needs was no problem

I had one last assignment I had agreed to at the request of an editor, an old friend who had helped me get started years before. It was an article on the early days of news broadcasting. I had already gotten most of my information together. I had one more appointment, an interview with Jeffrey Patterson, news anchor at CBS. He had been one of "Murrow's Boys," hired for his youth and his keenly analytic mind during those furiously intense days of World War II, days that shaped and stretched and defined radio news to a dynamic reality unheard of in earlier times.

As I headed for this last interview, I wondered if this man's path had ever crossed Douglas'. It seemed likely since both were in England during those perilous days of the war.

Mr. Patterson, face and voice familiar as an old friend's, was a heavy-set man with a genuine smile and an avuncular demeanor. He welcomed me warmly and, with the gracious tact I had found in most well known people, gave me his undivided attention. Somehow his manner conveyed that he had all the time in the world, that there was nothing he could possibly prefer to sitting and chatting with me.

He was forthcoming about his experiences, both in radio and in his climb upward to one of the premier positions in television. I asked him which personalities he thought were most instrumental in shaping broadcasting news into its present form.

"Well, of course, Ed Murrow. He practically created news as we know it today. Cronkite, Cameron in England come to mind. Our present day reporters are heirs of those first pioneers who brought the news to us directly from its source. They were willing to do whatever was necessary to get their story–fresh, alive, immediate. Before the war, newspapers were the only real news gathering agencies, and, of course, they can never be as immediate as radio and television, given our present technology."

"And you were one of those correspondents who did whatever was necessary, did you not?"

Jeffrey Patterson smiled in remembrance. "Yeah, I was a hell of a reporter. I'd take any risk, go anywhere by any means available to get a good story. You had to if you wanted to succeed in this business. Those were good days–tough, but, by God, great. You knew you were really alive. Lord, sometimes we'd be awake and on a story for forty-eight hours without sleep." He paused reflectively. "I have Ed Murrow to thank for my start. I was just a punk kid when he signed me on."

"Those must have been exciting times. Did you know Mr. Cameron?"

"Oh, yes. I knew him. He had a very forceful personality. You know, it was a dog eat dog climate in those days–still is, for that matter–and he fought it out with the best of them, hot to get the story first. Talk about taking risks–he was the most daring of us all. He courted danger repeatedly, verging on irresponsibility–to the point that NBC extracted a promise from him to use more caution. Not that he paid any attention. He lived life dangerously and to the hilt."

"Oh," I said noncommittally, hoping that he would continue. He seemed to be enjoying his reminiscences, and I was eager to hear about Douglas.

Mr. Patterson leaned back in his chair and sighed. "This is off the record, of course."

I nodded.

"It's hard to explain the urgency that infected us all–military as well as civilian. We acted as if we were absolutely invulnerable, as if nothing could touch us. At the same time, we lived life as if there were no tomorrow. You know, 'Live for today lest that's all there is'. We drank heavily, we caroused–we survived on coffee, cigarettes, and booze. Hell, none of us were saints; most of us forgot the restraints of ordinary life. We were in a man-made Hell and many of us acted accordingly. Contradictory behavior, but maybe the only way we could survive. Anyway, Cameron outdid us all, I think. At one point, his marriage almost collapsed because of his excesses. He could be manipulative and a bit ruthless, too. I remember one particular incident–"

Suddenly, he interrupted himself and sat up straight. "Well, that's old stuff. No point in rehashing it. Have we covered all your questions, Mrs. Parrish?"

"Yes, sir." I got up to go. "Thank you for your time. Mr. Patterson.

You've been most helpful."

As I walked to my car, I couldn't help but wonder just a little what the TV anchor had been about to say, but actually I was grateful that he had stopped himself. The young Douglas no longer existed; that desperate time had passed. I knew the depths of maturity and compassion that made up his character now, and I saw no value in resurrecting past indiscretions. I supposed that the deep regrets that Douglas had mentioned to me had to do with those early years.

As my life settled into a quiet routine, I threw myself into experimenting with various techniques in painting. I was consumed with the desire to capture on two-dimensional canvas a small hint of the gloriously Grand Design shown to me in my vision. I understood very well that I was undertaking the impossible in trying to translate the blazing lightning that had flamed from the hand of God, that shimmering splendor that I had witnessed, to the mundane reality of paint on canvas.

I worked at dozens of small canvases, underpainting, glazing, layering in an attempt to get that luminous glow that I had blessedly experienced. I worked with abstract designs, with swirls of color, with grids and slender threads of interwoven pattern. I wanted to image the effulgent, ethereal dynamism of the Universe, the vast ever-changing play of light and flame and radiance in which I had abandoned myself that sacred night. None of my efforts solved the problem I had set for myself

I studied the techniques of past masters: fauvism, impressionism, cubism. I was enchanted with Georges Seurat's pointillism, with the sense of infinity that he painstakingly created in his skies and limitless horizons; by the bold webbed greenery of leaves and foliage that spilled on to canvas from the fertile mind of Henri Rousseau; by Marcel DuChamp's efforts to suggest motion on a static surface. I found no definitive answers, but I was determined to find my own motif and idiom. To that end, I struggled relentlessly.

I struggled, too, for several weeks with choosing the most appropriate avenue for the gift God had seen fit to give me. I vacillated; I procrastinated; I dragged my feet. Finally I signed up to do volunteer visitation work at St. Joseph's Hospital several times a week.

One cloudy afternoon, I warily made my way through a warren of halls into the children's wing at St. Joseph's, a list of names clutched in my hand. This was my first foray into unknown territory. I decided to check out the general layout first so that I could determine how best to spend my time.

In room after room, I found wards of suffering kids. Some, enduring broken legs or minor operations, beamed with interest at this strange visitor who might help them while away a piece of their tedious day. A few shyly ducked their heads and smiled. Too many, though, hardly had sufficient vitality to lift their heads, much less pay any attention to me. Steeped in pain and misery, these kids' suffering was almost palpable. Their need seemed overwhelming. I saw that my only hope was to trust God and to ask for wisdom and judgment as I honed my nascent healing ability.

That first afternoon, I contented myself with visiting as many youngsters as I could. I patted their hands and smoothed their covers, held endless glasses of water and adjusted numerous hospital beds. I knew my approach must be low-keyed and unobservable; I wanted neither attention nor controversy.

As I went from room to room, from bed to bed, I was alert to any inner signal I might receive about how to begin. I was hoping that I might receive some kind of sign, that three or four youngsters would in some way be singled out–those who would benefit most from my hesitant attempts. I knew that inevitably some of these kids that I worked with would fade and die, no matter what I did. How could I, then, read each soul's intent so that I could be most effective?

Gradually, I worked out a routine. I centered my attention on the rooms that held two to four beds. In the larger wards, youngsters came for a short time, soon to be replaced by others. They quickly recovered and returned to their homes. I saved my efforts for the seriously ill, who were generally the most isolated. In each room I chose one small person on whom to concentrate though I spent some time with all of them. I made my choices by listening to my inner being and by asking nightly for discernment and direction.

My procedure was simple. I would sit by each child, making him as comfortable as possible. Sometimes I sang softly; at other times, we shared a game or a story or a joke. Then, I would hug him and stroke his hair before going on to the next bed. Sometimes, when it seemed appropriate, I would hold a youngster's hand in mine, sometimes putting my other on his forehead or his chest if I could do so without causing embarrassment.

For my specially targeted kids, sometime during each visit, I unobtrusively placed a hand closest to whatever organ seemed to be implicated and placed the other on the crown of his head, at the same time keeping up a gentle lullaby of conversation. Before leaving, I would hug him to me for as long as possible, letting my energy commingle with his. I had very little to go on in assessing how much my visits were helping these sick children.

As the weeks went by, I realized that I was being subtly directed to go at times into the larger wards as well. Sometimes, I felt drawn to a particular ward, to a particular bed. Other times, I just walked through and smiled, patting a child's hand here, smoothing another's rumpled hair there.

One day, as I walked through one of the larger wards, I felt drawn to a bed where a little girl, probably six or seven, lay quietly staring at the ceiling. Her blond curls were pasted to her damp head and her eyes were glazed looking; she occasionally gave way to terrible paroxysms of coughing.

I smiled at her. "Hi," I said. "My name's Kathleen." She looked at me but made no response.

"You aren't feeling so well, are you?"

She shook her head and started coughing again. I reached out and put my hand on her forehead; she was burning with fever.

"Is it okay if I stay here with you for a little while?" I asked.

She almost imperceptibly nodded her head, a look of relief on her face. I pulled up a chair and sat with her, lightly holding one hand on her forehead and the other on her chest. I knew she didn't have the energy even to listen to me talk, so I sat and softly hummed a simple tune. As I hummed, I mentally directed energy through my hands into her fiercely hot little body. Gradually, her rasping breathing quieted, her eyes drooped and she fell asleep.

Just as I was about to go, a worn-looking young woman came in. She eyed me curiously, no doubt wondering what I was doing by her child's bed.

I put out my hand. "Hello. I'm Kathleen Parrish I'm a volunteer here. I visit the kids and help to make them as comfortable as possible."

"I'm Patsy McClellan. I'm worried to death about Jeannie. She has bronchitis and the doctor can't seem to give her any relief. He decided to put her in the hospital so that she could be treated more easily, but she's no better." She looked down. "Thank God, she's sleeping. The poor little thing is completely worn out."

As I studied Mrs. McClellan, it appeared that she, too, was completely worn out. My heart went out to her. I knew how upset I would have been had the child in the bed been my own.

"How long has she been ill?"

"Almost three weeks–and she doesn't seem to be responding to anything." Her forehead wrinkled in a frown.

"She seemed glad to have me sit with her. I hope you don't mind."

"Oh, no, not at all. I spend as much time with her as I can, but I have a baby at home. I'm being run ragged. I'm grateful that there's someone here with her for a little while."

Mrs. McClellan reached up and rubbed her forehead. "I have a nasty headache, too. That's all I need." She looked harried and weary, her blond hair in disarray, her face pinched.

"Why don't you sit down and let me massage your shoulders and the back of your neck?" I suggested. "It might help."

Gratefully, she dropped into the chair I had just vacated. I stood behind her and put my hands on her shoulders, just letting them rest there quietly. Then I put one hand on her forehead and the other on the back of her neck. She sighed and I could feel the tension drain away. I gently massaged her shoulders and neck and then let my hands rest again on her head.

"Oh, that feels good," she said. After a few minutes, she looked up at me in surprise. "It's gone–my headache's gone. Oh, I can't thank you enough."

I was glad to see the pinched look clear from her face.

"I'm just glad I could help. Oh, look, Jeannie's waking up."

The sick youngster opened her eyes and saw her mother. "Mamma, mamma." She reached out her arms to be hugged. "I feel all better."

Her mother kissed her forehead. "Hi, darling." Her eyes met mine. "She feels cool. I think maybe her fever has broken. What a relief!"

Jeannie's face was a little flushed, but her eyes looked clear and bright. She grinned. "This lady sat with me and sang to me and now I feel good."

"Well, Jeannie, I'm glad," I said. "I'd better be going. I'll come and see you again in a few days."

"Oh, I won't be here–I'm going home," she said with blithe assurance. "Thank you–" Her little face screwed up in thought. "I know you told me your name, but I don't remember."

"Kathleen."

"Thank you, Kathleen." She reached up to hug me and I willed another stream of energy into her little body as I held her tight.

Her mother, thanking me again, had no idea that I might have speeded her child's recovery. I said a quiet thank you to God as I headed home, content that I had been instrumental in easing both mother and child's suffering.

After I had been going to St. Joseph's for about a year, I knew that some youngsters that I had worked with were regaining their health more quickly than their doctors had expected, and that a few had recovered from their illnesses against all odds to the amazement of their physicians. On the other hand, some that I had desperately wanted to save had slipped away like shadows in the night.

Slowly, I learned that I must leave the outcome to God, that I was only a tool for Him to work through. I also began to understand that there were many levels of healing and that emotional healing, being freed from panic and fear in the face of certain death or learning to accept a chronically debilitating condition, was just as valid as physical healing.

One day as I was walking by the nurse's station, I overheard a few of the hospital personnel talking.

"It's odd–I can't explain it." A trim little dark-haired nurse shook her head.

"What do you mean exactly?" a tired intern asked.

"Well, it seems to me that some of the kids are recovering far faster than anyone could reasonably expect–or faster than I would expect from my experience. I don't know–it's just a feeling I have."

I walked rapidly by and didn't hear the rest of the conversation, but it brought back to me my vulnerability. I didn't want to be singled out. I didn't want anyone catching on to what I was doing. I thought it was probably time to move on to some other place. Not wanting to abandon the two or three serious cases that I thought might be responding well, I decided to take on no new ones and eventually to disengage myself from St. Joseph's.

A few weeks later, Elizabeth, Dad's wife, called. We saw each other regularly and occasionally had lunch or dinner together. We had a date for dinner that night.

"I'm sorry, Kathleen. I don't feel very well. I guess I'd better cancel our dinner plans. Maybe I'm coming down with the flu or something."

"What's wrong, Elizabeth? Upset stomach?" I wanted to help her if I could so I kept her talking while visualizing energy pouring through her body. I had never attempted healing over a distance before, but I knew that others had done so successfully.

"Well, I don't know–my stomach does feel uneasy. I have a terrible headache and I think I might have a fever." Her voice had lost its usual resonance.

"Have you taken anything?" I asked.

"Just some aspirin. I've been lying down, but I thought I ought to let you know about dinner."

"Are you all right alone? Do you want me to come over?"

"Oh, no. I can manage by myself. There's no need for you to do that."

"Why don't you go back to bed and try to rest. If you feel better later, give me a call."

"All right–but I very much doubt I'll recover that fast."

"Well, take care–and if you're up to it, call me later anyway. If I don't hear from you, I'll come over and check on you toward evening–oh, and Elizabeth, try to imagine a big golden sphere of light surrounding you and healing you while you're resting," I added as we hung up.

At about 3:30 Elizabeth called. "I can't believe it, Kathleen. I feel fine–as if I'd never been ill at all. I want to go to dinner with you as we planned."

"Are you sure?" I didn't tell her that after we had hung up, I had spent ten or fifteen minutes mentally willing psychic energy to flow across space to her needy body.

"Positive. I feel wonderful!"

We ate dinner at the Fireside Inn, a warm, congenial place for conversation. Elizabeth looked radiantly lovely with no sign of any lingering illness. Always direct, she studied me as we sipped our wine.

"Kathleen, after you called, something happened while I was resting. I have a feeling that you had a part in it. Did you?"

I looked down, re-arranging my food. "What happened?" I finally said, buying time to think how to respond.

"Well, I did what you suggested. I tried to envision a radiant golden light surrounding me, but it was difficult to concentrate because I was aching everywhere. After a short time, I suddenly felt a tingling feeling all over and a warmth went all through my body."

"Then what?"

"I fell asleep for a couple of hours, and when I woke up, I felt fine. I waited a bit to call you to be sure I was all right." She looked at me curiously. "You tell *me*. What happened?"

Over the last year, I had been learning to listen very carefully to my inner voice for direction when I was uncertain about the best course to take. I was very slowly coming to the realization that, much as I dreaded the idea, I couldn't continue to hide this amazing gift and still use it appropriately.

It was clear that I needed to develop courage as well as compassion if I were to follow the guidance of my inner being. The fears that beset us all at times, the fear of being cast out of the group, of being isolated, the fear of being misunderstood–these fears I realized I would have to face and deal with. I sat quietly for a moment and then, prompted from within, I met her questioning eyes and answered honestly.

"Yes, I probably did have something to do with your rapid recovery. I willed some energy to you."

"That's remarkable. Tell me about it; from whence comes this ability?" Elizabeth looked genuinely interested.

And so I told her a little of my interlude with Ultimate Reality. I told her how I had come to realize that I had been given this amazing gift and about my work at St. Joseph's. I also told her about my fears. She of the generous heart comprehended immediately the stigmas, the aspersions that were all too likely to come my way, the notoriety and relentless importuning that I feared would be inevitable that made me even more uneasy.

"Kathleen, my dear, I understand your anxiety, but surely if God saw fit to give you this beneficence, He will direct you in appropriate paths."

"I've heard horror stories, Elizabeth. People sometimes willfully misunderstand this kind of controversial issue; it's a very volatile one."

"When Stephen and I went to Europe the summer before he died, we became aware that England is very much more supportive than America about all things psychic. The whole climate is different; in fact, psychic healing is almost institutionalized. I'm not suggesting that you go to England, dear, but I wonder if you could work in conjunction with some doctor or some hospital with their full knowledge and consent. You know, others wouldn't need to know your full name. That might provide you some protection and yet give you a wider arena in which to work. You'd have better feed-back, too."

"Hmm–I'd like that. I could be more open. It would certainly be helpful to have medical input, too. I'm really flying blind. But how do I find a sympathetic ear? Someone ready to risk this kind of intervention?"

"I don't think it will be easy, but if you're alert and a little more visible, you might be surprised. There must be someone out there who's frustrated with medical limitations and wants to push the parameters a bit. "

"I've been aware for quite awhile," I confessed, "that I have to muster up the courage to be more open, but it still really scares me. Before I discussed this with you, I was planning to leave St. Joseph's; instead, I think I'll stay there for awhile and see what happens."

As I stopped in Elizabeth's driveway after driving her home, I hugged her. "Thanks, Elizabeth. You've given me a lot to think about."

"I should be thanking you. After all, I'm well tonight because of you. I appreciate your confiding in me, dear. I miss Stephen dreadfully, but your love is a great comfort to me."

That night I thought seriously about Elizabeth's suggestion. I urgently requested that God grant me courage and help me find the right doctor to work with, and I determined to keep my eyes open for any opportunity that might come.

A good beginning, I thought, would be to change my routine a bit. Visitation volunteers were pretty much able to come and go as they chose, so I began to venture into the rest of the hospital, making visits to patients of all ages. I began to drop in at odd hours, sometimes in the morning, sometimes at dinnertime or even later. Children, even if they noticed, were unlikely to tell anyone what they felt at my touch, while most adults would be sufficiently aware of the unusual heat of my hands to comment both to me and to their physicians.

I was now ready to give up my low profile and become more visible to the doctors on the staff–a complete turn around from my previous attitude. At first, I was filled with trepidation. I thought it quite possible that some doctor might take exception to what I was doing and politely ask me to leave and never come back. That was a chance I'd have to take.

I made my usual rounds, looking in where I felt led to intervene. Several patients caught my attention. One older man, his face pale with pain, looked at me and managed a weak smile.

"Hello. I'm Kathleen. Is there anything I can do for you?"

He looked to be about sixty-five years old, with sparse gray hair, a prominent forehead and large, beaky nose.

"Hell, yes," he grinned. "You can cut off this damned leg." He gestured to his right leg. "It's giving me fits."

"What's wrong with it?" I asked as I reached out to hold his hand.

"Mmm–it's been a long time since a pretty girl like you held my hand." He gave my hand a light squeeze. "The doc says I've got myelitis–transverse myelitis–it has something to do with my spine. My leg is almost paralyzed. No feeling in it."

"Are you here for surgery?"

"No, not yet, anyway–just for a lot of tests–but the pain in my lower back is pretty bad. I hope they can do something."

I took a deep breath. "Maybe I can make you feel a little better. Would you like me to try?"

"Hell, yes. What will you do?"

"I'm just going to rest one hand on your forehead and put the other on the back of your neck. Will that hurt?"

"I don't think so. Believe me, I'll let you know if it does."

I cradled the back of his head in my right hand and rested the other on his forehead. I didn't make any effort to talk but focused my thoughts on sending golden energy all the way down his spine, visualizing each disk in perfect alignment, intact and whole. After a few moments, I placed both hands on his damaged leg, willing unhindered blood flow through it. As I worked, I watched his face. He closed his eyes and visibly relaxed.

As I removed my hands, he turned his head to me. "Hey, young lady–whatever you did, I'm not feeling the pain I had before."

"That's great. Sometimes a little help with relaxation is almost miraculous."

"Relaxation? " He looked at me quizzically. "I felt some tingling in my leg when you were resting your hands there. Come on, it's more than relaxation."

"Well, I envisioned energy circulating down your spine and into your leg.

Sometimes the warmth of my hands helps."

"Your hands felt really, really hot, even through this blanket." He smiled. "Can you come back tomorrow and do it again?"

"How long are you scheduled to be here for tests?"

"Several days. I'd sure appreciate it if you could come."

"I'll do my best, Mr.–?"

"Middleton. Robert Middleton. And many thanks, Kathleen. I feel much better."

"I'll see you tomorrow, Mr. Middleton," I gave his hand another light squeeze and left the room.

For two more days, Mr. Middleton took his tests and I gave him daily healing. Each day found him more enthusiastic and relaxed. He reported that the pain had disappeared from his back.

"This old leg feels like it's a part of me again," he laughed as he slapped it vigorously. "You know, Doc Jenner can't quite figure it out. He says that the tests are all negative–I guess that means good instead of bad–and that my sensory capacity has improved. How about that?"

"Great. Does that mean that he won't have to operate?"

"Yep. Not for now, anyway. He's releasing me tomorrow." His pale eyes filled with tears.

"How can I thank you, Kathleen? Doc Jenner may not understand, but I *know*. Your hands healed me.

"You take care, Mr. Middleton," I said as I hugged him and said good-bye.

Chapter 15

My changed visitation routine at St. Joseph's made it difficult to find enough time for my painting. I usually restricted my hours at the hospital to three times weekly, but every so often someone like Mr. Middleton needed to have daily treatment for a few days. I persevered, and worked in a few hours here and there as best I could.

I felt that my paintings were coming closer to what I envisioned, but I still was far from satisfied. Subject and technique were symbiotically intertwined in my mind, and I was having difficulty getting a clear grasp on either. Transcendent experience is almost by definition untranslatable; neither words nor paint can do more than palely hint at the awesome grandeur that lies just beyond material existence. Nevertheless, I felt impelled to keep trying.

One afternoon, I got a call from my old friend Andy of the Marshall Anderson Gallery.

"Kathleen, Andy here. Why don't you ever come to see me any more?" His plaintive tone was an act; he loved to tease.

"Oh, Andy–I'm sorry. I've been busy with this and that, and the painting I've been doing wouldn't be what you want–it really wouldn't."

"Well, you can come and see a friend anyway, can't you? I miss you." He paused a beat. "Besides, you know I'm interested in your work. Exactly what have you been painting that you're so sure I wouldn't want?"

"I'm trying out different techniques–impasto, glazing–all kinds of things. I'm not really satisfied with the results I've been getting."

"Why don't you bring a few things in and let me have a look? Day after day, I see tediously repetitious stuff, the same things over and over again. Damn it, I know what sells, but maybe it's time I try something a little different. I'm perishing from boredom."

"I promise I'll come to see you in the next few days. I'll see if I can find a canvas or two for you to see, but, Andy, don't get your hopes up. They're strictly experimental; they aren't your kind of thing."

I looked my work over, and after much hesitation, I chose two canvases. One was a painting of five whirling dervishes wearing short crimson jackets, long white robes swirling, feet flying as they circled arm in arm, crimson-fezzed heads proudly lifted to Allah. Each dervish had one arm on his brother's shoulder, the other lifted to heaven in devotion. One celebrant was raising a scarlet rose, symbol of Sufism, in praise. I had underpainted the background with a silver-blue impasto of small swirling brush strokes, letting it dry in ridges, almost as a plasterer would swirl a pattern on a fresh surface. The figures were boldly colored–red jackets and fezzes, the dervishes' skirts thickly white. In an effort to suggest great vitality and movement, I had painted a pale, almost indistinguishable, blurred figure behind each celebrant, as if the dancers' auras were striving to catch up with their turning bodies. I then painted over the background with intermingling strokes of hunter green and black, occasionally letting the silver-blue underneath show through, circles within circles, around their dancing feet.

The other painting was an attempt to bridge the material world with the world of spirit. I used an old sketch of Dylan that I had drawn last time she was home as a basis for the painting. I had mixed abstract and representative figures with reckless abandon. This was a large canvas, suggesting twilight edging into darkness. A girl in a gauzy kind of white dress was swinging, delicately balancing on her toes, one hand holding the rope of the swing lightly. Her marigold hair spun out behind her as she perched, poised between earth and heaven, as if to soar into infinity at any moment. I had painted her on the right side of the canvas in very small scale compared to the firmament that arched over her in all its glory. The heavens were alive with slender threads of light, with barely seen geometric forms of various size and shape, with subtle weavings of color and texture. I hoped I had not crossed the fine line that separates art from sentimentality. I hadn't been able to decide whether or not the painting was successful. Andy would know in an instant.

My usual trepidation anytime I showed new work accompanied me to the Marshall Anderson Gallery even though Andy was an old and supportive friend. I knew how keen his eye was, how competent at finding flaws of balance or design or the smallest hint of bathos. I considered both of these canvases to be uncharacteristic of Andy's gallery. They were so far afield from my former paintings that I hadn't shown them even to Gentry, preferring to struggle in solitary isolation.

After the usual hugs and pleasantries, Andy unpacked the canvases. He placed them on two easels at eye level. He studied them; he backed up; he moved up close and carefully examined the brush strokes; he stepped back again, looking at first one, then the other in quiet contemplation. Finally, he turned to me, his bright eyes eager.

"But they're very good, Kathleen. I like both. Each has a numinous quality uniquely its own."

"I m thrilled that you approve of them, Andy. I've not been sure how successful they are–especially the one of the girl swinging."

"I think it's extremely successful. You've managed to capture the immensity of the universe in relationship to humankind and yet you suggest that, huge and undifferentiated as it is, it's benevolently supportive of us. Come, let's go back to the office and talk."

I agreed that he could hang the canvases. I was reminded of the first time he had hung a few of my paintings as a kind of test to see what kinds of comment they drew. Those had been successful beyond my most fanciful dreams; I hoped these would do as well.

"How is Dylan, Kathleen?"

"She's doing really well. She'll graduate this spring, you know."

"Amazing–I still think of her as about thirteen years old. What will she do after she's through with school?"

"She's planning to stay in New York. She wants to take more classes at Martha Graham's School of Contemporary Dance–at a professional level. She has an audition lined up and she'd really like to get into Graham's company."

"Well, she's a beauty and I know she throws herself into everything she does with real passion. I'm sure she'll make it."

"Oh, I hope so. She'll be devastated if she doesn't get a place in some prestigious company." I rose to leave.

"I like the direction you're going in your painting, Kathleen. Keep at it," Andy said as he walked me to the door. "I'll let you know what my patrons have to say."

A few days later, hot summer sunshine dazzling the air, I was making my usual rounds at Saint Joseph's Hospital. As I came out of a ward, a round-faced, red-haired nurse approached me.

"Could I have a word with you, Mrs. Parrish?" she said hesitantly.

"Of course."

"Do you have time for a cup of coffee in the cafeteria?" she asked.

"Yes, I could use something to drink about now." I noticed by her nametag that her name was Lacy.

As we settled over our drinks, coffee for her, lemonade for me, I looked at her quizzically, wandering what she had in mind.

"Uh–I've been noticing, Mrs. Parrish, that many patients improve after you've been visiting them. I hope you don't mind, but I've been watching you–and I see you either hold their hand or place your hand on their forehead." She flushed slightly. "Forgive me for seeming nosy, but I'm really interested in what you're doing."

I temporized. "Do you really think patients get better because I hold their hands?"

She grinned at me. "Yes, I do–somehow you're helping them get well.

155

Please, I mean no harm. It took all my courage to speak to you. If there's something that can help people beyond what our medicines and surgeries can do, we need to take advantage of it."

"Lacy, this is a very complicated issue. You're right, I do have some talent for making people feel better. My hands give off an inordinate amount of heat that, in some cases, heals them and, at the least, almost invariably makes them feel better. But the problems are enormous–" I sighed. "I'd love to work with a doctor or two. I think a lot of good could be accomplished, but how do I go about finding one that wouldn't think me crazy? And how do I protect myself from being overwhelmingly inundated, if the general public should find out, by requests that I can't possibly handle? Then, too, there are real crazies out there who could make my life downright hellish–it could all too easily turn into a witch hunt."

She mulled over what I had said. "Yes, I can see your problem. I hadn't particularly thought of it that way. You know, I work with lots of different doctors. After a while you begin to understand where they're coming from–some are really hard-nosed; others are more open. If it's all right with you, I'm going to casually discuss this–I don't quite know what to call it–with one or two of them."

"I guess the best term to use is 'intentional healing' or 'psychic healing' though some people call it spiritual healing–but, Lacy, I could get into real trouble."

"Oh, I'll be careful, Mrs. Parrish. I won't say anything about what you're doing until I find the right doctor."

"Please, call me Kathleen. I've wanted to find someone. I'm grateful for your interest."

She looked at me uncertainly. "Something just occurred to me. I don't know if I should ask this of you–but I slipped and fell on a wet patch of floor the other day, and my shoulder's bothering me a lot. Am I being really pushy if I ask you to use your healing ability on me? That's not why I spoke to you," she hastened to add. "I've been trying to get up the courage for several weeks."

"No problem." I saw a deserted courtyard outside the cafeteria. "How about if we go out there and sit on one of those benches?"

I sat side of her and quietly placed one hand on her sore shoulder, the other on the back of her neck. As soon as they were in place, I could feel the typical rush of warmth I usually experienced. I held both hands quietly for a few minutes and then gently massaged her shoulder.

"Wow, that's incredible." She lifted her shoulder and shrugged it a few times. "The pain is completely gone. Wow," she repeated. "I could really feel the heat pouring off your hands." She straightened up. "I'm going to find someone, Kathleen–someone that you can work with. I promise you, I'll find the right doctor for you."

A few weeks later, Lacy stopped me in a hospital corridor. "I've found someone," she said excitedly. "Doctor Jerome Wolfe. He specializes in internal medicine. He's here on the staff. I don't know him that well but I know his office nurse, and I brought up psychic healing to her. She told me that her boss was really interested in alternative healing methods, especially in healing energies sent through the hands. I haven't mentioned you to her yet. Is it okay with you if I talk with her and see what she suggests?"

"Yes, I suppose so," I said hesitantly. "I guess I've got to start somewhere."

On my next trip to the hospital, Lacy stopped me again and elatedly told me that Dr. Wolfe would like to meet me. He had suggested that I drop in at his office at 5:00 some afternoon at my convenience.

I prayed for guidance and listened carefully to any direction my inner being might choose to deliver. A few days later, sensing an 'all clear' from within, I stifled my qualms and walked into Dr. Wolfe's waiting room. Looking around, I saw that the large room, airy and light, was attractively furnished in muted tones. There were several large plants here and there and some interesting original art on the walls.

His nurse ushered me in to his office almost immediately. Dr. Wolfe rose and held out his hand then motioned to a couple of chairs flanking a low coffee table. He was a man of modest stature with dark curling hair, clipped quite short, and tortoise-framed glasses. I was surprised to see that he was dressed casually with open necked shirt and rolled back sleeves; his official hours were obviously over. His face had a look of sharp intelligence.

"Mrs. Parrish, my nurse tells me that you're a healer," he said as we settled into comfortable tan leather chairs.

I grinned at him. "I guess you could call me that though I'm not entirely comfortable with that label. It seems a bit ostentatious, don't you think?" I could see that he approved of my reluctance to make too much of my ability. "To tell you the truth, I'm a little nervous about this conversation," I added.

"You don't have to be. I'd like to ask you a few questions and then see if we can work out something that would be satisfactory to you and helpful to my patients." He shook his head. "I get terribly frustrated sometimes with how often our treatments are completely ineffective, of how many we really can't help. I'm always looking for better answers, better methods." He studied me appraisingly. "Can you describe to me what you do and what effect you think you're having?"

I told him about my experience with Mr. Vittorio and explained how I had been working, *sub rosa*, at Saint Joseph's for more than a year. He then asked if I would be willing to give him a demonstration.

"Sure–though I think it might work better if I had some problem in mind. You see, I have no control over this at all. I'm just a channel for the energy that comes pouring out of my hands; it takes its own course. Is there some particular area that I could help you with?"

"I have a sinus condition that never seems to clear up completely. You might try your hand at that."

I suggested that he take his glasses off; then I went through my usual routine. As I placed one hand on Doctor Wolfe's forehead and the other on the back of his neck, I opened myself up to the energetic current that swept from the crown of my head down into my hands. I always tried to be aware of guidance as I worked, to any hunch about where to place my hands. This time, I felt constrained to move one hand over his eyes. I held it there for a few minutes and let the heat go where it would.

When I was through, he replaced his glasses and smiled. "I certainly felt the heat, Mrs. Parrish. For the moment, at least, I feel really good–almost magnetized. I have no doubt that some kind of energy was transmitted to my body." He paused, thinking. "If you're willing, I'd like to give it a try. How do you think you could best work with my patients?"

As we explored various possibilities, I told him about my fears, particularly my concern for my anonymity. He understood, suggesting that I use only my first name when meeting people; he promised to be very selective in the cases he chose.

"Well," he finally said, "if it's all right with you, let's just leave it this way: when I have a case that seems appropriate, I'll call you and we'll arrange a time. Probably sometimes it will be in the office, sometimes in the hospital. I should be there to introduce you each time. By the way, how many times do you usually work with a patient?" he asked.

"Sometimes just once is enough; other times I get the sense that I should see the patient several days in a row. I somehow seem to know when I've done all that can be done. I'm sure I don't have to tell you that there are bound to be failures."

Dr. Wolfe sighed. "I would that it weren't so, but I know all too well. Doctors face failure with distressing regularity."

After a few days, Teresa, Dr. Wolfe's nurse, called and asked if I could come to the office the next afternoon. When I arrived, she took me immediately into his office. An elegantly dressed older woman, perhaps sixty, looked at me with interest as I came in.

"Ah, Kathleen. Come in and sit down." Dr. Wolfe motioned me to the other chair that had been pulled up to the desk.

"Mrs. Clifford," he said simply, "this is Kathleen."

As we shook hands, I saw that she had a well-defined chin and broad forehead. Her graying hair was swept back in a chignon, a style that suited her patrician face that was dominated by large hazel eyes. She didn't look particularly ill.

"Kathleen, I told Mrs. Clifford about you and she has agreed that she'd like to work with you. We've recently discovered that she has a large tumor in her stomach. She's reluctant to undergo surgery, so I suggested that we might first try your healing hands. Do you think you can help her?"

I turned to her. "You know that I will be placing my hands on your head, and perhaps on your stomach?"

"Yes, Dr. Wolfe explained it to me. The idea of an operation is repellent to me. My mother died from cancer after she had surgery. It only made her suffering worse, as far as I could see. I'd like to try this first, if you're willing."

"All right. Doctor, why don't I give her an initial treatment right now and then perhaps I'll know whether or not we should schedule more treatments?"

He nodded assent. I centered myself and breathed a silent prayer for guidance. I had never tried to heal a cancer patient before and I had little idea of how to begin. I placed my right hand, as was my custom, on her forehead, my left on the back of her neck, just above her chignon. As usual, my hands begin to heat up.

"Do you have a low stool I could sit on?" I asked after a bit.

Dr. Wolfe quickly went into an adjoining room and returned with one. I pulled it in front of Mrs. Clifford and, sitting down, placed one hand on her solar plexus, the other on her stomach. I could sense that there was a large mass on the left side of her lower torso. I willed light into it, first gold, then green, then pearl white. I received a clear impression that she should have several treatments, each a week apart.

When I finished, she smiled. "Well, I certainly feel good. Do you think I need more treatment?"

"I think more would be helpful," I said cautiously. "Doctor Wolfe, do we have serious time constraints here?"

"I think we could give it a few weeks. Mrs. Clifford, how do you feel about it?"

"Whatever you think, Doctor. What did you have in mind, Kathleen?"

"I'd like very much to see you several times, a week apart."

"Here in the office?" she asked.

I looked inquiringly at Doctor Wolfe. He nodded imperceptibly.

"Yes, here in the office. Let's see, this is Wednesday. Could you come next Wednesday at the same time?"

"That would be fine, Kathleen." Her eyes teared slightly. "Thank you so much, my dear. Is there anything I should be doing at home?"

"It would be really helpful if you would lie down and imagine a golden light coming into the top of your head and vibrating through every cell in your body. Then focus on the area of the tumor and bathe it with more golden light and imagine it disappearing. It doesn't have to be for long; do it before you go to sleep at night or before you get up in the morning for ten minutes or so."

"I'll do it." She thanked me again, shaking hands first with the doctor and then with me. "I'll see you next week, Kathleen." Her head high, she sailed out of the room.

After she had gone, Doctor Wolfe asked if I could stay for a few more minutes. "I just got an idea that I want to run by you," he said, leaning against his desk.

"What do you have in mind?"

"As I was watching you and then listening to you talk to Mrs. Clifford, it occurred to me that we have a small diagnostic room down the hall that we don't use. It's being used for storage right now. Would you like to have your own place to meet with people? You know, if they need to be seen several times?"

I sank down into a chair. "That would be wonderful! I wouldn't have to tie up your office or your other rooms that way."

"Come on, let's go look at it."

The small room was crammed with boxes and what appeared to be old equipment. It boasted a window and a small sink in the corner.

"This would be ideal," I said.

"Okay–how would it be best to furnish it?"

"I really need nothing but a place for the patient to lie down and a stool like the one I used earlier. If it's possible, a couch would be more conducive to relaxation than an examining table or a hospital bed–less clinical. But whatever you have on hand would be greatly appreciated."

"A couch it is," he said. "I'll have it ready for you by Wednesday."

When I arrived the next week and walked into the room, I was astonished. It had been painted a lovely pale apricot, the floor gleamed, the window was freshly washed and the furniture looked new to me. A small desk had been placed in one corner with a few yellow cards on top; a very large cream-colored couch dominated the room, and an oak cupboard stood on the other wall. I opened it curiously. It contained five or six neatly folded pink sheets, a light blanket, and a pillow. The sink was scrubbed clean and there were paper towels and soap dispenser at the ready along with a supply of paper cups. The message was clear to me; hygiene and record keeping were important.

When Mrs. Clifford arrived, I had her remove her shoes and lie down. I had already folded a sheet and spread it on the couch with the pillow on top. As I covered her, I asked how her week had gone.

"Very well, Kathleen. I did the exercise you suggested every day–both morning and night. It's very relaxing if nothing else." She wore gray flannel trousers and a blue silk shirt and, rather than the tight chignon, had her hair fastened back with a silver barrette.

After washing my hands and centering myself, I repeated the same movements that I had done the week before. As I placed my hand on her abdomen, I sensed that the tumor had shrunk some. I couldn't actually feel anything–it was a knowing I had. And again, I received the impression that she needed at least two more treatments. I decided I'd say nothing to her; I didn't wish to raise false hopes. I concentrated on sending the same green, gold and pearl colors to the tumor and envisioned it dissolving away. Mrs. Clifford's breathing became very relaxed and even. I glanced at her. She had fallen asleep, a peaceful look on her face.

I tiptoed from the room, leaving the door ajar, and went to find Teresa. I found her at a nurse's station filling out some kind of record.

"Any chance of seeing the doctor for a few minutes?" I asked.

"He's just finishing with a patient. Wait here and I'll find out."

In a few minutes, Dr. Wolfe appeared wearing a white medical jacket over an open-collared shirt, a stethoscope dangling from his neck.

"Are your furnishings okay, Kathleen?"

"Okay? They're terrific; everything's beautiful. I have a question, though. Those cards on the desk–I gather you want me to keep some kind of record?"

"Umm–yes, I think it would be a good idea to keep track of the various appointments you have along with a few observations. Will that be a problem?"

"No, not at all. Do I fill out a separate one for each patient?"

"Yes–just leave it with Teresa before you go, and if you let her know when you're coming in, she'll have the appropriate record on your desk each time. I think it will be better if your notes are separate from my medical notes. How did it go?"

"Very well. Mrs. Clifford is sleeping right now. I didn't have the heart to wake her."

He grinned, patted my shoulder and went back to work.

I sat quietly at the desk, filling out the record card for Mrs. Clifford. I thought back and filled in the time of our first appointment and was working on what I had just done when I heard her stir. I went over to her. "You've had a good sleep. How are you feeling?"

She looked bemused, not quite awake. "Oh," she stretched, "I feel wonderful–completely relaxed. I guess I haven't been sleeping too well the last few weeks."

I handed her some water. "This should help you to wake up."

She sat up and sipped it slowly. "Thanks, Kathleen. Your hands are unbelievably soothing. Even if the tumor doesn't go away, the relaxation is worth it."

"Well, we'll just have to wait and see how it goes."

We agreed to meet again in another week, and to my astonishment, cool Mrs. Clifford hugged me close as she said goodbye.

I quickly became accustomed to spending one day a week at Dr. Wolfe's office. We agreed that all of the cases he wished me to see would be scheduled, whenever possible, on Wednesdays. I worked on a diversity of problems, some serious, some quite easily alleviated by just one treatment. Usually, I knew ahead of time what the day would bring, but occasionally the doctor would walk a patient over to my little healing room on the spur of the moment. Not all of my efforts were successful.

Over lunch, I discussed my failures with Gentry.

"As I understand it, Gentry, the soul has an agenda that may be quite different from that of the conscious personality. Perhaps, in some cases, the physical organism's suffering or even his death is completely appropriate from the point of view of that person's spirit. That's not something that can be readily explained to the individual. At least, I don't think so."

We were eating in Mary's café. Gentry, dressed in denim shirt and blue jeans, stretched out his legs and leaned back in his chair.

"I agree," he said. "A great many people wouldn't understand. Their perception of life is too narrow to grasp any explanation you might offer; they aren't inclined to look at the larger picture; they'd think you were being simplistic."

"Of course, many accept that it's God's will that they should not be healed. I guess that's not so different from saying that the soul has deliberately chosen some particular direction whether the ego wishes it or not."

"True–and that's what most people come to, I think. If the patient can understand that, rather than a punishment handed down by God, it's a

162

learning process initiated by his own inner being–his own unique link with God–and can surrender to it, he'll fare much better emotionally. Long-term attitudes have so much to do with the healing process, as you well know. Without a clear understanding of the complexities that go into any outcome–illness or death or accident, actually any of the many vicissitudes of life–," he paused and shrugged.

"Yes. That's exactly it. All the interwoven threads of choices upon choices upon choices that individuals have made in their lives, intermingled with a host of emotions, both positive and negative–all of those have brought them to the place where they now find themselves."

"Yes, most have no idea how toxic negativity is–fear and guilt and self-indulgent attitudes like resentment and self-pity," Gentry observed as he sipped his coffee.

"Hatred and self-loathing, too" I added.

We ate quietly, reflecting on our conversation.

"Don't you find that most dying people, after they get over their 'why me?' attitude, come to some kind of interior acceptance of death?" Gentry asked.

"Yes, blessedly the soul somehow prepares them."

As we walked down the street after lunch, Gentry turned to me. "Is your affiliation with Dr. Wolfe still working well?"

"It couldn't be better. He tells me he's been talking to a few other doctors about what I'm doing. He's unbelievably generous. He wants me to feel free to use my little room for anyone I might want to see, even the patients of other doctors. Isn't that amazing?"

"It is, but you're very generous, too, Kathleen. I know how much time you devote to helping others. Do you notice any difference in the way you work, now that you've been doing this for awhile?"

"The only difference I can see is that I seem to get more inner guidance–an inner knowing. I often can define the problem before the doctor tells me, and also I get more direction these days. Now, I usually place my hands a couple of inches away instead of actually touching the patient." I thought a moment. "Sometimes I know the outcome, as well."

"Hmmm–interesting. Your gifts keep growing. Oh, by the way, Andy tells me that your work is selling well."

"I guess it is. It's very surprising to me–probably because I can't capture what I envision."

"Hah, who can?" Gentry laughed. "Still, I like what you're doing."

"And your work sells well too, so we're both blessed."

We hugged each other, and went our separate ways, back to our studios and the frustrations and delights of painting.

Mrs. Clifford came in exultantly the week after her last appointment. "Kathleen, my dear." She hugged me. "I've just come from Dr. Wolfe's office. A few days ago he suggested new x-rays." She smiled widely. "The tumor is gone, Kathleen! It's gone!"

"I'm overjoyed for you, Mrs. Clifford. I suggest you keep on doing your exercises of envisioning light going through your body."

"Oh, I will, Kathleen. They make me feel wonderfully rested and relaxed. I don't know how to thank you." She took my hand in both of hers. "Is there anything I can do for you? Anything at all?"

I smiled. "Your good health is payment enough for me."

"Dr. Wolfe told me that you don't want too much made of your amazing healing ability, but I wonder–," she paused uncertainly. "Would you mind if I get in touch with you if I think there's someone you can help? I'd be very careful about whom I recommended," she hastened to add.

"Yes, of course," I told her. She smiled brilliantly and hugged me in goodbye.

* * *

"Hi, pretty Peggy," I called as I crossed the lawn to the garden where my aunt, on her knees, was digging up richly dark soil.

"Hi, darling." Aunt Peg wiped her wet brow with a dirty hand, leaving a trail of mud behind. "I'm just trying to loosen this soil up a bit. I want to plant some ranunculus here."

"Ah, I love those. I thought I'd see if I could bum some iced tea from you."

"Ooh, sounds heavenly. It's really hot today. Come on, let's go inside; I'm ready for a break." She got up, her back wet with sweat, and headed for the house.

Peggy and Richard had just returned from another jaunt, this time to Italy. Every summer they traveled to some new destination for a month or two. I was so glad for Peggy with her obviously compatible marriage.

"How's Richard?" I asked.

"He's just fine. He's over at his office checking up on all the mail that no doubt accumulated while we were gone. Gosh, it will be time for school to begin before I know it."

We sat in her kitchen, sipping iced tea and eating home-baked sugar cookies. Peg, inveterate homemaker that she was, always had a sweet of some kind to offer.

"Hmm–these are delicious, Peggy."

"What do you hear from Dylan?"

"That's one reason I came over. She called me last night and asked me to tell you her news. She's gotten a place with the Paul Taylor Dancers. She's beside herself with excitement."

Peggy smiled. "Good for her. That's what she's wanted for so long. But, gosh, it's a hard life."

"I know–I don't know how she stands the discipline; dancing is such a tough profession. Well, she's strong–strong-willed, too. She'll make out all right."

"Sure she will." Peggy eyed me with concern. "How are *you* doing, Kathleen? Everything okay? You're looking a little thin, it seems to me."

"I'm fine. I'm frustrated right now because I can't get the effect I'm striving for in my painting. I guess I'm a little obsessed by it."

"Knowing you, you probably forget to eat."

I laughed. "Maybe once in a while–but not for long, Peg–not for very long."

I left my aunt to her planting and went back to my uncertain attempts to commit infinity to canvas.

Chapter 16

1968, year of infamy. Probably one of the most tumultuous times of our nation's history. Looking back, it's difficult to piece together the actual flavor of that time. Cultural upheaval, political dissent run amuck. This was the year of protest, of outrage. Disaffected youth, often from prosperous homes; college students, increasingly militant; civil disobedience rife across the land; vast disparate groups taking to the streets to protest the war in Vietnam, to march for civil rights, to riot in formerly peaceful city streets.

The killing of our youngest president, John F. Kennedy, in 1963 was a precursor of more horrors to come: Martin Luther King gunned down on an April evening in Memphis, Robert Kennedy assassinated in Los Angeles the night in June that he won the California Democratic primary. The horrific confrontations between police and citizen that marked the infamous Chicago Democratic Convention in August.1968 was the bursting point in a festering sore of divisiveness that marked the agitated sixties. Disbelief rapidly turned to horror. This was the year that shattered America's innocence beyond redemption.

As the death toll passed the 30,000 mark in Vietnam and as formerly respectful students organized sit-ins at college campuses across the nation, my own life continued its even passage. I was exceedingly grateful that I had a daughter rather than a draft-age son. I was firmly against our involvement in that far away land, but I tried to be a silent witness to the events that were unfolding before my eyes rather than become a part of the problem.

Dylan, fiercely anti-war, was preoccupied with her budding career. She sensibly chose to make a difference through the ballot box rather than through civil disobedience. I kept abreast of the news as best I could, hoping that Douglas had given up his dangerous profession. There was no one I could ask.

On a dreary, cold Sunday morning in November, as I settled in to eat breakfast in front of the fireplace in the family room, I reached for The Book Review, my favorite section of the Sunday Times. To my surprise, on the second page was a review, a new book by Douglas, *Voices of War: Tales from the Trenches.*

The review included a short biography. I read it avidly. As I read, I could see that Douglas had compiled stories from all of the major wars of the 20th century, including stories from soldiers in Vietnam. This was the book he had talked of writing if *Voices of Destiny* proved to be successful. It was a very favorable review. The article indicated that he now spent his time in his country home outside of London studying history and writing. He no longer reported the news, the article stated; his interviews of soldiers from Vietnam were gotten in camps and hospitals well away from the front lines. His next book, he thought, would address the possibilities of peaceful co-existence among the nations of the world. I sent a silent thank you to God that Douglas was safe and well and productive. I wondered whether I would receive a copy of this book as I had the first.

During this time, several of Dr. Wolfe's colleagues began sending me patients. Soon I was working with several general practitioners, an ophthalmologist, and a pediatrician. I kept to my Wednesday schedule as much as possible though hospital visits were not always so easily managed. I hoped that my caseload would remain at a sustainable level. I couldn't handle much more, but I hated the thought of turning anyone away.

One day, I was asked to see a patient at Saint Joseph's Cancer Center who was suffering from leukemia. I was surprised to see a boy, perhaps sixteen years old, lying pale and still in the narrow hospital bed. His doctor had told me that he was seriously ill, that he probably would not make it. I was shaken to see a teenager looking so enervated.

"Hi, I'm Kathleen," I said; it was my standard greeting to youngsters.

He turned his head and put out his hand. "Hi. I'm Mitch Tavener." A brilliant smile lit up his thin face. "Dr. Steurben told me that you would be coming to see me. He asked me if it was okay–me and my folks."

"So he explained to you that I can sometimes help people to feel better?"

"Uh huh. What are you going to do?" He seemed more curious than nervous.

"Oh, I'm just going to hold my hands close to your body and try to send you some energy. I might put my hands on your head, too. If you want to talk, it's okay."

He smiled again and closed his eyes. Listening for any inner guidance I might receive, I placed one hand on his forehead and the other in the area of the medulla oblongata at the back of his head. As I worked, I noticed dark lashes on his pale cheeks, crisply curling dark hair very, very short–the results of chemotherapy, I supposed. As I moved my hands along his body, he opened eyes that were intensely blue. "I feel heat. Heat and tingling."

"Good." I decided to keep him talking. "What do you like to do when you're feeling up to it?"

"I like to read; I read a lot. And I like basketball and swimming and stuff like that."

"Hmm–what kind of thing do you like to read?"

"Oh, history and biographies of famous people—and science fiction. I love science fiction." He smiled diffidently. "I play the guitar, too."

"Ah, wonderful. Do you feel well enough to read here in the hospital?" I looked around but didn't see any books.

"I get pretty tired. My mom's going to bring me a couple tonight. I'm going to try."

I placed my hand on his. "Well, Mitch, if it's all right with you, I think I'll come back and see you in a couple of days again."

"Sure. Thanks a lot for coming."

Over the next several weeks, I made a point of visiting with Mitchell every few days. He seemed to be responding well. He was reading some and had even asked that his guitar be brought to the hospital. Something about his gallant courage and his quick intelligence struck at my heart.

One afternoon, I brought him a copy of Douglas' first book, *Voices of Destiny.* I thought he would enjoy the short pieces on famous people that Douglas had compiled. His face lit up as he paged through the various chapters.

"Thank you, Kathleen." His dazzling smile reminded me of Douglas. "This looks super. I know I'll like it."

I patted his hand. "I think you will, too. The man who wrote it is a friend of mine."

"That makes it even better—more personal, somehow."

I gave him my usual hands-on treatment, hugged him and told him I'd see him in a few days.

As I was walking down the corridor, feeling good about Mitchell's progress, Lacy flagged me down.

"Kathleen—do you have a minute?"

"Sure—can you take a break right now?"

At her nod, we headed for the cafeteria. Lacy said nothing until we were seated. I could see that she looked terribly distressed.

"What is it, Lacy? Is there some kind of problem?"

"I hate to tell you this, Kathleen, but I think you should know. Early this morning a nurse found some graffiti on the wall, right outside Mitch's room; it looked like it was written in blood, she said, though it turned out to be rust colored paint. It seemed to be aimed at you. Anyway, the gist of it was that there would be serious problems if you kept on with your work here."

"Oh, my God." I felt my stomach lurch. "Can you tell me exactly what it said?"

"I really hate to tell you." She gulped. "It said, *'the she-devil is a tool of Satan. Get her out of here, or else…'* It was all streaky and running down the wall. I didn't see it because they cleaned it up immediately, but it sounds vile." She shook her head in dismay. "I can't believe it! Who would do such a thing?"

"Someone who's very sick, I should think." I thought a minute. "Is this going to make trouble for me with the administration?"

Lacy shook her head in misery. "I don't know."

"Well, until someone tells me I can't do this anymore, I'm going to continue. Mitch seems to be responding well. It would be a tragedy to quit."

"But, Kathleen–don't you see? You might be in danger. This person is crazy–just like you were afraid might happen. I think you should talk to someone about it."

"Yes, but *who?*"

Lacy wrinkled her forehead in thought. "Maybe Dr. Wolfe?"

"I suppose that would be a good idea–and maybe Mitch's doctor needs to be told as well."

"It wouldn't hurt, but I have a feeling the Administrative Office will do something about alerting the staff."

As we left the cafeteria, I put my arm around the concerned nurse's shoulder and hugged her. "Thanks, Lacy, for telling me. Would you do me a favor?"

"Anything, Kathleen."

"Just keep your eyes open, and maybe you could ask some others to do that too. We need to find this person before this escalates into something really ugly."

"I'll do that, and if anyone looks the least bit suspicious, I'll get someone to review his record, see if it sounds all right."

"You're a dear, Lacy. Thanks again."

With some reluctance, I talked over the problem with Dr. Wolfe, who told me that the hospital executives were naturally very concerned. At first, he said, they had suggested that I should stop my visits for a while. He had pointed out to them that Mitch was doing exceptionally well with my ministrations, that it would be lunacy to discontinue and, second, that they really didn't want a crazy running around loose, did they? Furthermore, Mitch's parents were adamant that, if I were willing to take the risk, I should continue working with their son.

"You do realize, Kathleen, that there is some danger involved here?" Dr. Wolfe asked. "It seems that this person's spite is directed only at you."

"I understand. But anyone who is that unstable surely is not safe to be working in a hospital. I think it *must* be an employee, don't you?"

"The only other possibility would be someone in Mitch's family. That

170

seems highly unlikely to me. I don't think any other visitor would be aware of the purpose of your visits. The hospital is increasing its security for a while, and all personnel have been alerted to be watchful–but, of course, that means that the perpetrator has probably been warned, too."

"Well, I'm going to continue. I couldn't abandon Mitch at this point."

"I was pretty sure that would be your answer. Let's just hope we catch this guy soon."

My next few visits were uneventful, but a couple of weeks later, as I headed for my station wagon in the parking lot, I saw that someone had painted: *Warning! Whore–go home!* on the driver's side of my car. I stared in disbelief, feeling as if someone had slapped me. Terrified, I went back in to report this new mischief. The idea that this person knew which car belonged to me was distinctly unsettling; I realized that he could easily follow me home.

All the way to my house, I checked and re-checked my rear-view mirror. No one appeared to be following me, but I took extra turns and wandered around the neighborhood before turning into my own driveway and, quickly, into my garage. I felt as if I had been physically violated. I tried to think what steps I might take to protect myself. The best I could come up with was to vary my route to and from the hospital as much as possible and to be unpredictable in choosing my hours of visitation. Small comfort.

Surely, whoever was so upset by my activities couldn't get my home address from my license plate or from the hospital, could he? I was thoroughly unnerved.

In desperation, I called Gentry and asked if he could meet me for dinner at Mary's Café.

"Sure, Kathleen. You sound a bit agitated. Problems?"

"Yes, Gentry–I *do* have a problem. I'll tell you when I see you."

As we waited for our dinner, I filled him in on the ugliness of the last days. His eyes clouded with concern. "I don't like this, Kathleen. Someone is really over the top. He could do *any* crazy thing if you don't accede to his demands."

"I know. I'm really scared, but I refuse to be intimidated by him. Everyone says 'him', but it could be a woman, I suppose."

"Yes, we really don't have anything to go on yet."

We interrupted our conversation as Mary brought our orders and refilled our coffee cups.

As we ate, Gentry offered to help with ferreting out the culprit.

"If I go with you to the hospital a few times and wander around the halls, I may be able to sense who is responsible for this. Sometimes I seem to be able to tune in to subtle signals from people. No guarantees, but I'd like to try; that is, if it's all right with you." He looked at me quizzically.

"I'd appreciate your help, Gentry. There's so little I can do to protect myself. It's making me paranoid."

"If I can get a feel of the guilty party's identity, then we will have to decide what to do about it."

"Right. I know it's going to be difficult. Even if we have a suspect, proof will be hard to come by, but at least he can be watched. Maybe he'll tip his hand."

"He's bound to make a mistake sooner or later, Kathleen. When are you planning to go to the hospital again?'

"How about Friday afternoon at about three o'clock?"

"Fine. I'll drive."

That next Friday afternoon, I visited with Mitch and did my usual healing routine. Gentry wandered around listening and sensing what he could. It was an uneventful day. No leads, no traumas.

The next couple of times, Gentry accompanied me. Then on the next visit, Lacy met us in the hallway outside Mitch's room.

"Well, he's struck again. Here." She held out a dirty looking folded piece of paper. As I reached to take it, Gentry intercepted me. "Let me hold it, Kathleen. Maybe I can pick up something from it." He gingerly opened it and read in block letters: *Devils Daughter, go home. I will soon loose paitiens with you.*

"Well, he's not much of a speller, is he?" I remarked, trying to lighten the horror I was feeling.

Lacy craned her neck to look at the message as Gentry, quiet and withdrawn, held it by a corner. He looked up. "Let's go to the cafeteria. You, too, Lacy, if you can take a break."

"Sure."

We settled at a small table with our coffee. Gentry again held the paper by the edge and lapsed into a reverie. We waited without speaking; Lacy seemed to realize that quiet was essential though she didn't have any idea what Gentry was attempting to do.

Finally he looked up. "Where did they find this?"

"It was left on the table in Mitch's room. He didn't see it, though. It was half hidden under the tissue box."

"It's a man who wrote this, I'm pretty sure. Probably a youngish man, maybe twenty to twenty-five. I get a sense that he has long blonde hair tied back."

Lacy's eyes widened at Gentry's ability to describe him. "Off hand, I

172

can't think of anyone who fits that description," she said after a moment's thought, "but I'll certainly keep my eyes open."

"You might tell anyone you're sure you can trust. I wouldn't announce it publicly though. We don't want him to know we're on to him; he could dye his hair or cut it if he got suspicious." He smiled at Lacy. "Just tell them that someone had a hunch about it."

"Right. Well, I'd better get back to work."

"Thanks, Lacy," I said as she got up to leave. "Don't you think Lacy should turn this note in to the administration, Gentry?"

"Yes, by all means. They need to be kept up to date on everything."

Lacy promised that she would deliver it to the office herself.

"What's the next step, Gentry?" I asked after she had gone.

"I'll keep prowling around. That's about all we can do unless someone recognizes my description. I'm worried. I pick up an urgency about this; he's about ready to explode. Be doubly careful, Kathleen. Don't go anywhere alone here at the hospital."

We returned to Mitch's room, Gentry to wander the halls, me to give Mitchell his usual treatment.

"Hi, Mitch. How's it going?" I asked as I stepped into his room.

He looked up from his reading with a radiant smile "Great, Kathleen. I feel pretty good. I got to get up today and walk around for a little bit."

"Hey, terrific."

I was pleased to see that his coloring had improved. He was propped up in bed reading the book I had given him.

"Good book," he announced. "Boy, Mr. Cameron certainly got to meet lots of interesting people, didn't he?"

"Yes. His reporting took him all over the world."

"Gosh, that would be a great job. I think I'd like to be a foreign correspondent." His eyes sparkled with enthusiasm. "What would I have to do to be good at it?"

"Well, first of all you have to be a keen observer. Then you have to be able to speak well without much time to prepare your words." My hands were moving over various areas of his body as I kept him talking. "I should think you'd need a good memory too, and you'd have to be well-informed about history and international affairs. Do you ever read the newspaper, Mitch?"

"No—just the sports page and the comics. But I'm going to start. I'll ask my mom to bring the newspaper in when she comes."

"Good. You know, you might try writing little essays about the people you see here in the hospital. That would give you good training in being observant and in getting your observations down clearly."

"Neat idea. I kind of like to write anyway. I've got a notebook here somewhere. I'll begin right away." He grinned at me impishly. "I'll begin with you."

"Will you let me read it?"

"Maybe–it depends if I think it's any good."

"Even if you don't think it's very good, maybe I should read it. I could possibly give you some suggestions to make it better. I used to make my living writing magazine articles."

"You did? Cool. Okay–it's a deal." He paused. "If I continue to improve, the doctor's letting me go home soon. I have to get a little stronger first."

"That's great news, Mitch."

"But then you couldn't read what I wrote," he said with disappointment.

"Probably it would be a good idea if I gave you treatments at home for a little while yet. I'll need to talk with your parents."

He relaxed. "Cool."

I helped him find his notebook, waved goodbye and went to find Gentry.

Mitch was eagerly waiting for me when I visited him again.

"Hi, Kathleen. I've been walking every day and sitting in a chair for an hour or so. I feel ever so much better."

I bent and hugged his shoulder. "I'm so glad. This bed must get pretty tiresome."

"Yeah. I hope I can go home soon. I'm anxious to see Casey."

"Casey?"

"Yeah–he's my dog. He's a mix, part Irish setter and part retriever."

"Pretty color?"

"Really pretty–kind of a reddish gold."

"I'll bet you get to go home pretty soon. You look terrific. Did you do any writing?"

"I tried to write about you, Kathleen, but I had trouble making it sound right." He flushed. "I threw it away. It was awful."

"Well, sometimes it takes awhile to get the hang of things."

"I did write something, though. Do you want to see it?"

"You bet. Soon as I'm finished here."

When I had finished with his treatment, he shyly handed me his notebook. I began to read.

It takes a lot of different kinds of people to run a hospital. Doctors and nurses of course. But then there are all kinds of support people who are necessary to make it all work well: cooks, dishwashers, nurse's

174

aides, orderlies. I don't see much of those support people, but there's one man who comes into my room every so often to clean it up.

I don't like him. He makes me feel weird. He has dirty looking blonde hair that he has fastened back and a pimply face. He's supposed to be doing the floors, but he keeps looking at me. He kind of scares me, but I don't want to make a fuss.

I guess he's twenty-five or thirty. His eyes have a kind of wild look, and he bites his fingernails. He has a high forehead and he's very pale. He mumbles to himself as he works. Maybe he doesn't like his job but can't get a better one. I'm glad I'm going home soon.

I looked up at him. "Pretty good, Mitch. You've been very observant."

"It's really hard to do, isn't it? I mean–I don't know how to begin or end."

"Well, this is a tough assignment. To do a thumbnail sketch isn't easy. After all, you don't know this person at all. If you keep working at it, you'll become even more observant and will have practice in getting your thoughts down in words. It doesn't have to be a person. It can be a scene, an event–anything."

There was no doubt in my mind that the subject of Mitch's essay was the man Gentry had described. I didn't want to add to my young friend's discomfort, so I was careful in my questioning.

"I guess you don't like this guy much?"

"No–there's something creepy about him. I didn't know how to describe it."

"You got that across very well. I could sense his weirdness. Tell me, does he come in at the same time usually?"

"I'm not sure. Usually, he comes in kind of early in the morning, I think. Why?"

"Well, if you're uncomfortable with him, maybe we could get him assigned to another wing or something. I don't suppose you know his name?"

"No. He kind of keeps his head down and looks at me out of the top of his eyes. I try to ignore him."

"Well, I'll talk with Lacy. She'll know if there's anything we can do."

"Yeah, I guess. But I'd hate for him to be mad at me. I wouldn't trust him."

"Mitch, don't worry. We'll be sure he has no idea that you have anything to do with it, if we're able to get him transferred."

"Thanks, Kathleen. I'm not too worried. I probably will get to go home soon."

I said goodbye and went to find Gentry and Lacy.

"Umm," Lacy said after I had told her about Mitch's essay. "I have an idea he's on the early morning shift. I come in later."

"But how would he know about me? I never come in 'til afternoon."

"It's possible he's had a change of shift recently. Maybe he even asked for it so he could go into Mitch's room when there was no one about."

"That's creepy. We've got to find out who he is."

"Do you know any of the nurses on the early shift, Lacy?" Gentry asked, a frown on his mobile face.

"Yes, I know several. I'll call them tonight." She wrinkled her brow. "I wonder if the personnel office could be of any help."

"If necessary we can go through all their files. I'm sure we'd be allowed to, but it would be a lot simpler if we had a name. Why don't we hold off on that until you check with the women you know?" Gentry suggested. "I don't think I'd be allowed to roam the halls early in the morning, do you?"

"No, probably not," Lacy agreed. "I'll try to find out who's in charge of assigning personnel on the early shift." Her face brightened. "Oh, I know, I can talk to Mildred Corey. She assigns the personnel for this shift. She should know if anyone recently asked for a change. Maybe she'll recognize this guy."

"Good idea, Lacy. I'll probably come in next Tuesday afternoon, as usual. Maybe we'll have a lead on who it is by then," I said.

"I'll do my best to talk to those nurses. Surely someone will recognize him."

I thanked Lacy for her concern and we left her to her duties.

On our next visit, she was on the lookout for me and hurried over as soon as she saw Gentry and me.

"We've found him!" she said exultantly. "His name is Will Watson."

"How did you identify him?" Gentry inquired.

"Mildred Corey recognized his description. She said that he *did* ask to be transferred to the early morning shift a few weeks ago. He hasn't worked here very long—only a couple of months."

"Does the Administration know? Have they done anything about him?" I asked apprehensively.

"Yes. We all knew that we had a problem, so as soon as we identified him, she immediately reported him to the Administrative Offices. She tells me they gave him two weeks pay and fired him."

"Did they question him at all?" Gentry asked, looking worried. "This man really needs help. They may have loosed a ticking time bomb."

Lacy shrugged helplessly. "I don't know."

"I think we had better talk to someone in charge. Come on, Kathleen, let's

176

go talk to the hospital administrator."

After a short wait, a heavyset man approached, hand outstretched.

"Good afternoon. I'm Bryce Miller. What can I do for you?"

Gentry introduced us and explained our interest in Will Watson.

"Oh, yes. Why don't we sit down and talk about it?"

He motioned us into his office. As we seated ourselves, I noticed that the room was comfortably furnished. Mr. Miller, a congenial looking man, was well barbered and expensively dressed. His fleshy face was flushed, suggesting that he enjoyed his liquor.

"It's a difficult situation," he said as he smoothed his gray hair back with his hand. "We let Watson go, you know. Can't have that kind of thing in a hospital, can we?" He beamed at us, seemingly proud of a job well done.

Gentry leaned forward toward the desk. "Mr. Miller, Mrs. Parrish and I are concerned that this man may need help. He should have a psychiatric evaluation. We think he's a very dangerous individual."

"Oh, do you really think so?" Bryce Miller nervously played with a paper opener. "I talked it over with Dr. Morrison–he's head of the medical staff–and we felt it would be better to get rid of him. We told him we were forced to cut back on staff because of budget constraints. He seemed to accept it all right."

Gentry and I looked at each other in disbelief.

"But Mr. Miller," I said, "he knows my car. Didn't your secretary tell you about that?"

Mr. Miller nervously nodded assent.

"He could be waiting for me anywhere." I was thoroughly alarmed at the incompetent way the whole thing had been handled. "I'm the one who's in danger–and I don't see that firing him has helped at all. For all you know, he's managed to get into the hospital records and found out where Mitchell Tavener lives, too–and Mitch will probably be going home soon. He's afraid of him. So am I, for that matter. He could follow *me* home."

"Oh, I'm sure this Watson will forget all about it, now that he's not working here anymore." Bryce Miller waved his hand airily. "He'll just drift off somewhere else." His attitude of denial was making me increasingly angry.

Gentry, too, was visibly upset. "Mr. Miller, in my opinion the hospital has acted very irresponsibly. You should take steps to find him and have him evaluated."

"Oh, we couldn't do that, sir. What reason would we have?"

"You got that note he wrote, didn't you? Did you have it checked for fingerprints?"

He spread his thick hands in apology. "No, we didn't think to do that."

"Do you still have it?" Gentry asked sharply.

He cleared his throat. "I believe it's around here somewhere."

"Well, I suggest, sir," Gentry spoke with quiet authority, "that you turn the matter over to the police and have that paper tested. He should be brought in and questioned. That's what should have been done as soon as he was identified. You're letting a menace to society walk around loose."

"I think you're both making too much of this. We don't want a lot of adverse publicity here." He could see that we were far from satisfied. "All right, all right, I'll contact the police and give them the paper." He shrugged. "That's about all I can do."

He speedily ushered us out of his office and peremptorily closed the door.

"Well," said Gentry with annoyance, "that seems to be that. I find it hard to believe that they didn't turn this over to the police. Too worried about their reputation, I suppose."

"I guess I should have made more of a fuss earlier, but I have no authority even to be here. It puts me in a pretty ambiguous situation."

"No, there's not much that you can do except stay away and I know you won't do that."

"No–I think there's a much better chance that this crazy will be caught if I keep coming. Besides, as long as Mitch is here, I'm going to be here too."

Before I went home, I visited with my young friend and gave him his healing treatment. He had written a competent essay about his dog, Casey. I made a few suggestions and left him to figure out the next subject he wanted to tackle.

An ecstatic Mitch greeted me the next time I came to the hospital. "I'm going home tomorrow!" he told me excitedly.

"Oh, Mitch–I'm so happy for you." I tousled his short hair affectionately. I talked with your mom, you know, and she'd like me to visit you a couple of times a week at your home."

"I know. She told me.' He turned serious. "Kathleen, I haven't properly thanked you for all you've done for me. I *know* that without you I wouldn't be going home. Dr. Stuerben says sometimes leukemia goes into remission and that I might get sick again, but I don't believe him. Gosh, I don't know how to thank you."

"No thanks necessary, Mitch. You just stay optimistic about life and stay well. Come on, let's get going on your treatment–the last one here, isn't that wonderful?"

After I had said goodbye to Mitchell, Gentry and I started for the parking lot.

"Do you mind if I go say goodbye to Lacy, Gentry?" I asked. "I'm not sure how soon I'll be coming back."

"Sure. I'll wait for you by the door."

I found Lacy at the nurse's station, filling out some papers. I hugged her goodbye, promising to keep in touch. I was not sorry to be leaving this place–at least for a time.

As I came down the hall, I could see Gentry waiting just outside the large glass doors to the hospital entrance. I hurried to join him. Suddenly, a man came running from a side hallway straight at me. He had an open knife in his hand, a wildly demented look on his face. There was no way I could escape his crazed assault. Just as he stabbed at my heart, I managed to clutch my leather purse to my chest. I screamed as the knife buried itself in the purse.

Suddenly all was confusion. Several people came running; Gentry from the front door, a registration clerk, a man who had been sitting there.

His eyes wild, the assailant turned and ran out the door into the parking lot. I heard a screech of brakes, a sickening thud, and suddenly all was quiet. As soon as Gentry was assured that I was all right, he rushed out the door. I shakily followed.

The driver of a large black Buick that was wedged at an angle against the curb was on his knees beside my assailant who had obviously run in front of the car in his frenzied flight. I could see that he was still breathing, but he looked crumpled and broken. While Gentry ran back to get help, I kneeled down next to the dying man and put my hand on his forehead. He opened his eyes and gazed at me.

"It's all right," I said. "Just take it easy." I did my best to send him some energy, but I knew that his life was slipping away.

He tried to lift his head and say something, his eyes dark with confusion and pain.

"Shh–it's all right." I smoothed his hair back from his face.

He struggled to speak. "Sorry," he managed to gasp. Then his head fell back as he lapsed into unconsciousness. His struggle was over before help could arrive.

After a long and weary time, a detective finally came and took our statements and told us we were free to go. I asked if the police had found any of Will Watson's family, but all I could get from him was that a full investigation would be made and that I would be notified at some future time.

About a week later, a pleasant, open-faced young police officer appeared at my door one afternoon.

"Sergeant Porter, ma'am," he said as I opened the door. "I've come to fill you in on the Watson case."

I ushered him into the living room and offered him coffee. Placing his cap on his knee, he shook his head no.

"Sergeant, did Will have any family?" I asked.

"No. From what neighbors say, he lived with his mother until she died this last spring. That may have contributed to his instability. We found out two other things about him. He really wanted to be a soldier but no branch of the military would accept him. It seems he had a heart murmur and couldn't pass the physical. I guess he was pretty bitter about it."

He consulted his notebook. "One old lady who lives next door remembers that his younger brother had died when he was about thirteen. He had leukemia like Mitchell Tavener. His mother, in desperation, had tried some kind of quack remedy after it was clear that the doctors couldn't save him. When the kid didn't make it, Will really went to pieces, according to this neighbor. The police psychologist thinks that's why he turned on you with such hatred."

He sighed. "Apparently losing his mother on top of everything else was just too much for him to handle." He looked up. "That's about all we know. There's not much doubt that he's the one who harassed you. Unless you have other concerns, we will consider the case to be closed."

A picture of that young, crumpled body lying broken in the hospital driveway rushed into my mind. "It's so sad. If the hospital administration had turned this over to you sooner, Will might have gotten some help. There's no point in pursuing it further now. Thank you for telling me. "

After Sergeant Porter had gone, I reflected on this tragic conclusion. Will Watson's pain and rage–at whom? at God? –had compulsively propelled him to desperate action. In the end, he was more a victim than I whom he had victimized. I was infinitely relieved that all the confusion and fear were over, but I knew that the whole thing had been tragically mishandled. With tears in my eyes, I prayed for the repose of poor Will Watson's soul and gave thanks for my own survival.

Chapter 17

After Douglas' second book came out, I searched out a newsstand that carried the Sunday London Times and began to pick it up regularly. I couldn't believe I hadn't thought to do so before. Just turning the pages and seeing the headlines and pictures from London made him seem closer. My eyes were seeing the same scenes that he saw; I was reading the same words that he read.

I followed the Book Review with special interest. I learned that *Voices of War* was hugely successful in Great Britain and that his publisher was sending him on a three-week tour of the United States. Douglas was to do interviews with TV and radio stations. I knew that he would not try to see me; he would abide by our mutual agreement not to seek each other out.

He had sent me a copy of his book, signed as before, and again I had lingered over his photograph, this time a larger picture on the back of the book jacket. His hair was graying, his forehead higher, but his intense eyes were bright, his mouth as beautifully modeled as ever. He was still a remarkably attractive man. My heart melted with love.

Some weeks later, on a cold, damp morning, finding myself near the Marshall Anderson Gallery, I decided to drop in to say hello to Andy. As I opened the door, a man with a wrapped painting in his hand stepped aside to let me enter. With surprise, I realized that it was Douglas. Both of us were stunned. We stood speechless for a moment, staring in disbelief.

"Kathleen," he finally said. His eyes met and held mine.

My brain went numb with shock. "Douglas," I managed to gasp.

We stood motionless, uncertain of what to do. I longed to throw myself into his arms but I was aware, suddenly, of where we were and of Andy standing back watching us with unabashed curiosity.

"I didn't expect to run into you like this, Kathleen," Douglas finally said. He turned slightly so that his back blocked Andy's view of our conversation. "I had no intention of seeing you."

My wits were slowly beginning to return. "I read that you were coming to this country, Douglas, but how do you happen to be here? In this gallery?" Every cell in my body seemed to radiate toward him.

"I knew that this was where you showed your work. You mentioned it, remember?"

"Did I?" His brilliant smile tore at my heart

"I was hoping to find something of yours to buy." He grinned and nodded toward the cumbersome parcel he held. "Kathleen, now that we've run into each other, I can't just walk away. Will you have lunch with me?"

"Yes, of course. Give me a minute to say hello to Andy."

"I'll wait for you in the parking lot. I'm in turmoil. I couldn't face making small talk right now."

"Mmm–me, too. I'll make it quick."

As I approached, Andy reached out to hug me. "A friend, Kathleen?"

"Yes, I've known Douglas for several years." My heart seemed to be galvanized as I struggled to present a calm I didn't feel. "I didn't know he was in town. He said he just bought a painting of mine. I guess I mentioned to him once that this is where I show my work"

Andy looked at me appraisingly. "Yes. He came in and asked if I had anything of yours here. He didn't mention that he knew you."

"No, he wouldn't. Douglas is pretty reticent."

"He bought the only painting of yours that I have left–you know, the semi-abstract one with creation spilling from the eye of God. I sold your other last week."

"I'm glad he bought that particular painting."

"Do you have anything else in the works? I could use a couple of canvases."

"I'm trying to work out the idea for a series. I'm just beginning to formulate my ideas, so I won't have anything for you any time soon."

"I'll be waiting eagerly, Kathleen."

"I'll let you know when I have something. I just dropped in today to say hello. I've got to run."

I hugged Andy again and made my escape.

We pretended to eat the excellent lunch at the Bistro, but it was an effort that neither of us managed. We didn't even say much to each other. We were content just to sit and absorb each other's presence. My joy was overwhelming.

"Mavourneen," Douglas murmured as his eyes absorbed me, "I feel as if God has handed me a precious gift–a gift I never thought to have again in this life."

"A gift of grace."

My mind, my soul, my body could only respond to his. I was without volition, centered in a boundless, perfect time warp. I studied his face. He looked fit, but very thin. His features had a chiseled quality as if carved out of the rock of disciplined endurance. I knew that his choice to return to Rosalind had cost him dearly; I sensed that his payment had been in the coin of enormous soul growth.

As in days past, my eyes fastened on the endearing small mole on his upper lip. Involuntarily my mouth curved in a smile. "You are so infinitely precious to me."

Douglas reached across the table and put his hand on mine. In silence our beings absorbed each other, life-giving water refreshing a parched desert land.

"I just thought of something, dearest. Sometime around Christmas, a couple of years ago, I had a most amazing dream. It's a little hard to explain, but it touched me deeply." His eyes were soft with memory. "You and I were on some other plane–another dimension, I think–and as we approached each other, we floated together, blending into one another. We merged completely. I woke up feeling joy beyond any I have felt since we parted. It seemed miraculous to me."

My eyes widened in surprise. "Douglas, I had a very similar dream. I understand exactly what you're saying. It was as if all of our cells were intermingling for a few glorious moments in an epiphany of oneness, as if we met center to center. I had a feeling of completion that I've never experienced before. Then I woke up." I paused to reflect. "That feeling of completion and joy stayed with me for days. I'm not sure when I had that dream, but the time you mentioned sounds about right. That's incredible!

"The older I get, the more I realize that we don't understand very much about the human psyche at all, nor life itself, for that matter. What's that quote from Shakespeare? 'There are more things in Heaven and Earth, Horatio, than are dreamt of in your philosophy.' Something like that."

"Do you suppose we sometimes actually meet in another realm while we sleep and don't remember? I'm not too good at recalling my dreams."

"I'd like to think so, love, I'd really like to think so, but we'll never know this side the gates of Heaven."

In all too short a time, Douglas, looking at his watch, said sorrowfully that he had to go.

"I have an interview at CBS at 2:30, Kathleen. I really must leave you." He looked at me questioningly. "My feeling is that we must keep our pact. Do you agree?"

I sighed. "Yes, Douglas, I do. God knows, it's not what I want, but I'm beginning to understand that the imperative of the soul is the determining factor. Otherwise, everything turns to dust."

"In the end, we choose spiritual integration or alienation from the ground of our being." His intense blue eyes held mine. "In that light, it seems to be the only possible choice for us." He smiled tenderly. "I'm so glad we're in agreement, Kathleen. It's devilishly hard, even then."

"Yes, it's very hard–but I have the maturity now to rejoice in the blessing of this day without demanding more, like a spoiled child." I leaned forward and touched his mouth with my fingers. "I love you, darling. I'll always love you."

"God bless you, my dearest Kathleen." He raised my hand and kissed it.

And so we parted yet again, renewed in spirit by this brief but precious encounter. And once again, I marveled at the slender threads of God that seemed to shape our destinies.

* * *

At Christmas the next year, I flew to New York City to spend a few weeks with my daughter. She had gotten engaged to a young intern, Neville Grant, a few months before and was planning to be married in the summer. I had yet to meet him.

Her own career was flourishing. She was now a premier dancer, already inspiring admiring ovations whenever she performed. I had seen her dance several times in the last years and was awed and overcome with admiration for her fluid grace and luminosity.

Dylan met me at the airport, wild red curls brushed up on top of her head, long legs flying to greet me, arms outstretched to enfold me in hugs and kisses. She was a dizzying, dazzling delight, my exquisite daughter, clad in burnt orange trousers, burgundy boots, and a caramel-colored faux fur sweatshirt. With laughing eyes, she finally disengaged herself from me and drew forth a slightly bewildered-looking young man. I got a quick impression of light brown hair, glasses, an infectious smile.

"This is Neville, Momma. Isn't he cute?" She grinned wickedly as he blushed.

"Mrs. Parrish, I'm glad to know you." He held out his hand. "Pay no attention to your daughter. She's over the top with excitement."

"I'm pretty excited myself, Neville," I said as I clasped his hand. "I'm glad to meet you. It will make me feel awfully old if you don't call me Kathleen."

I liked him immediately. His hazel eyes were bright with intelligence. His rather long face, though not really handsome, lit up with a ready smile. He had an engaging, modest manner that I found most attractive.

Neville and Dylan deposited me at my hotel with the stern admonition to take a nap until dinnertime. Later, we went to a small restaurant close to the hotel for a lovely evening of good food, wine and conversation.

The kids determinedly kept me entertained. Each day they had something new to show me, some place that I had to see, some gallery to explore. One evening, they took me to see *George M.* with Joel Gray and a young Bernadette Peters. It was a joyful and lively show.

Another evening I had the pleasure of being escorted by Neville to see Dylan dance in a new piece called *Meditation.* Her radiance and delicate strength combined to make a compelling and inspired performance. As I watched my daughter, polished professional that she was, my heart glowed with pride. I wished that Matthew were here to share this lovely moment. Gentry and Richard, Peg's husband, had been her only male role models since my dad had died. I found myself praying that Neville, sitting quietly beside me, would be as strong, as gentle, as honest as the father that Dylan had never known, as passionate and yet compassionate as her beloved grandfather.

On Christmas Eve, through lightly falling snow, we went together to Midnight mass at St. Patrick's Cathedral, a glorious celebration awash with red and gold vestments, twinkling candlelight, and the sweet, pungent smell of freshly cut pine. The choir, angelically sublime, resonating through the high-vaulted cathedral, filled me with ecstasy:

Gloria in excelsis
Et in terra pax hominibus
Bonae volentatis

Glory to God in the Highest, and on earth peace to men of good will.

"So might it be," I thought to myself.

As in the words of an old carol that I knew from childhood, there were surely angels hovering near. Almost I could see them. It was a night to remember.

On Christmas Day we drove to Newark, New Jersey to have dinner with Neville's family. On the way down, I learned that Neville's father was a CPA and his mother, a high school English teacher. Neville had grown up in Newark; he had gone to Columbia University both for undergraduate work and for medical school.

The Grants lived in a red brick two-story house with tall pine trees at each side, rising like sentinels out of the snow-covered lawn. A circular driveway curved up to the front of the house that had white painted shutters and trim. There was a solid substantiality about it.

As Neville pulled up, he honked the horn and a young boy came running out.

"They're here! They're here!" he cried.

Neville jumped out and grabbed the youngster up in his arms.

"Neil! How's it going?" As he swung him up over his head, the youngster squealed with delight.

Dylan was next to greet the tow-headed boy with a hug and kiss.

"Mum, this is Neil, Neville's nephew. He's my buddy."

"Hi, there, Neil. I'm glad to know you." He shook hands with me gravely then danced ahead of us into the house.

"They're here! Grandpa, they're here!"

Neville's father, a middle-aged man with thinning hair and wearing glasses, rumpled the boy's hair with affection.

"I see that they are, Neil. Let's let them come in, shall we?"

After hugs and introductions, we settled in a comfortable living room graced by a roaring fire. Norman and Marilyn Grant were quietly pleasant people. Neville's older sister Carrie and her husband Joe, parents of young Neil, along with Neville's grandmother, made up the rest of the party. I liked the easy interchanges of badinage and affection that flowed between parents and siblings. Dylan, only child, was clearly delighted with her intended's family, and just as clearly, they welcomed her as a second daughter.

After a delicious late afternoon dinner, everyone gathered around the piano and sang Christmas carols, Marilyn at the piano while Carrie played the flute. We sang all of the old traditional carols: *God Rest Ye Merry Gentlemen, Joy to the World, Silent Night* and, finally, *Rudolph the Red-nosed Reindeer* for little Neil. Then it was time for pumpkin pie, exuberant hugs of farewell, and hurried piling into the car to return to New York City where Neville had to go on duty at midnight.

My future son-in-law, caring and intelligent, had carefully explained to me the first night we met that he was very much in love with Dylan and that he was thrilled with her career. His earnest efforts to convince me that he would in no way stand in her way were endearing. My visit with the Grants had satisfied me that my daughter was already an accepted and loved member of his family. They seemed eager to include her in their warm embrace. My mind was at ease about her; she had chosen wisely.

* * *

Back home, I continued with my painting and a greatly curtailed healing practice. I worked almost entirely at Dr. Wolfe's office or, on rare occasion, at my client's home. I stayed away from hospitals except in extreme emergencies. I had no wish to repeat my traumatic experience with Will Watson.

That summer, on a clear and sunny day, Dylan and Neville were married in a small, elegant ceremony in Peggy and Richard's back yard. Dylan wanted the simplest of weddings with only her family and Neville's and our closest friends present. In spite of the fact that she chose to make her living on the stage surrounded by admiring audiences, she had always wanted personal events to be intimate and unpretentious.

In a simple white ballet length dress, with her exquisite dancer's grace, Dylan joined Neville under a trellised arch to consecrate their union. I struggled to keep my composure as my daughter became Mrs. Neville Grant.

After the guests had gone and Neville had taken his bride away, I asked Gentry to come home with me for a drink. Though I had lived alone for many years, I didn't want to spend that evening by myself. Dylan's marriage seemed terribly final; she was now truly gone. After the busy days of wedding preparations, of having the house full of people, of presents being delivered and of last minute fittings, the house was too quiet, too empty. I needed the comfort of Gentry's compassionate company for a while even though I was exhausted both mentally and physically.

We sat, shoes off, feet propped on the coffee table, and sipped our wine as I slowly unwound. At first, talk centered on the wedding–how beautiful and radiant Dylan had been, how perfect the ceremony and the reception. We agreed that Neville's family had fit in happily; already the extended family connections were strong.

"It was all Dylan wished for, I think," I said as I put my head back and tried to relax. "In some ways it's a relief it's over–but now that she's married, I'm feeling pretty alone. You'd think I'd be used to it by now."

"It's natural that you'd feel a bit despondent, Kathleen." Gentry scrunched down lower on the couch. "You've done an awfully good job of bringing up Dylan; you've raised her mostly on your own and she's a fine human being. I love her dearly. Tonight you must wish that her father were here."

"Matthew would have been so proud of her." I sighed. "To tell the truth, it's difficult to remember him clearly. I can't comprehend what it would have been like if he had lived."

Gentry refilled our glasses. "I know. Even with people we love very much, after they've been gone awhile their unique qualities, their endearing idiosyncrasies, seem to slip through our fingers like sand. Their crisp edges blur." He paused to sip some wine. "You're exhausted, you know. Sometimes we need just to slump back and forget everything for a while; we need to allow ourselves to lie fallow. Actually, if we can do that, the quiet period often becomes a time of gestation. You're beginning a new segment in your life." He looked at me intently. "It's important that you give your inner being time to assimilate and refine–to transmute–to wait to see whether some rare fruit may be developing."

"Gentry, you have a genius for gently prodding me forward whenever my spirit fails. What would I do without you, dearest friend?"

That night after Gentry had gone, I seriously considered his words. He never offered his wisdom lightly. I decided to follow his advice, to take a hiatus from everything–painting, healing work, socializing, though, in truth, I did little of that. I determined that I would nurture my spirit and see what green and growing thing might come forth.

I spent long hours in meditation and contemplation. I read spiritual literature of one kind or another. I tried to approach the necessary tasks of life with a Zen-like attitude, to 'be here now' as Ram Dass recommended. My agile, very active mind objected strenuously at first to being ignored for such long periods. Gradually, though, I found a new clarity of being, a centered state that was neither passive nor active, but rather, quietly alert. After my mystical experience a few years before, the ecstasy I had experienced had been hard to contain in my unseasoned physical body. Now I was grounded in a more tenable feeling of joy.

Chapter 18

In the early days of 1974, I began struggling with a series of paintings that had come to me in a dream. I had been searching for a long time for a subject that could stretch itself into a spiritual statement and could accommodate itself to a series.

The dream that I had been graced with dissolved so quickly that I was able to grasp and retain only glimpses of a vast, breathtakingly panoramic vision. I seemed to be encircled, no matter where I turned, in a dazzling display of light and movement. Nothing was static. All was motion and crystalline light and swirling darkness: glittering motes of matter coalescing into planets, nebulae, asteroids, each swirling through endless space; then, lands and waters with luminous skies arching overhead; then beasts and fields and verdant forests stretching into infinity. And I heard in my dream the humming frequency, the vibrant song of God as the universe imploded and enfolded on itself and imploded yet again and curled in and spewed out in constant movement, spiraling into a dazzling dance of creation. I awoke awed and humbled and I knew that I must try to capture something of that dynamic vision on canvas.

After much thought, I envisioned seven large panels, each delineating a day of creation as told in the first chapter of Genesis. I was aware that I was setting up a problem for myself that was well nigh impossible to capture with integrity, artistry and originality. How to avoid the sentimental and the banal? How to express the tremendous dynamism and movement that I experienced in my dream?

I was faced with the same conundrum that I had struggled with after my mystical experience at the cliffs in Santa Monica. I hadn't solved the issue to my satisfaction then. It was time to try once more.

Weeks went by as I painted, repainted, scrapped canvases and tried once again. Sometimes I forgot to eat. Sometimes time disappeared completely. At night when I couldn't sleep, colors and shapes drifted through my mind in dizzying panoply. I was a woman obsessed

As I read the beginning chapters of Genesis once more, musing about the sequence, it became clear to me that I could not follow events exactly as they were told in the Old Testament. I realized that pictorial expression could not accommodate seven panels. The imagery would be too diluted. I closed the Bible. I would take liberties with the material.

Gradually, after endless experimentation, I began to see the direction I wished to go. I finally began serious work on the first canvas and began to have hope that it might be successful.

My labor was interrupted by a phone call from Mrs. Clifford, the first patient referred to me by Dr. Wolfe several years before.

"Kathleen, I'm reluctant to intrude this way, but I have a friend about whom I'm extremely concerned. I wonder if you would be willing to help?"

"What seems to be the problem?"

"Well, she's the wife of a state senator and, to put it bluntly, she has a drinking problem. Someone needs to intervene before she destroys herself and her family. I'm at my wit's end."

"I've never attempted anything like that, Mrs. Clifford. I'm not sure how successful I'd be. Can't you get her into some kind of treatment program? Alcoholics Anonymous, or something like that?"

"She's in heavy denial. When I talk to her about it, she says there is no problem, that she can handle it. But the fact is that she can't and she's getting worse. Please, Kathleen, if you could just come to lunch and meet her. I'd be so grateful."

"Uh–this could be awkward. Have you talked to her about me at all? It would be pretty hard to do anything without her knowledge and consent."

"Yes, I told her about you–what you did for me–and she's agreed to meet you and at least talk with you. If nothing else, maybe you can get her to seek professional help. You know, she's panicked at the thought of adverse publicity."

"Yes, I can see that she would be. All right, I'll give it a try," I reluctantly agreed. "When do you want me to come?"

"Could you come Friday at about one o'clock?"

After giving me directions to her home, she said goodbye.

Lois Parkhurst, the senator's wife, was a very thin, brittle woman with hair dyed black and a nervous agitation about her. Her dress was high fashion, her jewelry a bit ostentatious for a small luncheon. She wore crimson lipstick and dark liner around her eyes. To me, she seemed frantic to appear youthful though she must have been at least sixty. Her brown eyes assessed me anxiously as Mrs. Clifford introduced us.

We were served a delicious lunch in a glass-enclosed garden room. I noted that no alcohol or wine was offered. Instead, we drank iced tea from beautiful Waterford crystal goblets. We made desultory conversation about the latest books, the headlines of the last few days, music. I discovered that she had one son who was married, living in New York. I talked a bit about Dylan and her progressing career as a dancer and about the charms of living in that great metropolis. We had a pleasant enough time, but in spite of Mrs.

190

Clifford's social expertise, the three of us were well aware that this meeting was more than an agreeable social luncheon.

Finally, after we had finished eating, Mrs. Clifford suggested that I might like to talk with her friend privately and directed us to a small parlor that was comfortably furnished with rose-covered chintz chairs and couches and small white wicker tables.

I was at a loss about how to begin. "Mrs. Parkhurst–,"

"Oh, please call me Lois," she interrupted. "We both know you're supposed to convince me that I need help. No use pretending otherwise." Her hand fluttered vaguely.

I smiled at her directness. "How do you feel about it?"

Lois lit a cigarette and puffed nervously. "Oh, Marta means well. She's my best friend. I know she worries about me. If it makes her feel better, it's fine with me."

"But you don't think you need any help, is that right?"

"I sometimes drink too much, I know that." She shrugged. "But I can handle it. I can stop if I want to."

"Why don't you want to? Doesn't it sometimes cause problems?" I tried to keep my voice low and nonthreatening.

She ground her half-smoked cigarette into the ashtray. "Yes, sometimes, I guess." She furrowed her brow. "I embarrass my husband on occasion. That's not good." In a sudden spurt of honesty she added, "Hell, I embarrass myself too."

"I'm sure Mrs. Clifford told you that I sometimes can help people. I want to be up front with you. I've never worked before with anyone who hasn't had a well-defined physical problem. Would you like me to give you my usual treatment? At the least, it will be very relaxing."

"Sure; go ahead. I admit I'm curious about it."

I asked her to lie on the couch and I pulled up a rose-covered upholstered footstool for myself.

"Just close your eyes and try to relax."

As I placed my hands on her forehead and the top of her head, I breathed a prayer for guidance. She took a deep breath and sighed; I could literally feel tension drain from her body. Slowly, her breathing became even and her face smoothed out. After working with her for perhaps ten minutes, I sensed that she had drifted into an altered state of consciousness.

I spoke quietly to her. "Lois, what are you afraid of?"

Her eyelids fluttered but remained closed, as if it were too much trouble to open them.

"Afraid of getting old–unattractive." She sighed deeply. "I'll be all

191

alone." Her voice was so low that I had to strain to hear.

"You'll be all alone?" I repeated her words hoping she would amplify them.

"Yes–all alone." Tears began to seep from her closed eyes, making black smudges below them. "I'm all alone now." She wiped her hand across her eyes, increasing the devastation of her makeup. "All alone." She sniffed. "Paulie's gone–never comes to see me–hardly ever calls–too busy with his life in New York. And Walter–he hasn't any time for me. It's always committee meetings and fund-raisings–and other women, too, I'd bet. He probably has a bimbo hidden away somewhere. He's hardly ever home." She struggled to control her tears. "And when he is, he closes himself into his study to work. I can't stand it. I really can't stand it." She thought for a moment. "Booze helps me to stand it."

I paraphrased her last words. "You drink too much to deaden the pain; is that right?"

She opened her brown eyes, still drenched with tears, and looked at me with surprise. "I've never told anyone that before. I'm not sure I realized the connection myself until now." She smiled faintly. "It's shattering to admit it–but maybe I understand myself better now." She struggled into a sitting position and smoothed her hair. "God–I must look a mess."

"It's okay. There's a lavatory right next door. You can repair the damage."

"Yeah," she grinned mockingly. "I can repair the outer damage. How do I repair the mess inside?"

"Lois, I hope you don't think I'm presumptuous. Just tell me to shut up if you want to."

"Go ahead. Say whatever you want. Maybe I'm getting ready to listen now."

I felt my way cautiously. "I've come to realize, over the years of helping others, that a good many physical problems and virtually all serious emotional problems stem from spiritual malaise, an emptiness that usually expresses itself in some kind of fear. In your case, the fear of being alone and unloved. That spiritual emptiness must be filled some way, any way, so the person can feel better. There are lots of ways to do it. Overworking, overeating, overbuying, alcohol, drugs, oversleeping, keeping frantically busy–"

"I do that, too," she interrupted. "I keep busy at stuff I don't enjoy."

"Listen, Lois. I can't heal you. Only you can decide to do something for yourself now that you understand a little better. Would you be willing to go to a treatment center?"

"God, Kathleen, the senator would have a fit. Think of the publicity."

"There are good reliable places that would guarantee your anonymity–and are you sure the senator would object?"

She frowned. "No–I'm not sure. It's another excuse I've used."

"I have an idea that Mrs. Clifford knows someplace that would be good for you to go–and I'm sure the senator could handle any questions concerning your whereabouts."

"I'm sure he could. He's very facile when it comes to misdirection." She reached for her cigarettes and lit one. "Hmm." She shook her head as she closed her lighter, staring unseeingly at her cigarette "–another way I fill the emptiness?"

Then she smiled at me with determination.. "All right, I'll do it. Could I ask you something?"

"Anything."

"Could I come and talk to you again when I've finished my treatment, if I need to?"

"Of course. I'd be happy to see you anytime."

"God, I've got to fix my face."

She grabbed her purse and fled to the bathroom.

A short time later, I said good-bye, leaving the two ladies pouring over brochures of various rehabilitation centers, intent on choosing the best. I was relieved that my efforts had laid the foundation for possible recovery for Lois Parkhurst.

The next day, back in my studio, I again picked up my brush and continued my struggle with the first panel of the Creation series. My self-imposed task of creating order from chaos on canvas seemed to me to be a pale reflection of God's gigantic whirlwind creation of the universe from the formless void. I knew that I needed to draw on every ounce of courage I possessed. My efforts could so easily fail miserably.

The first tentative strokes on empty canvas are always intimidating to me. At first hesitant, and then with growing confidence, I painted an inky black background overlaid with midnight blues, blue-blacks, luminous purples, touches of silver gray, swirling the colors in a profusion of patterned whirlwinds, hurricanes of boiling activity, chaotic tumblings suggesting matter coalescing into tentative form. Dark on dark on deepest dark. Days sped by as I added subtle intertwinings more sensed than seen, ghost planets and phantom shapes barely visible.

Next, I spattered gold charily in a moving free-fall of light piercing the nascent cosmos. I cracked the darkness apart with long, slender jags of lightning grounded in an incandescent purple-blue ovoid, the phosphorescent blue that I often saw in meditation. Finally, after days of aching labor, I blended, within the ovoid, luminous gold surrounding the white, hot heart of a primordial birthing sun, the daystar that nurtures all living things.

In exhaustion, I stood back and studied my work: abstraction moving from confusion to incipient unity. After several months of backbreaking effort, the first panel, I realized, was finished. I was exhausted but satisfied.

I took down the large canvas from the wall where I had secured it–it had been too large to fit on my easel–and propped it against the wall under the window. I tacked up another clean, white canvas, again experiencing a frisson of excitement mixed with apprehension. A new beginning, new problems, a new vision springing from the limitations inherent in any creative endeavor. I sat on the floor and stared at the untouched surface, willing it to show me the way, to impress on my mind's eye a viable treatment for the next subject, the dividing of the firmament from the waters.

What I needed before I began, I realized, was sleep–healing restorative sleep. I wearily took a shower and tumbled into bed, promising myself that I would relax and take my time with the rest of the paintings I envisioned.

The next morning, taking my coffee with me, I again sat on the floor in front of the empty canvas. As I quieted myself, I imaged slender rays erupting from a fixed point, symbol of the One Primal Source. I sensed beams of light reaching across the whole empty white surface. Picking up a large compass, I drew a semi-circle at one side of the canvas with blue chalk. From a point behind it, I lightly marked five lines raying out that potentially divided the canvas into five planes. I then carefully painted cobalt blue over the chalk marks with a slender brush. Images of fragmented mountains and seas sprang to my mind, of ice and crystal, of clouds and luminous space, of caverns and rocks and chasms, of vast tunneled formations with waters flowing around and through them.

I prepared my palette with cerulean blue, with more cobalt, with ultramarine. Then I added greens: phthalo, hunter, terra verde; finally I squeezed out a great gob of white and small amounts of black, umber, and burnt sienna. It was a ritual I never tired of–choosing from the many jeweled and viscous colors and then arranging them to my satisfaction on my palette. Their brilliant purity would soon be smeared and blended and blurred, but I savored their pristine beauty as I dipped my brush into vivid blue and began to paint.

Time vanished. I found myself in a space where there was only inner seeing and visceral spreading of color that seemed to flow intuitively from brush to canvas. My mind was alert but strangely quiescent. Ideas, forms, images seemed to flow through me without conscious volition.

At noon, I forced myself to take a break and call my friend Annie whom I had neglected shamefully while I was painting the first panel. We agreed to meet for a late lunch at Meredith's in Studio City.

As usual, she rushed in immaculately turned out, but late. She leaned down to hug me. At fifty-two, she was, if anything, more attractive than ever.

"Gosh, Kathleen, it's good to see you. It seems like ages."

"Umm, it has been awhile. I'm sorry. I get so caught up in my work that I forget there's a world out here."

"Yeah–me, too. It's no more your responsibility than mine, Kath." She dropped into her chair and sighed. "Ah–it feels good just to relax a bit. My head's been spinning all morning, trying to come to grips with a new plot. I'm glad one of us had the sense to call a halt to our madness."

I grinned at her. "Madness, indeed. So, how are you?"

"Oh, I'm fine. You should see your godchild! She'll soon be taller than I am. Of course, that's not saying much–I'm such a runt."

"Yes, you are, a small package, but an alarmingly efficient one. Allison will be a teen-ager before we know it."

"And how is little Matthew Stephen Grant doing?"

"He's absolutely wonderful. Six months old now. Darn, I forgot to bring any of the pictures that Dylan bombards me with. He's adorable, of course."

"Of course," she said with an impish grin. "And what about Dylan? Is she ready to hang up her dancing shoes?"

"Not a chance. She's getting ready for a new role as we speak. Neville is wonderfully patient with her."

"Well, he understands that talent needs an outlet. We're lucky; we can do our creating at home. She's blessed to have such a perceptive guy."

"No question about it. She says she wants another child in a couple of years. She probably misses not having had brothers or sisters."

"I suppose so–but I'm an only child, and one chick is plenty for me."

We chatted happily for an hour and then we both went back to our own endeavors, refreshed and nourished. I reminded myself that while there were seasons to be alone, there were also seasons to be connected, to seek out the comfort and stimulation of family and friends.

As I put finishing touches on the second canvas a few weeks later, I stepped back to assess the results. Picking up my brush, I added a touch of burnt sienna in one area, a shimmer of silver gray in another, and then, highlighting a formation with white, I set down my brush and decided it was finished.

Gentry came to dinner the next night. He knew I was working on a new project, but I had said little to him about what I was attempting. I couldn't decide whether to show the canvases to him at this stage or not. I knew that sharing work before completion could drain the vitality from a project. It was perilously easy to dilute the creative process with talk and explanation, to take the driving energy out of it. And yet, I trusted Gentry to understand and to restrain himself from asking too many questions. I decided to see how the evening unfolded.

After dinner, we listened to a Rachmaninoff Concerto, sipped wine, and talked desultorily. Conversation with Gentry was sometimes quiet, sometimes wise, sometimes high-spirited, but it was never dull. Tonight, we enjoyed each other's company in peaceful silence.

I treasured this singular friend of mine more each day. I loved watching the subtle movement of expression across his mobile face. I loved his quick fluctuations from confidant to mentor to clown. He seemed to me to be, above all else, God's holy fool. He never worried about what tomorrow would bring; he never rushed to judgment; he never concerned himself about what others might think. He was complete in himself; he needed no other. He lived secure in his knowing that the Universe would smile on him and sustain him in every way. I smiled at my rare and special friend.

"What, Kathleen? What are you smiling about?" He looked at me quizzically.

"Ah, Gentry, I was just thinking how unique you are and how much I appreciate you."

"Thank you," he said simply, a puckish smile lighting up his face. "We've been close in many, many lives, you know." He stretched out his legs and leaned back. "This isn't the first journey we've shared."

"How do you know that, Gentry?"

"There are hints along the way: the sense of connectedness we feel, what I can read when I look into your eyes, little flashes of past lives together that come to me now and then. I just know."

"There's no one I'm more peaceful with than you–and no one I trust more. It's hard to express, but I feel as if I'm more sure of who I am when I'm with you. Maybe it's because you make no demands and have no expectations."

"Perhaps." He stood up and stretched. "Time to think about going. How is the project you're working on coming along?"

"Pretty well, I think. I was debating whether or not to show you what I've done. Would you like to see?"

"Yes, of course I would."

I led him to my workroom in silence and turned on the lights–strong lights that I had installed a few years earlier. The first panel was propped under the window; the second was still tacked on the wall.

He looked at both carefully, hands in pockets, an enigmatic look on his face. Silence. I wondered what he was thinking. Finally, he turned and smiled. "They are truly magnificent. This is the best work you've ever done, Kathleen."

"Thank you, Gentry. Your validation means everything to me. I'm planning to do several more panels."

"Creation—yes, a series. Great."

We walked to the door. "You've arrived as an artist, Kathleen. You've found your unique voice." He kissed my forehead gently. "I'm so proud of you. Goodnight, dear friend." And with a smile, he was gone.

I slowly walked into my study and sank down in my favorite chair. I looked at Douglas' portrait. My dearest, dearest Douglas. How was he? Was he happy? Was he writing? Was his life going well? I longed to share Gentry's observations with him, to share the euphoria I was feeling at his praise.

My love, my love. Do you sit under my paintings and think of me? I'm happy; I'm content; my life is good; but, oh, I miss you so.

* * *

The other three panels were finished by spring of the next year. The third in the series was of verdant plant life and birds—birds of many colors with fluttering wings aglow. The canvas was filled with loosely drawn flowers and leaves and trees spiraling up into the sky. I angled the upward sweep so that the trees seemed to form a delicately holy cathedral embracing the exuberant life below. It was a glory of various greens and celadon and mauve.

The fourth was of Eden before God created male and female. Again the animals, the plants, the abounding vegetation were loosely drawn and colored in the pale, shimmering colors of the dawn of a perfect new day. The animals were stylized and elegant, the canvas awash with dripping peach and pink, pale lavender and apricot.

The final panel was of incipient humanity coming from the heavens. The background was dark, sparked with lights and spatters of gold and dazzlingly white stars. From out of the cosmos stepped male and female luminous golden beings, transparent and featureless. Again, I arched the firmament; and at the top, looking downward, I painted hosts of angels, jubilantly singing praise in honor of those first souls descending into an earthly Paradise.

A year and a half had gone into painting this Creation series. My small studio was ablaze with the drama of five large canvases leaning against every available surface. I looked around me and was awed at what I had translated into materiality.

There was no doubt in my mind that I had been an instrument of some Force beyond my own insignificant ego. As I turned quietly to view the totality, a Presence seemed to fill the room, wrapping me in indescribable love and joy. I slowly left the room with tears streaming down my cheeks, knowing that something still fragmented within me had been made whole.

Chapter 19

"They are splendid, Kathleen–they're glorious." Andy had been going from one large panel to the other and then back again. He slowly turned in a circle to take in all five canvases at once. "These were well worth waiting for."

The paintings were leaning against the pale gray walls of his main gallery. His eyes roamed again; I knew he was imagining them properly framed and lighted.

"We have to have an exhibition," he exclaimed, "a reception, advertising, the whole nine yards. Those canvases belong together. They should go to one buyer."

"Andy, much as I like the idea, five paintings aren't adequate for a show; you know that, and I have nothing else to give you. It would never work."

"Hmm. Let me think." He paced back and forth, his forehead furrowed in thought. "Ah, I've got it!" He beamed at me. "We'll do a retrospective of your work. I'm sure most people would loan their paintings for a short time. I'll send out a letter to everyone who has one." He walked to the doorway of the next room and studied it. "We'll hang all of your past work in sequence in the secondary rooms and have only the Creation Series in the main gallery. What do you think?"

"I'm thrilled with the idea, Andy. I'd love to have the series stay together, and that would give it the best chance of doing so." I ran through some of my past work in my mind. "You know, I've given Gentry and Aunt Peggy and Annie several paintings. I'm sure they'd let us use them temporarily. Oh, Elizabeth has a couple, too. She has a portrait I did of her and one of my father, and I have several of Dylan at different ages."

"We'll do it, Kathleen. I'll get started on it right away. Let's aim for the last week of September."

"Fine. It will be exciting to see my old work all in one place." I reached up and hugged Andy. "You're wonderful! Thank you for all your support, past and present. I know I'll be nervous–I don't much like being the center of attention–but it will be great!"

Several weeks later, as I sorted through the mail, I came upon a letter addressed in Douglas' distinctive handwriting. As I sank into a chair, I stared at it in disbelief. Chaotic emotions that I couldn't sort out momentarily paralyzed me. Finally, I pulled myself together and slowly opened the envelope.

Dearest Kathleen,

> *I hardly know how to begin this letter to you. I have reached for the phone to call you several times but finally decided that it would be best to write to you instead so that you could think about what I have to say.*

> *Rosalind died a year ago on June 24th. She had cancer; after a long illness, she finally was released from her suffering. It has been a difficult time for Craig and me. As you well know, grieving takes its toll. I am at last able to think about the future.*

> *I received a letter recently from the Marshall Anderson Gallery asking me to loan them your paintings for a retrospective of your work. What an important milestone in your career! That letter propelled me to action. I am considering bringing my paintings in person to California for I long to see you.*

> *I love you, mavourneen, and I want to be with you for the rest of my life. I feel strangely diffident in saying this because I don't know what your feelings are. It's been a long, long while. Perhaps you are married. Perhaps you are committed to someone else. Your beauty and lovely spirit must have drawn many admirers in these long years. Dare I hope that you are still free?*

> *I find myself overcome with fear that you may no longer share my feelings nor wish to share my life. If you still love me, but say the word and I will come. Regardless of your answer, you have my abiding love.*

> *Forever yours,*
> *Douglas*

I reread his words, smiling foolishly. A surge of joy flooded through me; I was ecstatic. Without hesitation, I reached for the phone.

"Douglas," I said without preamble, laughter bubbling up as I recognized his voice, "dearest Douglas, please come."

"Kathleen! I didn't expect to hear from you so soon. Dear, are you sure?"

"My heart hasn't changed, Douglas. I'm ecstatic; I can scarcely contain myself."

"You don't know how I've been agonizing over your answer. I'll come as soon as possible." He paused. "Kathleen, I've had a lot of time to think about this. I think it best if I come first just to visit. Then we can talk things over and decide what we want to do."

"All right, dearest–if it makes you feel better. But come soon."

"I'll aim for the first of September. I'll call in a day or two."

Radiantly happy, we finally reluctantly said good-bye.

A surprising number of people were crowded into The Marshall Anderson Gallery on a pleasantly warm evening in late September. They were here to see and be seen and, hopefully, to look at my work. Waiters wove through the throng with trays of hors d'oeuvres and champagne. Beautifully dressed people, wine glasses in hand, wandered around, talking, looking, visiting the elaborate buffet table that Andy had provided. Murmured comments of approval, criticism, gossip, high-pitched laughter.

I met and greeted people and accepted their congratulations. Most of them I had never seen before. As I moved through the press, I caught fragments of conversation. "Excellent... Superb use of color, especially... What do you think she was trying to–" The exhibition appeared to be successful.

As the evening wore on, the crush of bodies and the confusion of raised voices increasingly overwhelmed me. I excused myself from a rather overbearing older gentleman and looked around for Douglas. Impeccably groomed, he leaned against a wall talking with Gentry. He smiled as his eyes met mine. I was so grateful that he was here with me.

* * *

He had come, as he had promised, a few weeks earlier. I had impatiently watched groups of people pouring through the gate at the airport the day he had arrived, hardly able to bear the wait. When I had finally spotted him, tall and straight and lean, a rush of joy had overwhelmed me. My beloved. He was incredibly beautiful to me. When he saw me, his stunning smile had lit up his eyes. For a very long time, we had just held one another, content to be again in each other's arms.

Now I walked through the crowded gallery to his side. It pleased me excessively that he and Gentry were comfortable with each other. In honor of the evening, Gentry had changed from his usual cords and sweater to a blue denim shirt and cream linen trousers.

"Are you two getting bored with just hanging around here?" I asked.

"Not at all, Kathleen. I'm enjoying the passing parade. How about you, Gentry?"

"I'm not much of a partygoer but I wouldn't think of missing this. I'm happier for you than I can say, Kathleen. It's a great success–and you are looking radiant this evening." He grinned and hugged me against him. "Ah, here come Peg and Richard."

"Kathleen, have Anne and Mark found you yet?' my aunt asked, as she hugged me. "They just got here and were looking for you."

"No, Peggy, love, but they'll find me. I've got to relax for a bit. This crowd is getting to me. Everyone wants to meet me, it seems."

"Too bad Dylan couldn't be here," Richard remarked. "She would be so proud."

"Yes, I'd love it if she were, but she's off on her European tour. I think she's in Vienna right now."

"Ah, there you are, Kathleen." Annie, gorgeous in apricot silk, Mark trailing in her wake, threw her arms around me. "Gosh, what a display. What do you think, Douglas? To see all her work together is pretty impressive, isn't it?"

Douglas had met my friends at dinner a few nights before. He grinned at Anne and shook hands with Mark. "Indeed it is. This is the first opportunity I've had to see much of it. I'm in awe of Kathleen's talent."

"Did you know that Nigel Capshaw is here?" Annie asked, her voice rising with excitement. "I saw him chatting with Andy a few minutes ago. I wonder if he's interested in buying your Creation series."

"Well, that would be great but I'm not going to hold my breath. They could be talking about his next movie for all we know."

"But you're aware that he has a really magnificent art collection, aren't you?"

"Yes, I am. In fact, I read in the paper the other day that he just finished remodeling part of his house so that he can display his paintings more effectively."

"Oh, that's right. I saw that, too. The article said he had himself designed a small hexagon-shaped gallery with a long hall opening out on one side of it. That sounds fascinating."

Just then, Andy hurried over. "Kathleen, come with me. Nigel Capshaw wants to meet you."

He grabbed my hand and pulled me unceremoniously back into the melee. I soon found myself looking up into Mr. Capshaw's distinguished, well-known face.

"Mrs. Parrish, it's an honor to meet you," he said as he took my hand, his deep voice vibrating with eloquence. "I'm very taken with your Creation series. I want to compliment you; the paintings are spectacular. I'm seriously considering purchasing them. If I do, they will be the focal point of my collection."

I took a deep breath to calm my fluttering stomach. "I'd be honored, sir, if you chose them. They really should be kept together."

"I agree, and not too many individuals could accommodate five such large pieces. I'll give the matter serious thought–and you must come to see them if I decide on them."

"Thank you. I'd like that."

After he had excused himself and turned away, Andy and I grinned at each other conspiratorially. "He'll buy them, Kathleen," he whispered. "You can count on it."

The next day, Nigel Caphart purchased the Creation series, and a week later in the Los Angeles Times, there was an article complete with photographs of him displaying them. They were indeed the focal point of his collection; they had pride of place in his new hexagon-shaped gallery.

* * *

Douglas and I had been discussing the pros and cons of where we might live as we ate a late lunch one crisp and clear day in early October. I had asked if he wouldn't prefer that we return to England to live.

"Craig and Laura and their daughter, Ashley, live in the big house on the estate," Douglas told me, taking a bite of his sandwich. "Craig runs everything with expertise and he's totally devoted to the land. I'm not needed in any way. It's time I come home, mavourneen. I want to live in this country again."

"Shall we sell this place and buy something larger?" I asked.

"If you want to, love, but I wouldn't mind living here. Your house is charming; I feel so at home."

"But is it big enough? You'll need a place for your desk and probably other things I haven't even thought of."

"I'm going to leave almost everything with Craig and Laura. I would need a desk and some bookshelf and closet space; that's about it. Can we cram another desk into your study, do you think?"

"I don't know. We'll figure something out."

"Mavourneen, how soon can we be married? I was thinking that we could go together to England so that you could meet my family. It wouldn't take much of my time to put my affairs in order once I got there. I've already seen to most of it."

"That would be wonderful. I've always wanted to see Great Britain. To tell you the truth, I don't care if we marry or not; I just want to be with you. I suppose Dylan and Craig would be upset, though, if we didn't do it properly."

"Craig would be, I'm sure. Kathleen, I'm going to transfer the estate to him–and the other properties Rosalind inherited as well. You don't mind, do you?"

"No, I think that's the right thing to do. He shouldn't have to be concerned for his future."

Douglas' face lit up. "I have a wonderful idea, mavourneen. Let's get married in Paris. After a few weeks there, we can return to England to wind up my affairs, and you can meet my family. Unless you'd rather have a formal ceremony?" He looked at me questioningly.

"No. Paris–just the two of us. That will be perfect!"

We were married in an old chapel tucked away in a quaint little neighborhood on the outskirts of Paris. The priest, our innkeeper's uncle, was round and benignly accommodating. Once he saw that our papers were in order, he obligingly went to the local bakery across the way and returned, triumphant, with the owner and his wife both laughing and chattering with excitement as they untied well-floured aprons from their comfortably plump middles and tossed them on a bench at the back of the church, quite ready to stand up for us. Prêtre Jean conducted the short service in broken English, our improbable witnesses nodding and smiling throughout.

As we exchanged our vows, Douglas' intense blue eyes caressed mine with such love that they almost undid me, but, clutching my sheaf of white roses, I managed to meet his absorbing gaze with a smile. We exchanged our vows and rings, and then the little priest said a prayer and pronounced his blessing on our union.

After we kissed, he offered his congratulations. "Félicitations–eh, congratulations." He beamed as he shook our hands and kissed us on both cheeks.

The baker and his wife, their faces alight with cheerful humor, sent us on our way with shouts of delight: "Félicitations! –Adieu, bonne chance!"

Their calls echoed down the street as, laughing and happy, we got in our car and drove off. We were officially husband and wife.

* * *

I lay in bed and watched the sunlight drift through the open casement windows, making bright sunlit squares on the rug. Sighing with contentment, I turned to Douglas and watched him as he lay sleeping.. Such a dear face! I would be able to absorb all its planes and lines at my leisure for the rest of my days. I could bask in his presence endlessly. No timetable. No constraints. None other to consider. Nothing could tear us asunder again.

My heart sang with joy as I realized that the rent deep in my being, un-acknowledged but still subtly present since we had parted, had vanished. Apart, our hearts had been fractured; together we were gloriously whole.

My thoughts drifted lazily to our weeks in Paris. We had walked its boulevards hand in hand, sometimes arm in arm, exploring quaint side streets, eating in small cafes, strolling down the Champs Elysees. We had wandered through the Louvre; we had loitered in gracious parks; we had visited Montmarte and Montparnasse. We had tasted Left Bank nightlife. It was as delightful a city as I had been told, a city of charm, a city for lovers, a city that was hard to leave.

Now, though, it was time to move on to England to meet Douglas' son and his granddaughter and daughter-in-law as well. The ranks of my extended family were growing rapidly.

As we drove from London to Atherton House, Douglas talked about his son and family. Craig had completed his education at Oxford but was quite content to be a part of the landed gentry, he told me. He wanted only to care for his estate; He was a farmer through and through.

"He's never happier than when he's mucking about, checking the livestock, or exercising his horses. He has three–and a pony for Ashley."

"How old is Ashley?" I asked.

"Umm–she's almost five." He smiled at the thought of her. "She looks like Rosalind, I think."

"And Laura–does she ride, too?"

"Yes. Horses are very much a part of their lives. She's a good countrywoman. Thank God. Craig would be miserable with a wife who would be pestering to be in London all the time."

"We're almost there," Douglas remarked as he turned down a small side road. Soon we were driving up a long circling driveway flanked by bare trees. It would surely be beautiful in spring.

Atherton House was a stately Tudor-style mansion, built, according to Douglas, sometime in the mid-1880's by Rosalind's great grandfather. It was brick with timber cross-sections and high-pinnacled gables. Mullioned windows winked in the clear light and smoke drifted up from several chimneys. Its grandeur made me a little nervous.

Douglas left the car in the driveway and led me to a great arched entrance. An elderly looking woman whose hair was scraped back in an uncompromising bun opened the ancient-looking oak door.

"Mr. Douglas," she beamed, her round face wreathed with smiles. "Welcome back."

"Thank you, Mary."

"Kathleen, this is our housekeeper. Mary's been with us for years; she keeps us all in line. We'd be lost without her."

Mary blushed and grinned. "Ah, go on with you, sir. And you'd be Mr. Douglas' new wife. Welcome, ma'am. Mr. Craig is in the library, sir. And

I'll have tea for you in a jiffy."

"Thanks, Mary. Will you ask George to bring in our luggage?"

Mary bobbed her head and hastened away.

Before I could take in much of the entrance hall and the sweeping staircase that curved upward, Douglas took my hand and pulled me toward the library. He knocked lightly and opened the door.

When Craig saw his father, he leaped up and gave him a crushing bear hug. "Dad, I thought you'd get here about now." He was a large man, an inch or two taller than Douglas, with broad shoulders and a muscular build.

"Ah, and you'd be Kathleen. Welcome to Atherton House." His light blue eyes were warm and smiling. "Come, let's go and find Laura and Ashley. They're probably upstairs."

I met the rest of the family in a lovely, small sitting room–Laura, petite and slender, and Ashley, a sturdy little girl with large blue eyes like her father's, and flaxen hair. They quickly embraced me. I realized that Craig was genuinely thankful that his father had found someone to share his life. It was clear that he adored him and was glad that Douglas could move forward into a new future. I saw no sign of jealousy, no questioning about my suitability, no fear that I might usurp his mother's place. He accepted me wholeheartedly. I was vastly relieved.

The next morning, we had a huge English breakfast, served buffet style, in a lovely paneled dining room. Craig, Laura and Ashley already were eating when we came down.

After good-mornings, Craig looked at me with interest. "Kathleen, do you ride?"

"Not much, I'm afraid. I've had very little opportunity."

"Would you like to give it a try? We have a lovely gray filly, quite gentle. She'd be perfect for you."

"But I understand that you have only three horses. I'd hate to deprive Laura of her ride."

"If it's all right with you, Kathleen, I thought I might go see my solicitor," Douglas interrupted. "I have a few things to take care of." He reached over and touched my hand.

"Fine–then I'd love to ride."

Later, as we dressed for dinner, Douglas pulled me to him and kissed me gently. "Did you have a good time today," he asked.

"I had a wonderful time, dearest. I enjoyed riding more than I had expected. Ashley is quite the little horsewoman, and the countryside is breathtakingly beautiful. Your estate, Douglas, won't you miss it unbearably?"

He walked over and looked out the window. "I suppose I shall, a little. I've lived here for over thirty years. I'll miss Craig, too. And Ashley. Isn't she a bright one?"

"She is. She's a beautiful little girl. She came creeping into my room after we got back from our ride and shyly asked me if I'd like to come and see her toys. We had a grand time admiring her things."

"That means she's really accepted you. It usually takes her awhile." He looked out the window again. "Yes, I'll miss this, but it's time I go back to America." He pulled me to him again. "Besides, home is where you are, mavourneen. As long as we're together, that's all that really matters to me. We'll just have to come back often to visit–and if I can pry Craig away from his land, we'll get them to come to see us once in awhile."

A few days later, we said our good-byes, hugging, kissing, Ashley hanging unto her grandfather's leg. He hoisted her up and kissed her. "Ashley, love–you'll come to see us in America, won't you?"

She wound her arms around his neck. "Yes, gramp–but I don't want you to go away again." She buried her head in his coat. "I missed you when you were gone."

Douglas set her down and tousled her hair. "I missed you, too, sweetheart, and I'll miss you when I'm in America, but you'll come to visit next summer. 'Bye for now, love."

On the way to California, we stopped briefly to see Dylan, Neville and baby Matthew in New York. An ecstatic Dylan, who had hoped for this for many years, was clearly thrilled that Douglas and I were married. After a few days, we returned home to settle into our life together.

Chapter 20

Our life with each other quickly developed its own rhythm. Douglas spent several days a week working in the study, a bit crowded with his desk and extra book cases, his portrait looking down on him as he worked. He was involved in research for another book, this one dedicated to persons who had in some way fostered peace among nations. It was tentatively titled *Voices of Peace*. His publisher had encouraged him to continue the 'voices' theme because his other books had been exceptionally well received.

We had agreed that four days a week, at maximum, were enough to spend on work. The others we spent together. Sometimes, we went to the big downtown Los Angeles Public Library where he could further his research and I could spend happy hours browsing. We went to museums and bookstores and art galleries; we had season tickets for the Philharmonic; we went to the theater. Some days, we packed a picnic lunch and walked the beaches or hiked in the canyons. Occasionally we saw Gentry, Peg and Richard or Annie and Mark, but we guarded our time together carefully.

Gentry was our most frequent companion. Douglas and he immediately became friends. They had much in common. Both were exceptionally intelligent and sensitive; both were verbally and psychologically astute; both enjoyed art and theater and music. They were generous of spirit. Gentry, though, was of a much lighter nature than my serious love. He was very good for both of us. His wisdom and deep spiritual insights did not burden him in any way. The laughter in his eyes matched his whimsical smile. In fact, everything about Gentry matched. Unlike us, he was complete within himself. His characteristic ebullience was an antidote to our more sober personalities, his clarity, a welcoming elixir to our spirits.

"What is it about Gentry?" Douglas asked after we had spent an evening with him. "I can't put my finger on what makes him so unique."

"I've tried to figure that out for years. The closest I can come is to say that he has a very deep comprehension and connection to both the material and the invisible worlds. He's completely at home in both. He says very little about his own interior life, but I get the sense that he has learned somehow to bridge this world and other dimensions. He's whole in a way that few are; I think perhaps he's able, at all times, to remember that he is a part of God, and he seldom forgets the God in others. He continually amazes me."

"He's never married–had children?"

"I don't know. As open as he is and as close as we are, nonetheless there is something in him that precludes asking a lot of personal questions. He never speaks of his past. I've often wondered if he might be truly androgynous. He once told me that he perceived humankind as progressing to an evolutionary point where the distinction between male and female would become less and less well defined. Perhaps he's kind of a prototype."

"Hmm–interesting. Well, he's certainly one of a kind and I enjoy him immensely."

"I'm so grateful that you do, darling. For me, life would be diminished considerably without Gentry."

As the days drifted by and we basked in each other's love, I continued with my painting. My work was now much in demand; the Creation series had made my name well known, but I refused to be stampeded into producing paintings that were clones of one another. My output was by no means prodigious. In spite of Andy's pleas for more inventory, I worked at my own pace in my own intuitive and often laborious way. I had always had a clause in my contract that allowed me to give away those pieces that I chose, so sometimes I relaxed by doing studies of Douglas or Dylan or some other who caught my fancy.

I still relished portraiture. For Christmas, the first year we were married, I sent a painting of Ashley to the English Camerons, based on the numerous sketches I had done of her when we had visited Atherton House the previous spring.

I still did some healing, but not in any systematic way–rather I learned to recognize and honor an inner nudge. The feeling might come at any time. "Here. This one is ready for healing," or "touch that one on the arm". I learned to trust my inner voice; it always gave me specific directions. Often, I simply held someone's hand or rested my hand on his shoulder, or hugged her with intent to heal.

Douglas, widely known in broadcasting circles, was often called on to be interviewed on television or to take part in some panel discussion or other. He enjoyed being a media presence in a limited way. Occasionally, he was asked to speak at universities and conferences. He was an excellent speaker and a charismatic figure. Both of us, however, were content to keep outside engagements to a minimum. We were in ourselves complete.

As the years of our marriage went on, I became increasingly aware of how blessed my life had been from my first breath to the present time. I was not naïve; since my youth, I had been cognizant of the degradation of poverty, the nightmare of familial dysfunction, the unbelievable cruelty against human and animal that pervaded every society, the greed, the corruption of power, the indifference to suffering. I marveled that my own life had been sheltered always in love and abundance. During the few rough periods that had come my way, compassionate family and friends had supported me unequivocally. I had never experienced alienation or true loneliness. I understood deeply how favored I had been. Now, with Douglas by my side, I wanted for nothing.

I had thought often in the past about the seeming inequities of life–how some could be so exceedingly fortunate in their parentage, their surroundings, and their basic abilities while others seemed to be tossed into a dark, precarious cesspool where they must frantically struggle to survive.

Now that my life flowed along joyfully day after day, the question took on a new cogency. I knew that this was an existential issue that was as thorny as any in the lexicon of man; still, I struggled to clarify my own position anew.

One afternoon as Gentry and I settled down for a chat, I broached the subject once again.

"Reincarnation, Gentry, seems to be the most viable answer. How else can we justify the randomness of life?"

"That answer seems to be the most satisfying." He paused to think. "Some would say that God is not required to satisfy our questions–that the world's suffering comes from man's unredeemed nature. Whichever way you look at it, it comes down to choice, does it not?"

"You mean the choice to love one another, as Jesus said? That alone would heal an infinity of wounds."

"Yes–and that's a choice that needs to be made over and over and over again. Every religion tries to deal with it–usually without much success–because for the most part, loving another applies only to certain groups or nationalities, not to all of God's creatures." Gentry toyed with his wine glass. "People tend to think in terms of 'better'. 'My religion is better. My political view is better. My family is better.' And on and on."

"It's really sad, isn't it? We still haven't learned. War, geopolitical turmoil, fanaticism, racial discrimination. Individual lives get swallowed up in forces beyond their control."

"But that's where choice comes in, Kathleen. The individual always has choices. I think each of us has three lives intertwined within our seemingly straightforward existence."

I leaned forward with interest. "Three lives?"

"In a manner of speaking, yes. There's our normal life–the day-to-day physical life that we take for granted. Then there is the spiritual life that entwines and enfolds the physical. For some, that life has great impact. For many, it's largely unconscious or even irrelevant even though it is the

211

absolute Source of our being. And then, there's what I choose to call our creative life: the place where emotions, attitudes, beliefs shape who we are and what we will become–indeed, whom we choose to become. That is an arena of absolute freedom, and most people never examine the ramifications of what they themselves call into existence. It's far easier to blame God or society or upbringing than to take true and honest responsibility for what we ourselves have wrought."

"You call it the creative life. Why?"

"Because it's ours to do with what we will–to create what we will–to become what we will. Our fears draw negative experiences into our lives–our doubts, our often faltering self-esteem, our reluctance to give up our disappointments and sorrows and petty resentments. Our negativity very literally cuts us off from that great creative pool from which we could choose more wisely. We could choose to love others and ourselves; we could choose to rest in God's benevolent Presence, confident that we need not fear nor worry nor struggle to protect ourselves against an alien universe. Isn't that what Jesus taught? 'Consider the lilies of the field, how they grow.'"

I nodded.

"Our lives, creative whether we wish them to be or not, are fraught with inconsistencies, Kathleen. All of the inchoate thoughts we have, moment by moment, fuse into an amalgamation that shapes our days. With every negativity we allow ourselves, we cut ourselves off from our Source; we block the flow–and after all is said and done, only we can control how we think."

"If I understand you correctly, you're saying that those three strands braid together, consciously or unconsciously, to form the tapestry of our lives: our physicality, our spirituality, our connection to the Source. That's where it gets tough, Gentry–continually keeping our connection to Spirit, staying awake and clear. Our world pulls us from God-awareness at every turn, and we can't all be hermits or anchorites."

"No, nor would that be God's desire. Understand, no one can actually break that connection completely, Kathleen. If anyone did, he'd be dead. But we surely can and do throw blocks in the way; that vast energy emanating from God often reaches us in a puny little trickle, barely enough sometimes to sustain life."

"And you're saying that it's our choice–how much of that energy we allow to flow through us."

"Exactly, Kathleen. We are, each and every one of us, essentially creators. Each person's environment is a reflection of his inner world. That, in turn, is shaped by his ability to access the munificent, benevolent Source of being.

The larger world we live in is shaped by group consciousness–the sum total of our individual contributions of thought, feeling, belief–a magnificent, heterogeneous mix."

"Ah, Gentry, what we need, then, is to raise our collective consciousness."

"Yes, we need spiritual transformation in every domain: economic, political– education, child-rearing–indeed, in every cultural pattern and in every institution in every country in the world. No small enterprise."

"It seems completely hopeless to me."

"Well, remember individual choice. There's a saying, Hindu, I believe–something to the effect that the forest is no greener than each individual tree. One by one by one, we green. I believe we are heading for a quantum leap in human consciousness, Kathleen."

Mulling over what he said, I got up and looked out the window. My attention was drawn to the pine trees that bordered my property–stately, strong shafts, ever green, reaching always upward toward the light. As I studied their quiet strength, in my mind's eye I envisioned immense stretches of trees, spruce, fir, pine, stand on stand, rank on rank, as far as eye could see, always and ever green, reaching, reaching to pierce the refulgent skies.

I turned to Gentry, gladdened by the image in my mind, "And with that evolutionary thrust toward transformation, God willing, some day we may have a green forest."

"God willing, yes," he said.

Sheltered in the sanctuary of Douglas' arms later that night, I pondered what Gentry had said. I looked at the face of my own beloved, so peaceful in sleep, and my heart swelled with deep love for him. Was it possible that God loved his children even more passionately than we loved each other? Could it be that He longed for each of us as a lover yearns for his beloved? Had He gifted us with the polarities of male and female so that, in our endless driving quest to mate, we could begin to understand the ecstasy of union with the Source of our being? Was human love, after all, a metaphor for the wildly passionate love God holds for His children?[6]

Awed and enthralled at my thoughts, I drifted into sleep, thanking God yet again for the gracious blessing of Douglas and his love.

---

[6] This concept is explored with compelling wisdom in the novels of Roman Catholic priest, Andrew Greeley.

Requiem

Journal Entry:

September 23, 2005
Douglas died in my arms one dreary morning in 1993. The flat slate skies were heavy with unreleased moisture. So too was my heart. I shed no tears as I looked at the face of my most beloved, peaceful and somehow younger looking in death. He had not been feeling well the night before. In the early morning hours of November 5th, clutching his chest, he had awakened gasping with pain. As I turned, alarmed, to gather him in my arms, almost that quickly he was gone. A sigh, a slurred 'I love you' and his spirit had flown away home.

I must try to put into words the poignant, eloquent state that overtook me moments after I realized that Douglas had stepped into that Far Country where I could not follow. Strangely enough, I was not panicked. My first thought was gratitude that his going was swift and merciful, that his pain was brief. Love for his dear being filled my heart. I traced once more his beautiful mouth. I kissed his forehead, momentarily grief-stricken that he should be taken from me so soon. I didn't want to let go his material form, so dear to me; I held him tight, almost paralyzed by this momentous finality.

Suddenly, unexpectedly, a deep peace flooded through me, transcendent and timeless, a crystal-clear awareness; I knew that I was surrounded by his loving presence. Filled with intense joy and with the certainty that death had not separated us in any essential way, I relaxed into the tender intimacy of Douglas' spirit; I was lovingly wrapped in a cocoon of warmth and love. After a bit, I got up, completely calm, and made the necessary calls.

I can't pretend to understand the how and why of my experience. It was numinous and awesome. Credibility is easily strained in the face of the unfathomable; others may not believe, but I refuse to negate the validity of my knowing.

Death is simply transfiguration-a metamorphosis into spirit. The veil between the other world and this solid and cumbersome reality can sometimes be strangely translucent. I bear witness that deep love can at times sift through the implicate order into the material plane, irresistibly making itself known to the beloved.

I do not grieve for Douglas. Even today, his loving presence enfolds me, ever shimmering just beyond my sight.

September 25, 2005
A few days ago, I came across a quotation written by the ancient Taoist, Chuang Tzu. He says it all:

"Birth is not a beginning; death is not an end."

I am now keenly aware that I am approaching my final years. The Golden World is just a heartbeat away. As I ponder the journey from whence I came to this place where I now stand, I know that my life has been good, more than good; it has been, in many ways, miraculous. Over the years, I have finally come to understand that I am complete within myself; I am whole. Yet, it has been glorious to share my life with Douglas and I am eager to see him once more.

I have made my share of mistakes. I have known sorrow and I have known joy. I am fulfilled; I am graced; I am held in the loving hand of God.

I don't know how many more years will be given me: five? ten? Possibly not even one. I do not fear death. I pray that when it comes, it will be swift and sure. Then I will go with eagerness across the threshold into that other far, fair land. I will go with joy; I will go with outstretched hand. I know that Douglas will be waiting for me, reaching out his hand to grasp mine. In that instant, I will be home.

*